THE BEST YEARS OF THEIR LIVES

A RESOURCE GUIDE FOR TEENAGERS IN CRISIS

SECOND EDITION

Stephanie Zvirin

American Library Association
Chicago and London, 1996

Project editor: Joan A. Grygel

Cover designer: Richmond Jones

Composed by Clarinda in 10/12 Garamond Light on
Penta DeskTopPro composition system.

Printed on 50-pound Arbor paper, a pH-neutral stock, and bound
in 10-point C1S cover stock by Edwards Brothers, Inc.

The paper used in this publication meets the minimum
requirements of American National Standard for Information
Sciences—Permanence of Paper for Printed Library Materials,
ANSI Z39.48-1992.∞

Library of Congress Cataloging-in-Publication Data

Zvirin, Stephanie.

The best years of their lives : a resource guide for teenagers in crisis / by Stephanie Zvirin.—2nd ed.

p. cm.

Includes filmography (p.) and index.

Summary: A selective, annotated bibliography of fiction and non-fiction self-help works for teenagers, arranged under such topics as "Family Matters," "Wellness," and "Sex Stuff."

ISBN 0-8389-0686-9

1. Teenagers—Juvenile literature—Bibliography. 2. Adolescent psychology—Juvenile literature—Bibliography. 3. Children's stories—Bibliography. 4. Children's films—Bibliography. 5. Adolescence—Bibliography. [1. Adolescence—Bibliography.] I. Title.

Z7164.Y8Z95 1996

[HQ796]

016.30523'5—dc20 96-14446

Printed in the United States of America.

00 99 98 97 96 5 4 3 2 1

To Mike, to Bob,
and to Mom,
the people
I most count on.

Cover illustration from *Truce: Ending the Sibling War* by Janet Bode, copyright 1991 by Janet Bode. Reprinted with permission of the publisher, Franklin Watts, Inc., New York.

Book jacket from *How It Feels When Parents Divorce*. Published by Alfred A. Knopf.

Book jacket from *Bringing Up Parents: The Teenager's Handbook* by Alex J. Packer, Ph.D. Copyright 1992 by Free Spirit Publishing, 400 First Ave. North, Suite 616, Minneapolis, MN 55401. (800) 735-7323.

Book jacket from *The Place I Call Home: Faces and Voices of Homeless Teens*. Copyright 1992, Shapolsky Press—S.P.I. Books, 136 West 22 St., New York, NY 10011.

Book jacket from *The Survival Guide for Teenagers with LD* by Rhoda Cummings and Gary Fisher, copyright 1993. Reprinted with permission from Free Spirit Publishing, Inc.

Book jacket from *Help! My Teacher Hates Me* by Meg F. Schneider. Copyright 1990 by Meg F. Schneider. Shown with permission by Workman Publishing Co., NYC.

Cover illustration from *Beating the Odds* by Janet Bode. Copyright 1991 by Janet Bode. Reprinted with permission of the publisher, Franklin Watts, Inc., New York.

Cover illustration from *When Food's a Foe: How to Confront and Conquer Eating Disorders* by Nancy J. Kolodny, M.A., M.S.W. Courtesy of Little, Brown.

Book jacket from *Social Savvy* courtesy of Summit Books.

Book jacket from *Safe, Strong, and Streetwise* by Helen Benedict, courtesy of Joy Street-Books/Little, Brown.

Book jacket from *The C-Word: Teenagers and Their Families Living with Cancer* by Elena Dorfman. Copyright 1994 by NewSage Press.

Cover illustration from *Risky Times: How to Be AIDS-Smart and Stay Healthy* by Jeanne Blake. Copyright 1990 by Jeanne Blake. Reprinted by permission of Workman Publishing Co. Photo by Walt Chrynwski.

Cover illustration from *It's Perfectly Normal*. Text © 1994 by Robie H. Harris. Illustrations © 1994 by Michael Emberley. Permission granted by the publisher Candlewick Press, Cambridge, Mass.

Book jacket reprinted with permission from *How Sex Works* by Elizabeth Fenwick and Richard Walker, copyright 1994. Published by Dorling Kindersley Publishing, Inc.

Book jacket from *Hearing Us Out: Voices from the Gay and Lesbian Community* by Roger Sutton, copyright 1994, by permission of Little, Brown and Company.

Book jacket reprinted with permission from *Teenage Couples—Caring, Commitment and Change: How to Build a Relationship that Lasts* by Jeanne Warren Lindsay, copyright © 1995, Morning Glory Press.

Book jacket from *Kerry, A Teenage Mother* by Maggi Aitkens, copyright 1994. Published by Lerner Publications Co.

Book jacket from *What Do I Do Now?* courtesy of Putnam.

Book jacket from *Teens Parenting—Your Pregnancy and Newborn Journey* courtesy of Morning Glory Press.

Book jacket from *Teens Parenting—Discipline from Birth to Three* courtesy of Morning Glory Press.

Book jacket reprinted with permission from *Straight Talk about Death for Teenagers* by Earl A. Grollman, copyright 1993. Beacon Press. Jacket photograph and design by Steve Snider.

Book jacket reprinted with permission from *After a Suicide* by Susan Kuklin, copyright 1994. G.P. Putnam's Sons.

Contents

Preface

"NEVER BEFORE has one generation of American teenagers been less healthy, less cared for, or less prepared for life than their parents were at the same age." These harsh words, issued in a 1990 report to the nation on America's teenagers, came from C. Everett Koop, former Surgeon General, and representatives of the National Association of State Boards of Education and the American Medical Association.[1] Their concerns are well founded. Suicide rates among young people have skyrocketed. The Alan Guttmacher Institute in New York tells us that although birthrates have declined slightly overall, one million young American women between the ages of 15 and 19 still become pregnant each year.[2] Drug and alcohol use among teens is once again on the rise according to a 1995 report by the Children's Defense Fund[3]; the Centers for Disease Control cites syphilis rates at their highest level since World War II, and concern about AIDS is growing. Also troubling is the state of America's economy; poverty strikes one out of every three American students.[4] What jobs will be available for teens when they graduate? Increasing violence among teens is a growing concern, too. The 1995 *State of America's Children Yearbook* notes that more than 5,000 young people were killed by firearms in 1992—that's one every 98 minutes, and each day, 135,000 children bring guns to school.[5]

Social scientists, medical professionals, and educators are responding to these disquieting revelations in a variety of ways. Up from a mere handful ten years ago, numerous school-based health care centers now exist across the country; adolescent parenting programs have been instituted on high-school campuses; day-care centers in some schools enable teen mothers to complete their educations; health studies curricula encompass mental health issues and AIDS; and drug-awareness programs are implemented as early as first grade in some areas of the country.

The publishing industry has also reacted to the statistics. Teenage novels dealing with issues such as alcoholism, sexual abuse, and divorce have a long established place in publishers' catalogs and on library and bookstore shelves. Nonfiction titles have also found a place, with writers now almost routinely tackling in detail subjects once considered taboo. Somewhat slower to gain acceptance, however, have been practical nonfiction books that help young adults directly and actively address personal crises in their lives. This too, however, seems to be changing. Self-help nonfiction for young people has begun to come into its own. Calls for such materials by the educational community, increased publicity about Twelve Step programs used by such organizations as Alcoholics Anonymous, and the continuing demand for self-help literature coming from adults have all contributed to the shift. Today, most publishers of juvenile materials have self-help books on their lists, including some titles for very young children; a few, such as Facts On File and the Rosen Publishing Group, even have their own self-help series.

While such books can be excellent resources for young people seeking a better understanding of the challenges they face and the choices they have, self-help books are not substitutes for professional medical or psychiatric care. Nor do most of their authors, many of whom are medical professionals, suggest that they are. Bibliotherapy, in which a facilitator directs the use of literature (fiction or nonfiction) to promote mental or physical health in the rehabilitative or clinical sense, is the province of specially trained professionals, not the majority of teachers, librarians, or the authors of books. Yet, self-help books can be effective in several ways when used by teenagers dealing with developmental concerns.

1. They provide young adults with a sense of what they have in common with others their age, whether that be an unplanned pregnancy, an abusive parent, or simply pimples on their face.
2. They provide background information and useful suggestions for more confident handling of situations that occur in daily life, such as dating or sharing a room with a brother or sister.
3. They help teenagers determine life choices and adjust to the consequences of their decisions.
4. They inform teens about the physical and psychological changes that come with adolescence.

The Best Years of Their Lives is a selective guide to nonfiction, accompanied by an assortment of related fiction and video titles, that can give adolescents, ages 12 to 18, a better understanding of what growing up in a rapidly changing world is all about. With the exception of a few outstanding or unusual titles, most of the material included has been published since 1990 and is currently available. Age-level designations, provided for all entries, are suggestions only. They are based on a variety of factors, including subject matter, format, depth of treatment, and writing style.

Were it not for the help of my colleagues at *Booklist*, this book could not have been written. Many thanks to *Booklist* editor Bill Ott for his support during this project and to Sally Estes and Hazel Rochman, friends as well as coworkers. I would also like to thank the *Booklist* Audiovisual Materials staff, headed by Irene Wood, for contributions to the video section of this new edition—in particular, Sue-Ellen Beauregard for granting permission to use excerpts from her interview with Michael Pritchard and Nancy McCray, who suggested a number of the new titles listed. Lastly, I acknowledge with gratitude Janet Bode, Jill Krementz, and Lynda Madaras, each of whom took time out of her busy schedule to speak with me.

NOTES

1. Felicity Barringer, "Found: Another Lost Generation. What Is Youth Coming To?" *New York Times* (9 June 1990): 24.

2. *Facts in Brief*, "Teenage Reproductive Health in the United States." The Alan Guttmacher Institute, 1994.

3. *The State of America's Children Yearbook*. Children's Defense Fund, 1995.

4. *The State of America's Children Yearbook*.

5. *The State of America's Children Yearbook*.

Family Matters

ADOLESCENCE IS A TIME marked not only by sexual maturation but also by changing relationships within the family. Teenagers naturally strive to break away from their parents and assume more responsibility for themselves. As they become more self-confident, their roles at home change. Old family ties are broken and new ones, based more on shared experience and mutual respect, are formed. The process is a slow, difficult, and often upsetting one for all concerned, but it is further complicated when a family is divided by divorce or burdened by internal conflicts such as serious sibling rivalry. The books in this chapter explore these special challenges along with other issues that may cause tension within families and between parents and teens.

NONFICTION

Getting Along with One Another

Bernstein, Joanne E., and Byrna J. Fireside. *Special Parents, Special Children.* 1991. Morton Grove, Ill.: Albert Whitman (0-8075-7559-3). Ages 9–13.

What's it like to live with parents who are physically challenged? Sixth grader Lisa Kavanaugh, seventh grader Angela Stewart, fourth grader Adam Holdsworth, and high-school sophomore Stephanie Rigert can tell you. They each have at least one parent who has to cope with a physical disability. John Kavanaugh is blind; the Stewarts are both deaf; Adam's father cannot walk; and Connie and Bob Rigert are achondroplastic dwarfs. Black-and-white photographs personalize family profiles in which parents describe the discrimination they've experienced and what their daily lives are like, while their kids talk about family relationships, personal goals, and the frustrations of living with parents who are different. The terminology is not always politically correct, but that won't matter to most readers. What they'll really care about are the strength and optimism that shine through the unusual family portraits.

Bode, Janet. *Truce: Ending the Sibling War.* 1991. New York: Watts (0-531-15221-9); Dell, paper (0-440-21891-8). Ages 13–18.

Bode sets aside "routine aggravations" that arise between brothers and sisters to concentrate on problems between siblings that turn homes into battlefields where emotional or physical injury actually occurs. Remarks from family counselors and others who work with the young add authority to the well-documented text, which explores how such factors as birth order, divorce, family coping mechanisms, and poverty influence relationships. The book is not easy to read: personal testimony awkwardly interrupts the narrative, and the family portraits Bode paints are very disturbing as teens recall how they were beaten, sexually abused, or viciously ridiculed by a brother or sister. But Bode tackles aspects of sibling rivalry not often acknowledged, and she offers teens trapped in harmful situations some reasonable strategies to reduce their stress, improve their communication skills, and raise their self-esteem.

"I'd really wanted a brother or sister since I was God knows how old. When it happened for real though, it all happened so quick. I was used to it being just me and my mom, and one morning she got remarried. Then it was me and my mom and my dad—now Xavier and Desmon and then Michael, the baby. . . . I didn't like it."

—Armando, 16, from *Truce*

Different Mothers. Ed. by Louise Rafkin. 1990. San Francisco: Cleis Press (0-939416-40-9); paper (0-939416-41-7). Ages 15–up.

"I am writing this introduction to parents but in my heart I have put together this book for kids," writes Rafkin, who has assembled the frank responses of twenty-seven individuals, many of them teenagers, who've grown up with a lesbian parent. Males and females, ranging in age from 5 to 40, speak frankly. Some remember how their parent "came out" to them or talk about their mother's lesbianism in relation to their own sexual identity; others explain how they feel about being shuttled back and forth between parents who've split up, keeping mom's lesbianism a secret, or having two "moms" and no dad. In many ways, the words demonstrate the extent that children "carry the burden of social stigma" for having a lesbian parent. Yet they also capture feelings and situations common to most parent-child relationships. It will be these revelations that push readers, especially those with lesbian mothers, beyond stereotype toward recognition of other more important things—about their parent, about affection, and about the nature of families.

"My mom's the best mom in the world, whatever she is."

—from *Different Mothers*

Koffinke, Carol, and Julie Jordan. *"Mom, You Don't Understand!": A Mother and Daughter Share Their Views.* 1993. Minneapolis: Deaconess, paper (0-925190-66-7). Ages 14–18.

A family counselor and her 15-year-old daughter take turns talking about areas of common parent-teen conflict. In alternating chapters they speak earnestly, often disagreeing, on issues ranging from boyfriends and house rules to money, privacy, and peer pressure. Not all the examples that come out in the discussion are general ones; the family's personal problems are also frankly aired to clarify the battle terrain. Though this lacks the immediacy of an ongoing dialogue or an interview, young adults will still gain a clear sense of the struggles that frequently mark parent-teen relationships and acquire a better idea of why grownups act and feel the way they do.

LeShan, Eda. *When Grownups Drive You Crazy.* 1988. New York: Macmillan (0-02-756340-5). Ages 10–14.

LeShan, a child advocate, family counselor, and the author of a number of perceptive books for young people, also recognizes the importance of successful adult-child interactions. Her chatty overview considers the relationships between kids and grandparents, teachers, and others with whom young people interact on a regular basis, but the real focus is on what happens between kids and their parents. Using specific examples, the author reveals what's behind many adult behaviors, providing enough insight to help children respond assertively to a parent's derisive behavior and lobby realistically for changing what they feel is unreasonable or unfair. LeShan describes and strongly condemns adult behaviors involving physical abuse and violence and motivates children to secure help from a counselor or trusted adult if they feel they are in danger. She also discusses verbal abuse and its negative impact on self-esteem. Self-esteem, in fact, is of vital concern to LeShan throughout her book, which encourages young people to respect themselves and acknowledge their own opinions and needs.

Packer, Alex J. *Bringing Up Parents: The Teenager's Handbook.* 1993. Minneapolis: Free Spirit, paper (0-915793-48-2). Ages 15–18.

Although not above coddling or resorting to caustic humor (and even an occasional insult) to gain attention, Packer offers a sober, very practical book that parents as well as teens should read. Impressive credentials in education and psychology serve him well

as he explores the fine art of parental manipulation and the reasons parents and teens act as they do. Important issues, such as establishing trust, are discussed, as are specific techniques teens can use to develop listening skills, defuse family power struggles, and effectively wage verbal battles with parents (it won't help to call Dad a "Butthead," even if he is). Packer openly acknowledges that bringing up parents won't be easy and that his strategies won't always work, but the ideas he presents here will help teens see things from a broader perspective and accept the idea that change making isn't always about giving up or giving in.

Rue, Nancy N. *Coping with an Illiterate Parent.* 1990. New York: Rosen (0-8239-1070-9). Ages 12–16.

Should young people try to convince their illiterate parents to learn to read? Absolutely, writes Rue, who opens this unusual book with a heartbreaking scenario in which a child accidentally discovers that Dad can't read. She then speaks directly to teenage readers, discussing some reasons illiteracy still exists today and looking at how a parent's inability to manage the printed word influences a young person's role in the family and changes family relationships. Running through the text is a strong message about the importance of teens' own educations. A list of words crucial to personal health and safety is appended.

Webb, Margot. *Coping with Overprotective Parents.* 1990. New York: Rosen (0-8239-1088-1). Ages 12–16.

Using examples of parent-child interactions many teens will recognize, Webb explains how and why parents may consciously or unconsciously repress their kids. She looks closely at the detrimental effects of using manipulative strategies to influence and discipline children and describes several techniques parents use, among them negative criticism, overindulgence, and false praise. Webb makes it plain to her teenage readers that she dislikes these particular methods of exerting control, but she never suggests that parents have no right to discipline or that the limits they set are unimportant. Questions scattered through the text will prompt classroom discussion, but the book will also arouse independent readers, whose overprotective parents may be making them feel more like "angry prisoners" than individuals ready to face adulthood.

Winjberg, Ellen. *Parental Unemployment.* 1994. Austin, Tex.: Steck-Vaughn (0-8114-3525-3). Ages 14–18.

A psychotherapist who specializes in family therapy, Winjberg here uses a combination of straight text, statistical tables, and interviews to help teens understand and cope with one of the most difficult family challenges. Although she answers many general questions—about unemployment compensation, changes in family dynamics, the ways job loss may affect parental behavior—her attention never strays far from teens themselves. It's their feelings and concerns she zeroes in on—the way the situation affects a teen's self image, the prospect of moving or postponing college, the need for helping out at home and handling the extra stress. As in other books in the Teen Hot Line series, this one emphasizes the necessity of opening communication lines with parents and suggests ways teens can go about it. A fine, practical book about a problem that frequently affects teens but isn't often discussed in literature written for them.

Adoption, Blended Families, Divorce

Bolick, Nancy O'Keefe. *How to Survive Your Parents' Divorce.* 1994. New York: Watts (0-531-11054-0). Ages 14–16.

Bolick makes herself a vital presence in this book, adding background and continually speculating about the feelings and situations described by the young people she's talked to. But her amateur psychologizing rarely gets in the way of the teens' accounts. Instead, it adds texture to the riveting testimonies and provides fertile ground for reader reflection. Bolick has managed to leave the voices of her teenage commentators strong and distinctive as they bring forth common concerns about such situations as being caught between two angry divorced parents or living with a stepparent. A final chapter suggests some specific ways teens can get beyond their parents' problems and start taking care of themselves.

Gravelle, Karen, and Susan Fischer. *Where Are My Birth Parents? A Guide for Teenage Adoptees.* 1993. New York: Walker (0-8027-8258-2); paper (0-8027-7453-9). Ages 12–16.

Noting that it is usually a feeling of disconnection or a wish to strengthen one's sense of control that drives a search for birth parents, the authors make a good case for adoptees' pursuing their heritage even before they come of legal age to gain access to records. Including comments from many adoptees and the personal stories of three young people who searched for their birth parents with varying success, this book adeptly and clearly defines the emotions and practical issues involved—grief, guilt, disappointment, joy, and plain old hard investigative work. With a lengthy, state-by-state listing of search-support groups and some follow-up readings, this book can serve as a good preamble to a life-changing step.

Levine, Beth. *Divorce: Young People Caught in the Middle.* 1995. New York: Enslow (0-89490-633-X). Ages 14–18.

Levine takes an earnest look at a painful subject, interspersing case studies with comments from teens and up-to-date statistics. Chapters consider expected topics, such as custody and emotional ramifications, but also touch on some things less often included in books of this kind—pre-divorce stress, for example. Although Levine is realistic about the pain and difficult adjustments that must be faced, she still manages to end the book on a hopeful note by reminding teens that divorce sometimes strengthen ties between parents and kids and can lead to new positive beginnings for everyone involved.

Krementz, Jill. *How It Feels to Be Adopted.* 1982. New York: Knopf (0-394-53851-4); paper (0-394-75853-6). Ages 10–15.

They range in age from 8 to 16. They are black; they are white; they are Korean or Puerto Rican. Some of their families are homogeneous; others are mixed. One child lives in a single-parent family; his father is a Catholic priest. What the nineteen young people who speak out have in common is that they are adopted and, despite a few problems, they are happy in their adoptive homes. They also share a common curiosity about their roots, though not all want to seek out their birth parents. As one of the boys explains: "I hate to blame them, but it truly is their fault, and they don't have the right to reexamine their decision later on." Other kids disagree. Several, in fact, talk about the birth mothers they have located and are getting to know. Krementz's excellent black-and-white photographs give life to the individuals behind the words, and her smooth editing allows each speaker to remain distinctive. It's a book filled with eye-opening perspectives, a book that has stood the test of time.

"I've always known I was adopted, and when I was real little, I would go up to every pregnant lady I saw and ask her if she was planning to keep her baby or to give it up for adoption. They would all just stop dead in their tracks and look at me as though I were crazy!"

—Philip, 15, from *How It Feels to Be Adopted*

Krementz, Jill. *How It Feels When Parents Divorce*. 1984. New York: Knopf (0-394-54079-4); paper (0-394-75855-2). Ages 10–15.

In this sensitive book, Krementz focuses her camera lens on nineteen children, who, like herself, have divorced parents. As in her book on adoption, she calls on young people representing a variety of ethnic, economic, and family situations to voice their feelings about a pivotal family issue. Ranging in age from 8 to 16, the children talk openly about their families and themselves in a series of nicely polished personal accounts. Whether describing the shock of their parents' break-up, ensuing custody battles, or being shuttled back and forth between households, their unstudied testimonies validate the trauma of family dissolution and reveal the kind of personal strength needed to adapt to new circumstances. Like Krementz's *How It Feels to Be Adopted,* this is an insightful documentary, both disturbing and comforting. Young people can read it on their own or share it with their families.

Pohl, Constance, and Kathy Harris. *Transracial Adoptions: Children and Parents Speak*. 1992. New York: Watts (0-531-11134-2). Ages 15–18.

The format indicates that this book will be used predominantly as a research tool, but comments from parents and children who are part of interracial families may invite personal-interest reading, too. Mothers of adopted African American children, Pohl and Harris, who are white, bring both personal experience and factual perspective to bear in their investigation. The positive aspects of transracial adoption are emphasized, though the authors also point out difficulties inherent in the situation, especially when the culture of the adopted child is ignored, and they are candid about objections to transracial adoptions raised by such groups as the National Association of Black Social Workers.

Rosenberg, Maxine. *Living with a Single Parent*. 1992. New York: Bradbury (0-02-777915-7). Ages 11–14.

There are no adult perspectives in Rosenberg's roundup of first-person profiles this time, as there are in *Talking about Stepfamilies,* following. What's distinctive about this book is the variety of kids' voices. Children residing with a divorced parent are included as are kids living with a gay parent, an unwed mother, or a widowed parent.

The young people talk frankly of problems—missing a parent who is no longer around, having to go to therapy—sometimes admitting that living with just one parent "isn't that great." There are a few too many voices in the mix, but that doesn't detract from the generally positive tone of the book, which confirms the value of common sense, caring, and communication.

Rosenberg, Maxine. *Talking about Stepfamilies*. 1990. New York: Bradbury (0-02-777913-0). Ages 10–14.

Rosenberg includes the responses of adults as well as children in her collection of personal accounts, with her sixteen interviewees ranging in age from 8 to 41. With Rosenberg filling in the background, they lend insight into stepfamily dynamics and the changes that come with such things as moving to a different house and altering routines and responsibilities. There is no sugarcoating: the testimonies express fear and hostility as well as the satisfaction of working to develop new friendships and stronger family ties. A brief afterword contains practical guidelines for refining family accord, and two bibliographies, one for adults and one for children, are provided. The book provides a frank, well-balanced view of a family phenomenon becoming commonplace.

Being Homeless

Artenstein, Jeffrey. *Runaways: In Their Own Words: Kids Talking about Living on the Streets*. 1990. New York: St. Martins (0-312-93132-8); TOR, paper (0-812-51354-1). Ages 14–18.

Interviews with ten runaways staying at a Los Angeles halfway house offer a poignant, also shocking view of life on the streets for "between 730,000 and 1.3 million youth . . . who live, most of the time, by their own wits." Artenstein provides descriptive commentary through the book, which reverberates with the tough street jargon of the teenage addict, the prostitute, and the gang member. The kids, ranging in age from 10 to 17, have much history in common. Many come from broken homes; often they were abused by parents or involved with drugs. They are candid about their feelings ("being a whore like that is still better than being a normal person who doesn't have anywhere to go") and about what they've had to face. Artenstein's epilogue, telling what happened to each of the teens he spoke with, serves as a grim, frightening reminder of how difficult it is to turn the hope for a family and a better life into reality. This is a cautionary book with a grim message.

Cwayna, Kevin. *Knowing Where the Fountains Are: Stories and Stark Realities of Homeless Youth*. 1993. Minneapolis: Deaconess (0-925190-71-3). Ages 15–18.

An advocate for homeless youth, Cwayna, a gay physician who has worked with AIDS-infected teens, contributes a sensitive and informative combination of social science research and the stories of kids who live on the street. A proponent of changes in social programs for teens, he stirs readers into looking beyond dress and behavior to recognize the exploitative street culture that keeps homeless young people captive. Cwayna writes mainly to adults here, yet the first-person experiences cited will call strongly to teens and give them some honest answers about why their peers run away and what happens when someone cuts loose with nowhere to go.

Greenberg, Keith Elliot. *Runaways*. 1995. Minneapolis: Lerner (0-8225-2557-7). Ages 11–15.

The subject matter, the clear jacket photo of an attractive teenage girl, and the case-study approach Greenberg employs all work together to give this book good browser appeal. Greenberg focuses mainly on two young people, Erin and Vicky, telling their stories, complete with photos from their family albums. Their stories end promisingly, with the girls finding sanctuary from desperate family situations with Sister Delores Garatanutti at a group home called Noah's Ark. Despite the success of these girls, there's no soft soap about what awaits teens on the streets, even though both the personal profiles and the background information are rather sketchy. Still, there's enough here to maintain teen interest, and Greenberg's devotion to destroying the stereotype of the runaway as a "bad" kid is commendable, as is his demonstration that there are, indeed, adults willing to help young people toward a brighter, safer future.

Stavsky, Lois, and I. E. Mozeson. *The Place I Call Home: Faces and Voices of Homeless Teens*. 1990. New York: Shapolsky (0-944007-81-3); paper (1-56171-071-7). Ages 14–18.

Teenagers participating in Stavsky's Manhattan dropout-prevention program interviewed peers who live on the streets for this disturbing collective profile. Language has

been edited to "keep the book appropriate for younger readers and school libraries," but the brief first-person accounts still vividly convey the violence, poverty, and disaffection so much a part of some urban teens' lives. The young people, from 14 to 22 years of age, speak matter-of-factly. Some express hope, but, like Tammy, a teen prostitute with AIDS, many sound discouraged and cynical; others seem unbelievably naive considering the experiences they describe. There are so many stories here (thirty-one in all) that eventually they begin to lose their impact. But the book still sends a message that compels attention: stay off the streets—any way you can. Teenagers already faced with going it alone may find help through one of the organizations listed in the appendix.

"I haven't had an address in years. I live in Riverside Park most of the time and go into the tunnels beneath the park when the weather's bad. There are old Amtrak tunnels in different parts of town that are underground cities. They have their own mayors and everything. In the salt mines near the piers, the boss is called the president." —Dave Frank, 22, from *The Place I Call Home*

Switzer, Ellen. *Anyplace but Here: Young, Alone, and Homeless: What to Do*. 1992. New York: Atheneum (0-689-31694-1). Ages 14–16.

Switzer, who begins with a personal anecdote about her own running away (she returned before she was even missed), is candid but not preachy in this exploration of the dreary future awaiting teens who take to the streets. Glimpses of teen runaways in Venice, California, and in New York City bolster discussions of who runs away and why, and there are hot line numbers as well as a full chapter listing help resources and supplying useful information about AIDS and other STDs.

Jill Krementz: Listening to Children

When she traded her sewing machine for a camera, Jill Krementz took her first step toward a career as a photojournalist. Hired by the *New York Herald Tribune* as its first woman photographer and later employed as correspondent for *Time,* she has since become a respected author of more than two dozen children's books that showcase her abilities as photographer and writer, among them *A Very Young Gardener* and *Lily Goes to the Playground.* She is also the author of the How It Feels series, an exceptional group of books about children and teenagers dealing with personal crises such as the death of a parent, divorce, chronic illness, and adoption. The newest in the series is *How It Feels to Live with a Physical Disability.* She is presently working on a book about learning problems. In "Listening to Children," which originally appeared in slightly longer form in *Worlds of Childhood: The Art and Craft of Writing for Children,* edited by William Zinsser (Houghton Mifflin, 1990), she explains how books for the How It Feels series are "born." At the same time, she reveals her fondness and respect for children and her devotion to her work:

When I think back to when I was ten, it was such a different life from what a ten-year-old lives today. There was no television, so what I knew about the outside world came mostly from books like the Nancy Drew series and *The Secret Garden.* I wasn't reading books like the ones I now write: I don't think there were any books like that. What girls of my generation were reading, in other words, was fiction and fantasy, and I'm sure all the work I've done, as a photographer and as a writer, has been a rebellion against that. I've been determined that children reading books today won't grow up as deprived of reality as I was.

I'd like to tell you how some of my books got born, especially the How It Feels books. I want to explain the process of how I choose and interview many different kinds of children and why I think their stories are helpful to other children and their families.

I started working and having heroes almost simultaneously—when I was nineteen. My heroes (and they still continue to influence me) were Jacob Riis, Lewis Hines, Dorothea Lange, and Gordon Parks—men and women who truly photographed people and did it with their heart. They used their pictures not only to gather information but to put it to constructive use. I've never been someone who would want to take pretty pictures and hang them on the wall and that's the end of it. I've always wanted to channel what I gather—to reprocess information in a way that's helpful to others.

Another one of my early heroes was Margaret Mead. When I was a young reporter for *Time* magazine I took Dr. Mead's anthropology course at Columbia, and I made a point of getting to know her. I think I realized very early that I wanted to do books about how people live. The course was basic anthropology, and that's what I've been doing ever since. What I like about anthropology is that it's nonjudgmental. In my How It Feels books, which deal with issues of loss that are highly complex—adoption, death, divorce, serious illness—I try to present every side of the issue without taking any side myself. What I learned from Margaret Mead was to be relentless and persistent in what I was going after, to work very hard, and to be a good listener. That course was the jumping-off point for my career as a writer of children's books.

My method is the same with every book. I take along two cameras (a Leica M-6 and a Nikon), a tape recorder, and a small spiral notebook. The notebook is for my field notes. It's never enough to just take pictures and to tape-record what a child says; I also need to know what the child was doing and observing and thinking and feeling, and what the people around him or her were thinking and saying. Then I convert all that information into a first-person narrative.

During this process I think of myself as the reader and try to make sure I understand the situation. I assume that if I understand it, any six-year-old will. All the children in my books have the final right of approval. I feel very strongly about that. Some people are surprised—they think it's unprofessional. But I feel the same way about my books that I feel about my photography: that it's a collaboration between me and the person I'm working with. If I photograph someone, I want to use photographs that will please him.

After I go over the copy with the child and we've got what we think is good, we let his parents see it. I do this because it would be too easy to exploit children; they're extremely honest. The reason you get them to say such wonderful things is that they don't edit themselves if they trust you, and you can't violate that trust. Also, it's one thing to talk about your parents, but when children see what they've said in black and white and realize that it's going to be in a book, they may want to soften their remarks a little. I don't want these kids to hurt anybody.

Also, I have to get the mother and father to sign off; that's a legal requirement because I'm dealing with minors. Fortunately, no parent has ever refused to sign; it's usually a question of some factual detail. They call us and say, "We have a few changes," and my heart is in my stomach. Then they say I've got it wrong about how old their dog is.

I think the reason parents are willing to stand by the material—even though it's often threatening to them—is that they respect what I'm trying to do. Let me explain how I happened to get started doing these books. A friend of mine, Audrey Maas, died suddenly and unexpectedly after a short illness. She and her husband, Peter, and their little boy, John Michael, who was only eight, lived near us in the country, and in the days after Audrey's funeral we would go over and visit the house. I noticed that Peter had friends who had gone through a similar experience. But John Michael seemed very isolated, with nobody to talk to. So I thought it might be nice to try to do a book for other kids who were going through this. It would help them know that some of the weird feelings they were having weren't inappropriate. For instance, I had heard that John Michael told someone that he didn't understand why, right after his mother died, this perpetual cocktail party was going on. He had no way of knowing that such gatherings are a kind of grieving ritual that almost all societies have.

Because I had done six books that focused on one child—Sweet Pea and five Very Young books—my first thought was to follow one young girl through the death of her mother, probably of cancer, so that I would be on hand when it happened. But then I had second thoughts. Would my book help a little boy whose father dies? I also wondered what religion I should use. If I had an Episcopalian funeral, would it be relevant for a Jewish child? And how about the burial—should it be in a cemetery, or would the parent be cremated? Should the child have siblings, or should he or she be an only child? And I hadn't even thought about suicide, which is a surprisingly frequent cause of death among relatively young people. I realized that I would have to think more broadly.

At about that time I was asked to give a talk about my Very Young books to a group of librarians in Westchester County, New York. I told them about my project and read them a few passages about the children I had begun to interview. I asked them if they knew of any children in their schools who had lost a parent and who might like to participate. Within a week I had heard from eight of those librarians, and they all had wonderful kids for me; librarians are really in touch with the kids in their schools. I also put a notice in my alumni magazine and called the Big Brother organization. In the case of two of the children, Nick Davis and Susan Radin, their mothers had been close friends of mine before they died.

Pretty soon I had the eighteen boys and girls I ended up using. I pick my children carefully. I look for an age range from six to sixteen; at seventeen you're moving into an adult book. In fact, I don't have that many who are sixteen or six—just one or two. I want to be able to reach down to the six-year-olds, and if there's one six-year-old in the book, they feel that they have a friend they can latch onto. But after that I'm going for a median age. I want the book fairly evenly divided between girls and boys. I also want certain demographics—some blacks and Hispanics and Mexicans, not just little white children. I want both Christian and Jewish kids. I want some children who have brothers and sisters and some who don't. I want children who have been helped by psychiatrists and children who hate psychiatrists.

Most of all I want a range of issues. My books are designed to show both sides of every question. In *How It Feels When Parents Divorce,* for instance, there are various custody arrangements. I wanted to include a wide variety of possible structures. In *How It Feels to Be Adopted* I wanted it pretty evenly divided on the issue of "to search or not to search" for the birth parent and also to cover children who had been searched for. My own opinion doesn't enter into it; nobody reading these books would know where I stand. I tried for the same diversity in *How It Feels When a Parent Dies.* Of the eighteen children, probably half want to go to the cemetery on Easter and Christmas, and the other half never want to go because it gives them the heebie jeebies and just reminds them of their own mortality, or it makes them worry that something will happen to the surviving parent. But on one issue—whether or not the child should go to the parent's funeral—without exception the children who went to the funeral were glad and the ones who didn't go regretted it later. I feel very strongly about that issue, and I think it's one of the most important lessons that can be drawn from any of my books. But there was one experience even worse for children than having a parent die. Divorce—as I found out when I was writing *How It Feels When Parents Divorce*—is the most painful of the traumas that my books deal with. Yet it's the most underestimated of all the injurious things that happen to children.

What makes divorce so long lasting in its effects has to do with self-image and ego. If a parent dies, he or she is all but deified by the surviving parent. It's always, "Oh, your father would have been so proud of you." It's a positive reinforcement of the missing parent, which, while it may sadden the child on one level, makes the child feel good about himself. Even in a "civilized" divorce, for example, it's not unusual to have one parent say to the child, "You'd better call your father and remind him to pick you up on Saturday." The implication is that the father doesn't care enough to remember. With *How It Feels to Be Adopted,* I was surprised by how many parents turned me down. Many of them felt they had gone very far by even telling their children they were adopted. I always approach the parents first: I don't want to ask the children first and have them want to do it and then find their parents opposed, so that the parents become the bad guys. My ideal subject is therefore the child of a parent who, when I say I'm working on the project, says, "Well, I know Melissa loved *A Very Young Dancer*—in fact, it's grafted onto her chest, she's been carrying it around so much. It's fine with me, but why don't you call her, because the decision is totally hers." Then I feel that I'm home free, because first, that's the kind of parent who lets her child make decisions like that, and second, it's a parent who allows her child to have her own feelings. I believe that all the children in my books have benefited from the experience.

Often their teachers have told me how much better they're doing in school, or the children have written me themselves. They were so proud to be in the book, as well they might be; it makes me proud that they were included just for being articulate and in touch with their feelings and not because they made the baseball team or got all *A*'s. Therefore one value of these books is that they enable children to listen to themselves. But their real value, I think, is that they enable children to listen to other children—to realize, often for the first time, that they are not alone in their situation.

Finally, I'd like to tell you about *How It Feels to Fight for Your Life,* which seemed like the natural fourth in the series. It's been by far the hardest and most painful one to write. I'm dealing with children who have a total of fourteen different illnesses and disabilities. Actually, it's not the illness that I've focused on. I'm dealing primarily with the issue that the children are coping with—sibling rivalry, overprotective parents, financial stresses in the family, religious doubts, pain, hope, doctors who don't always listen to them, their relationships with schoolmates, and their struggle for independence at a time when illness makes them more dependent than ever on their parents. As for the medical issues, that's why the book has taken me twice as long as the other How It Feels books. When I worked on the divorce book I at least knew what a divorce was; we all know that. But these illnesses are unfamiliar—you can't begin to interview a child until you've read the literature (and medical literature is a language unto itself). Before I could understand the problems that a child with lupus has, or a child with juvenile rheumatoid arthritis, I had to understand the disease, so that I would know what problems we were talking about.

I chose the title *How It Feels to Fight for Your Life* because it puts the child in an active, positive role. Even if the illness isn't literally life-threatening, what all these children are still fighting for is a normal life—one that is ennobled and that has a dignity they want and can reach for. My point is not to talk about a particular disease or to tell people what it's like to be sick. I'm using children who I hope will be role models for other children. I'd like some other girl with rheumatoid arthritis to read about ten-year-old Lauren Dutton and say, "I don't really like playing the piano, but I like it enough so that if it's going to be good for my joints and make my fingers exercise, that's more interesting than the dumb exercises I'm doing with the therapist. I might even learn to play the piano, too."

There's one young boy in my book, Spencer Gray, who had a kidney transplant. He's terrific. He can't do contact sports, and he's also quite small because all the steroids have stunted his growth, so he signed up with the ROTC program at school. I went to photograph him in his uniform, and this is what he told me: "Master Gunny Washington, who works with our group, told me right off to stop worrying about my size and not to think of myself as a novelty. What he said was, 'Size doesn't mean anything—it's the size of your heart that matters.' I go to training every day at seven-thirty, and on Tuesdays and Thursdays I have a drill at eight o'clock. We've won the city championship four years in a row. When I go to ROTC I forget that I'm smaller than the other kids, and a lot of the time I even forget that I'm sick. All I feel is real proud."

—Jill Krementz

FICTION

Blume, Judy. *Here's to You, Rachel Robinson.* 1993. New York: Orchard (0-531-06801-3). Ages 12–15.

Smart and responsible Rachel seems to have herself together; so does her 16-year-old sister, Jessica, despite a serious case of acne. It's middle sibling Charlie, dope smoker and school flunkout, who is testing the family's strength.

Brooks, Bruce. *What Hearts.* 1992. New York: HarperCollins/Laura Geringer (0-06-021131-8). Ages 14–18.

In four heartfelt connected stories, Asa grows up, exploring his relationship with his stepfather and his fragile mother as he confronts the concerns of everyday life.

Crutcher, Chris. *Ironman.* 1995. New York: Greenwillow (0-688-13503-X). Ages 14–18.

When Beauregard Brewster is remanded to the school's anger management group for spouting off to a rigid teacher, he discovers that much of his hostility and pain is rooted in his relationship with his father and that it will take more than running a triathlon to cure the problem.

Doherty, Berlie. *Granny Was a Buffer Girl.* 1988. New York: Watts/Orchard (0-531-05754-2). Ages 14–18.

Preparing to leave England for a year abroad at school, Jess describes the extended family that has gathered to wish her well, weaving their stories into her own.

Duder, Tessa. *Jellybean.* 1986. New York: Viking (0-670-81235-8); paper (0-14-032114-4). Ages 11–14.

Geraldine (nicknamed Jellybean) lives with her single-parent mother, a cellist whose rigorous practice schedules leave Geraldine on her own, sitting in rehearsal halls or auditoriums for hours on end.

Fine, Anne. *Flour Babies*. 1994. Boston: Little, Brown (0-316-28319-3). Ages 11–15.

None of the boys in Room 8 is enthusiastic about learning parenting skills by carrying around a six-pound "flour baby," least of all mischievous Simon Martin, who never had a dad to teach him about fathering.

Fox, Paula. *Monkey Island*. 1991. New York: Watts/Orchard/Richard Jackson (0-531-05962-6). Ages 10–14.

When his pregnant mother simply can't cope and disappears, 11-year-old Clay finds a home of sorts on the streets, where Buddy, an African-American teenager, and Calvin, a crabbed old alcoholic, manage to help him survive.

Grant, Cynthia D. *Mary Wolf*. 1995. New York: Simon & Schuster/Atheneum (0-689-80007-X). Ages 14–18.

Homeless and rootless after the collapse of the family business, 16-year-old Mary Wolf finds herself leading the family as her dad's depression tips over into madness and her mother withdraws into passivity.

Homes, A. M. *Jack*. 1989. New York: Macmillan (0-02-744831-2). Ages 14–18.

After Jack's father reveals he is gay, the puzzling aspects of Jack's parents' acrimonious divorce suddenly fall into place.

Johnston, Julie. *Adam and Eve and Pinch-Me*. 1994. Boston: Little, Brown (0-316-46990-4). Ages 12–16.

A history of foster-home life has taught Sara Moone never to let her feelings show and never to become too attached to anyone. When she moves in with the Huddlestons, however, she discovers that her strategy doesn't seem to work anymore.

Lynch, Chris. *Gypsy Davey*. 1994. New York: HarperCollins (0-06-023586-1). Ages 15–18.

A developmentally disabled boy escapes the legacy of his dysfunctional family to become a loving uncle for his baby nephew. A harsh but ultimately uplifting family portrait.

MacLachlan, Patricia. *Baby*. 1993. New York: Delacorte (0-385-31133-8). Ages 11–15.

Twelve-year-old Larkin and her family discover an abandoned baby on their doorstep with a note entrusting the child to their care. The act of taking in baby Sophie alters all their lives.

Maguire, Gregory. *Missing Sisters*. 1994. New York: Macmillan/Margaret K. McElderry (0-689-50590-6). Ages 12–15.

An orphan with both speech and hearing disabilities, Alice Colossus thinks she needs some sort of intervention from on high when her friend Sister Vincent De Paul is injured. Alice does receive a miracle of sorts—a twin sister she never knew existed.

Mahy, Margaret. *The Other Side of Silence*. 1995. New York: Viking (0-670-86455-2). Ages 12–15.

In a family where words and intellect are highly prized, rebellious Hero marks a special place for herself by choosing not to speak. Her decision to be mute comes into question when she meets eccentric Miss Credence.

Mori, Kyoko. *One Bird*. 1995. New York: Holt (0-8050-2983-4). Ages 14–18.

Divorce is a disgrace in Japanese society, even though it's 1975, but 15-year-old Megumi's mother finds it impossible to stay with her husband. Her departure leaves Megumi in the care of her distant father and dictatorial grandmother, with only the wounded birds she cares for and memories of her mother for comfort.

Myers, Walter Dean. *Somewhere in the Darkness.* 1992. New York: Scholastic (0-590-42411-4). Ages 12–17.

Having escaped from the prison hospital, Crab shows up at the New York tenement where his son Jimmy lives, hoping the boy will forgive him and learn to love him.

Nelson, Theresa. *The Beggar's Ride.* 1992. New York: Orchard/Richard Jackson (0-531-05896-4); Dell, paper (0-4400-2187-X). Ages 12–15.

With her mother's live-in boyfriend constantly trying to molest her, 12-year-old Clare runs away and finds a family in secretive Cowboy's gang of tough, homeless kids.

Newton, Suzanne. *I Will Call It Georgie's Blues.* 1983. New York: Dell, paper (0-440-94090-7). Ages 14–16.

The church congregation has no idea that their minister expects perfection from his family and metes out harsh punishment if he is disappointed. Fifteen-year-old Neal can cope with his father's demands. His little brother Georgie can't.

Okimoto, Jean Davies. *Molly by Any Other Name.* 1990. New York: Scholastic (0-590-42993-0). Ages 14–18.

Molly is Asian; her adoptive parents are white. After she discovers she can request a search for her birth mother when she reaches the age of 18, she decides to pursue answers to some long-suppressed questions.

Paulsen, Gary. *Harris & Me: A Summer Remembered.* 1993. New York: Harcourt (0-15-292877-4). Ages 14–16.

A boy is sent to spend the summer with his feisty young cousin on a farm and not only has the time of his life but also learns what it means to be a part of a real family.

Pfeffer, Susan. *Family of Strangers.* 1992. New York: Bantam (0-553-08364-3); Dell, paper (0-440-21895-0). Ages 13–16.

Conceived as a replacement for the brother who died as a toddler, Abby has grown up ignored and unloved in the middle of a busy, disconnected family that is ignorant of how troubled she is until she tries to kill herself.

Radin, Ruth Yaffe. *All Joseph Wanted.* 1991. New York: Macmillan (0-02-776641-6). Ages 11–14.

Though the fact that his mother can't read embarrasses Joseph, he's always been willing to help her. After she becomes lost on a bus because she's unable to make out the street signs, both Joseph and his mom realize things must change.

Sachs, Marilyn. *What My Sister Remembered.* 1992. New York: Dutton (0-525-44953-1). Ages 11–14.

Aunt Karen and Uncle Walter adopted Molly after her parents died, but they didn't adopt Molly's older sister, Beth. When Beth and her adoptive parents pay a visit, Molly finally finds out why.

Salat, Christina. *Living in Secret.* 1993. New York: Bantam (0-553-08670-7); Dell, paper (0-440-40905-0). Ages 12–14.

Although Amelia has wanted to live with her mother ever since her parents' divorce, the courts think Mom isn't a proper role model because she is a lesbian. Running away with Mom and Mom's partner, Janey, strikes Amelia as the perfect solution.

Taylor, Mildred. *Roll of Thunder, Hear My Cry*. 1976. New York: Dial (0-8037-7473-7); Bantam, paper (0-553-25450-2). Ages 11–14.

Unlike most black families in their small Mississippi town during the Depression, the Logans own the land they farm. Young Cassie tells the story of their struggle to keep it and to keep their family strong and together.

Thesman, Jean. *The Rain Catchers*. 1991. New York: Houghton (0-395-55333-4); Avon, paper (0-380-71711-5). Ages 13–16.

Abandoned by her mother as a child, Grayling, now 14, has grown up in a household of nurturing women, headed by her strong, loving grandmother. Although she loves her family dearly, she's no longer satisfied to sit with them over steaming cups of tea; she wants to know the secrets of her past.

Vail, Rachel. *Do-Over*. 1992. New York: Orchard/Richard Jackson (0-531-05460-8); Avon, paper (0-380-72180-5). Ages 12–15.

Whit's older sister is always with her boyfriend. His mom hides her unhappiness by cleaning house and cuddling her beagle, and his dad's making a play for his teacher. Where does that leave Whit?

Woodson, Jacqueline. *From the Notebooks of Melanin Sun*. 1995. New York: Scholastic/Blue Sky (0-590-45880-9). Ages 12–15.

Thirteen-year-old African American Melanin is shocked when his mother informs him that she has fallen in love with a student in her law school class—a woman, a white woman.

"If she [my mother] was a dyke, then what did that make me?"

—Melanin, from *The Notebooks of Melanin Sun*

School: For Better or Worse

COMPLETION OF SCHOOL has traditionally been considered one of the steps necessary to enter adulthood, but *The State of America's Children: 1995,* a publication issued by the Children's Defense Fund, reveals some alarming news about today's youth and their attitudes toward education. Among other things, it tells us that even in the face of new, stronger legislation, "2,217 teenagers drop out of school each day," and each year spent in poverty reduces the chance a young person will finish high school by the age of 19. The reasons for such grim revelations, some of which are beyond control of the students themselves, range from poverty and school violence to insufficient equipment and learning incentives. The following books explore some of the causes of student disaffection, including learning disabilities, and suggest alternatives to traditional education and learning strategies that can help individuals identify their educational priorities and make the most of their school years.

NONFICTION

Barrett, Susan. *It's All in Your Head: A Guide to Understanding Your Brain and Boosting Your Brain Power.* 1992. Minneapolis: Free Spirit (0-915793-45-8). Ages 11–15.

A resource teacher for gifted students puts her classroom know-how into action in a combination information-exercise book. First published in 1985, this could have used some new listings in the bibliography, but that doesn't negate the value of Barrett's tips for improving memory, enhancing creativity, and sharpening thinking and listening skills. That she's packed the book with brain-stretching exercises and facts about a host of brain-related stuff—from IQ to dreams to biofeedback—makes this clever, enthusiastic book an "instruction manual for the mind" that's hard to put down. Black-and-white cartoon illustrations make the book even more approachable.

Cohen, Susan, and Daniel Cohen. *Teenage Competition: A Survival Guide.* 1987. New York: Evans (0-87131-487-8). Ages 13–18. O.P.

Regarding competition as an inescapable part of life that can be detrimental as well as beneficial, the Cohens explain how to make certain that what a person strives for is really worthwhile. Using an easygoing, up-beat tone that will appeal to a teenage audience, they examine what's good and what's bad about competition and look at how rivalry shows up in family life, in peer-group and school situations, in sports, and in boy-girl relationships. Examples used to illustrate the discussion range from authentic sounding to simplistic and patronizing ("Let's imagine an intelligent observer from some distant planet, one who knows just about as much about human behavior as you know about the behavior of herring gulls . . ."), to just plain dated by today's standards. Despite that, the authors' view of how easily such things as SAT scores and popularity polls become false barometers of success makes intriguing reading, and their guidelines for setting more meaningful personal goals are grounded in common sense. Unfortunately, the book is now out of print, so hang on to the copy you already have: there's virtually nothing else on the subject.

Cummings, Rhoda, and Gary Fisher. *The School Survival Guide for Kids with LD.* 1991. Minneapolis: Free Spirit, paper (0-915793-32-6). Ages 10–14.

In this helpful companion to *The Survival Guide for Kids with LD,* following, the authors explain learning disabilities (LD) in a way young readers will easily understand, then discuss specific strategies that will make classroom learning experiences more successful. Cartoon drawings and the authors' encouraging tone make the suggestions seem more like fun than schoolwork, whether the subject at hand is math, language, or interpersonal relationships. Suggestions for better organizing time and work, memorization tricks, and guidelines for improving handwriting are presented, as are alternatives to try when reading itself is the problem. Sensitive to the difficulties LD children have with peers, the authors also deal with ways kids can cope with teasing and handle other types of conflicts in the classroom or at recess. Although their discussion of peer relationships is general at best, their advice is certainly good: think before you act.

Cummings, Rhoda, and Gary Fisher. *The Survival Guide for Kids with LD.* 1990. Minneapolis: Free Spirit, paper (0-915793-18-0). Ages 10–14.

While the *School Survival Guide* (Cummings and Fisher, preceding) concentrates on skills learning disabled students can use in class, this text focuses largely on facts about LD, or "learning different." Emphasizing that having a learning disability "does not mean you are retarded! It does not mean you are dumb!" the authors discuss several different types of problems and the rationale behind LD special education programs. They also lend insight into the particular stresses LD youngsters face and suggest ways to deal with pressure from parents, teachers, and peers who don't always understand the impact a learning disability has on everyday life. Cartoon drawings, an open format, and bold headlines provide browser appeal.

Cummings, Rhoda, and Gary Fisher. *The Survival Guide for Teenagers with LD* (Learning Differences).* 1993. Minneapolis: Free Spirit, paper (0-915793-51-2). Ages 14–18.

For an older readership than the two listed previously, this book alerts individuals with learning disabilities to their legal rights at school and explains how they can become advocates in shaping their own individualized education plan (IEP) and their futures. Fisher, a school psychologist, and Cummings, with background in education and an adult son with LD, go well beyond the high-school setting here, covering everything from preparing for college and getting a job and a driver's license to dating and living independently. They present a reassuring and effective merging of special needs issues with matters all teens have in common. Further readings are scattered throughout; a cassette is also available.

"Having LD means that you learn some things differently. It doesn't mean you come from a different planet."
—from *The Survival Guide for Teenagers with LD*

Dentemaro, Christine, and Rachel Kranz. *Straight Talk about Student Life.* 1993. New York: Facts On File (0-8160-2735-8). Ages 14–18.

For an older audience than Meg Schneider's *Help! My Teacher Hates Me,* this book in the Straight Talk series covers some of the same territory but in a less lively (the text is not anecdotal), less thorough fashion. The advice, which is aimed mostly at middle-class, college-bound youth, is intended to help teenagers make wise choices regarding their educational goals, whether involving study habits, extracurricular activities, social relationships, or problems at home that affect school performance. This is not a book teens will readily pick up—the format and dust jacket are unattractive at best—but it does contain some useful tips on getting the most out of school and using education as a tool for self-discovery.

"Learning what you want and how to go after it may be the most important thing you can learn from your time in school."
—from *Straight Talk about Student Life*

Goldentyer, Debra. *Dropping Out of School.* 1994. Austin, Tex.: Steck-Vaughn (0-8114-3526-1). Ages 14–17.

If you must leave school, don't leave it for the wrong reasons. That's the underlying message of this helpful book, part of the Teen Hot Line series. Although readers won't find the text as congenial in tone as Wirths and Bowman-Kruhm's *I Hate School,* the book does a respectable job of addressing the most common complaints about school—it's boring, it's difficult, it takes time that I could be using to earn money or to do something I like. Without lecturing, Goldentyer establishes a strong case for staying in school, not simply because of a dropout's dismal job outlook, but also because of the social and cultural opportunities that will be missed. She also recognizes that some kids are bound to drop out, by choice or by necessity. For them, she examines alternatives to leaving school and talks about the GED and other options for "getting ahead by going back." Black-and-white photos are fuzzy, but the book is loaded with statistics and contains some useful further resources as well as some interesting comments from teenagers who've dropped out or are seriously considering doing so.

Hall, David E. *Living with a Learning Disability: A Guide for Students.* 1993. Minneapolis: Lerner (0-8225-0036-1). Ages 11–14.

The format and tone of this book lack the kid appeal of Cummings and Fisher's Survival Guides, but this is still a useful book to have on hand. Hall, a pediatrician, presents current knowledge in no-nonsense, easy-to-understand text, explains what learning disabilities are (and are not) and what causes them, and notes basic characteristics of several of the more common types. His tone is encouraging, and he includes some valuable learning strategies. But like Levine, following, who writes for an older audience, Hall makes it plain that there are no easy answers. His book is a concerned response to familiar questions young teens ask about learning problems, written in a fashion that won't overwhelm them with details or sugarcoat the facts they want or need.

Landau, Elaine. *Teenagers Talk about School . . . and Open Their Hearts about Their Concerns.* 1989. Englewood Cliffs, N.J.: Messner (0-671-64568-4); paper (0-671-68148-6). Ages 12–18.

Personal testimonies based on interviews with a cross section of American teens are the core of a book that presents a grim, even alarming view of American high schools today. Twenty-three junior-high and high-school students reflect on the educational and social aspects of the school environment they've experienced. Some express a love for learning and school, but most view school as a boring place, a place where academic, parental, and peer pressures collide to cause them pain and even humiliation. Unfortunately, Landau has not managed to preserve much of the personal voice of her speakers. There's a sameness about sentence structure and word usage that suggests a heavy editorial hand. It's the individualizing details in the accounts that leave an impact. Through them comes a sense of what kids really experience, whether it's the struggle of an inner-city boy whose school is run by gangs or the appeals of an Asian immigrant who's desperately trying to find friends.

"Most of my friends have cheated on tests in school at one time or another. . . . Nobody wants to cheat. But if it's a choice of being honest or of getting a grade, most kids will try for the A. That may sound wrong, but we didn't make the rules, we're just trying to get by."

—Michael, a student, from *Teenagers Talk about School*

Levine, Mel. *Keeping a Head in School: A Student's Book about Learning Abilities and Learning Disorders.* 1990. Cambridge, Mass.:

Educators Publishing Service, paper (0-8388-2069-7). Ages 13–18.

A textbookish layout and 300-plus pages will scare off some teenage readers, but those who persevere will find a wealth of information on a topic frequently misunderstood. Levine explains a variety of difficulties and describes how they affect an individual in school and in social situations. He goes on to consider four basic operations—reading, writing, arithmetic, and spelling—identifying the particular problems students may face in each of these areas and suggesting simple strategies they can use when they are unable to process information in the usual way. Levine is realistic about the obstacles students with LD must overcome, but he urges them not to use their problem as an excuse to give up. He encourages them to look toward the future, assuring them that what they'll face in the post-school adult world will seem much less formidable than what they're dealing with now. More formal in approach than Cummings and Fisher's books but just as sensitive to the issues.

Llwellyn, Grace. *The Teenage Liberation Handbook: How to Quit School and Get a Real Life and Education.* 1991. Eugene, Ore.: Lowry House, paper (0-9629591-0-3). Ages 14–18.

Parents and teachers probably won't like this book. They'll argue that leaving school dooms a young person to a low-paying job and that Llwellyn's "experiential" approach to education is too unbalanced and too narrow. A former teacher, Llwellyn is familiar with the arguments, and she counters them nicely with a thought-provoking discussion that points to homeschooling as the best educational choice for most young people: "healthy kids can teach themselves what they need to know through books, various people, thinking, and other means." She's marshaled enthusiastic commentary from self-taught youth to help her prove her point as she explains how teenagers can overcome parental, legal, and practical roadblocks to home study. She even suggests creative activities and readings (a limited but excellent selection) to help teens come to grips with such subjects as math, English, and social studies. Because she's less pessimistic about the value of higher education than she is about compulsory schooling, she encourages teenagers to prepare for college and tackles the problem of college entrance without high-school credentials in a separate chapter based on information gathered from college admissions officers. Llwellyn's strident, recurring anti-school sentiments eventually become tiresome, but her enthusiasm for learning, her great faith in kids, and the wonderful educational possibilities she presents make her book tantalizing reading for teens who can't make it in school but have the discipline and the passion to learn on their own.

"Schools and schooling are increasingly irrelevant to the great enterprises of the planet. No one believes anymore that scientists are trained in science classes or politicians in civics classes or poets in English classes. The truth is that schools don't really teach anything except how to obey orders." John Taylor Gatto, New York State Teacher of the Year, 1991

—from *The Teenage Liberation Handbook*

Lucas, Eileen. *The Mind at Work.* 1993. Brookfield, Conn.: Millbrook (1-56294-300-6). Ages 12–15.

The terminology (kinesthetic learning, algorithm, etc.), the typeface, and the approach make this book a better bet for more sophisticated readers than Barrett's book. But formality notwithstanding, it still contains plenty that's practical—for example, tips for taking tests and managing homework and information for helping readers argue successfully and think critically. Lucas makes definite distinctions between perception, learning, and memory, and she encourages readers to have faith in their own ability to think clearly and effectively, quoting author Peter Kline: "Somewhere inside of you is your own sort of genius—waiting and wondering when you'll care enough to call it forth." An extensive list of adult and children's resources is appended.

Real Lives: Eleven Teenagers Who Don't Go to School. Ed. by Grace Llwellyn. 1993. Eugene, Ore.: Lowry House, paper (0-9629591-3-9). Ages 14–18.

Careful to differentiate homeschooling from dropping out, Llwellyn, author of *The Teenage Liberation Handbook,* cited previously, offers another, less direct push for autodidacts. Her gathering of eleven personal profiles confronts head on what it's like to learn at home. The length of the profiles is bound to put off some readers. A bit more editorial intervention would have helped. But the voices and personalities of the writers have been diligently maintained, and they shine through as the teens explain why they abandoned traditional education and what has taken its place. A scattering of information about newsletters, books, and other resources will be of interest as well.

Roby, Cynthia. *When Learning Is Tough: Kids Talk about Their Learning Disabilities.* 1993. Chicago: Albert Whitman (0-8075-8892-X). Ages 11–14.

Eight young people, ranging in age from 8 to 13, tell about their learning problems and their lives. Black-and-white photos show their earnest faces as they talk about what they do well—one is an artist, another a runner, a third a poet—and their problems in school. They recall cutting remarks from classmates as well as their relief at discovering that being learning disabled wasn't the same as being stupid. But Roby goes farther than simply introducing some pretty nice kids; she makes it clear that with the right resources, such as extra help from parents, a computer, or a special class, children with learning disabilities can be happy and successful in school.

Salzman, Marian, and Teresa Reisgies. *Greetings from High School.* 1991. New York: Peterson's Guides, paper (1-56079-055-5). Ages 12–18.

This lively paperback catchall relies on questions, student comments, boxed lists, and quick-reference tips to inform its readers. Chapters on subjects such as romance, schoolwork, and stress outline issues on the minds of most teens. The book also introduces some unusual topics: for example, the pros and cons of different kinds of high schools (public, private, single-sex). Though the book does address some matters of interest to young people entering the work force right after high school, the text is really targeted to middle-class college-bound students. Not all subjects receive equal attention. Health-related matters fare the worst: safe sex gets two paragraphs; steroids, a big concern in school sports today, aren't even mentioned. But teenagers will grab the book anyway. They'll like its attractive cover, and the fact that the text is broken up into small chunks will be a great inducement to browsers.

Schneider, Meg. *Help! My Teacher Hates Me . . . A School Survival Guide for Kids 10 to 14 Years Old.* 1994. New York: Workman, paper (1-56305-492-2). Ages 10–14.

Respect the school experience; think things through; accept responsibility for personal actions. To those reasonable basics Schneider adds good-sense advice on a host of school-related concerns, from cheating and teacher woes to slipping grades and sports hassles. In keeping with the changes in many of today's schools, she's also included information on AIDS as a factor in the student population, physical assault on campus, and sexual harassment by a teacher. If

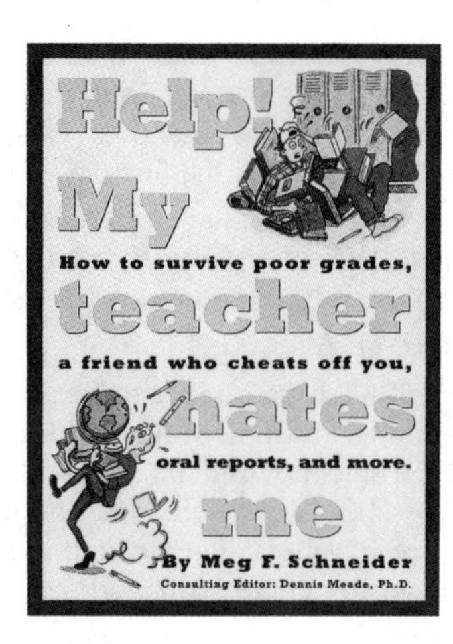

Schneider is a bit too wordy, she makes up for it nicely by presenting issues from many sides, not just the student's. She also speculates on how people involved in a given situation may be expected to act. Her book will help kids navigate school corridors with more awareness if not more ease.

Wirths, Claudine, and Mary Bowman-Kruhm. *Circle of Friends.* 1993. New York: Twenty-First Century Books (0-8050-2073-X). Ages 11–14.

———. *Your New School.* 1993. New York: Twenty-First Century Books (0-8050-2074-8). Ages 11–14.

———. *Your Power with Words.* 1993. New York: Twenty-First Century Books (0-8050-2075-6). Ages 11–14.

Written with the same humor and good sense as the authors' 1986 book *I Hate School,* following, these books in the Time to Be a Teen series tackle subjects of even greater interest among young adolescents. Written as dialogues between the authors and "an almost teen," they effectively and practically broach and respond to a host of questions about making, keeping, helping, and losing friends; interpersonal communication; and effecting the transition from elementary school to a middle or junior high school. A strong sense of values underlies the advice, which is neither patronizing nor judgmental as it touches on critical, common issues such as dealing with cliques, talking comfortably with grown-ups, and keeping up with the work in a new school.

Wirths, Claudine G., and Mary Bowman-Kruhm. *I Hate School: How to Hang In & When to Drop Out.* 1986. New York: Harper (0-690-04556-5); paper (0-06-446054-1). Ages 13–17.

A wealth of material exists for the young adult preparing for college or planning a career, but little is available for a teenager simply trying to get through a tough school day. Wirths and Bowman-Kruhm offer one of the few such support books. Their friendly and sympathetic book speaks to restless, unmotivated students, encouraging them to stay in school—if only to avoid a lifetime of dead-end, low-paying work. The authors look briefly at the impact of school social life on student performance and attitude, but their real concern is study skills. Cartoon characters expressing common gripes ("Trying to do homework in my house is impossible," or "Are there any shortcuts to reading?") inaugurate discussion of particular topics that the authors then explore in uncritical, reassuring terms. It's a serious attempt to help kids make the most of their classroom experience, with clever art that will attract kids who like to browse the shelves. *I Hate School* is an older title but still of value.

Wirths, Claudine G. and Mary Bowman-Kruhm. *Upgrade.* 1995. Palo Alto, Calif.: Consulting Psychologists Press/Davis-Black (0-89106-069-3). Ages 12–15.

Although there is plenty of talk about writing webs, source cards, and test taking, this book is definitely not a run-of-the-mill text on study skills. Computers, camcorders, and tape recorders are the focus here, with the authors explaining various, very simple ways the technology can be used to improve the way people learn. The book is not a how-to manual for hardware operation, nor does it plug specific software programs when it describes useful aids such as spellcheckers or outline-creating programs. It is mostly a time- and energy-saving idea book that shows teens how to add a bit of zest to routine chores such as memorizing material, producing reports, or taking tests. A useful glossary of technical terms is appended.

FICTION

Avi. *Nothing but the Truth*. 1991. New York: Watts/Orchard/Richard Jackson (0-531-05959-6); Avon, paper (0-380-71907-X). Ages 12–18.

When Philip Malloy is suspended from school for refusing to comply with a rather silly school rule, no one involved expects the incident to trigger a debate that hits the newspapers.

Barrie, Barbara. *Adam Zigzag*. 1994. New York: Delacorte (0-385-31172-9). Ages 12–14.

In a tale that harks back to her own life, Barrie tells poignantly of dyslexic Adam, whose inability to make sense of the written word affects his self-concept and the lives of his whole family.

Cormier, Robert. *The Chocolate War*. 1974. New York: Pantheon (0-394-82805-4); Dell, paper (0-440-94459-7). Ages 14–18.

When Jerry Renault refuses to sell candy for his parochial school, he makes a powerful enemy of Brother Leon, his instructor, who runs things by turning a blind eye on the activities of a vicious school gang. A sequel, *Beyond the Chocolate War*, set in the same school milieu, was published in 1985.

Hall, Lynn. *Just One Friend*. 1985. New York: Scribner (0-648-18471-0). Ages 14–18.

Following three years of special education, Dory Kjellings is not looking forward to being mainstreamed into regular high school. She thinks she can do it, though, if she can just get one friend to cross the threshold with her on the first day of class.

Hermes, Patricia. *I Hate Being Gifted*. 1990. New York: Putnam (0-399-21687-1). Ages 11–14.

Adults tell KT it's an honor to be in LEAP, the Learning Enrichment Activity Program for gifted students. But KT knows better. She's seen her "weirdo" teacher and heard "LEAP creep" taunts often enough to make her certain her entire sixth-grade year will be a disaster.

Lynch, Chris. *Slot Machine*. 1995. New York: HarperCollins (0-06-023584-5). Ages 13–15.

To prepare him for junior high school in the fall, fat kid Elvin Bishop is sent off to a Christian Brothers' camp that emphasizes what Elvin hates most: sports.

McCants, William D. *Anything Can Happen in High School (and It Usually Does)*. 1993. San Diego: Harcourt (0-15-276604-9); paper (0-15-276605-7). Ages 13–15.

After being dumped by his girlfriend, 15-year-old T. J. Durant starts the Radical Wave, a high-school club for outsiders, to try to win her back.

Mills, Claudia. *Dinah Forever*. 1995. New York: Farrar (0-374-31788-7). Ages 12–15.

This fourth novel about Dinah Seabrooke finds her beginning seventh grade with more than the usual zeal only to be put in her place by ideas that spring from her schoolwork, in particular the scientific prediction that the world will eventually come to an end.

Morpurgo, Michael. *The War of Jenkins' Ear*. 1995. New York: Philomel (0-399-22735-0). Ages 12–14.

Toby fears that his second year at Redlands School will be just as terrible as his first. He realizes he is wrong when he meets Wanda and falls in love for the first time and gets to know classmate Christopher, who convinces Toby he's a reincarnation of Jesus.

Peck, Richard. *Princess Ashley*. 1987. New York: Delacorte (0-385-29561-8); Dell, paper (0-440-20206-X). Ages 12–15.

Sophomore Chelsea Olinter feels wonderful when she's invited to join the most popular crowd in her new school—until she discovers she's been asked because her mother is a high school guidance counselor.

Rapp, Adam. *Missing the Piano*. 1994. New York: Viking (0-670-95340-2). Ages 14–18.

With his mother and sister in New York and his father and shrewish stepmother totally unprepared to care for him, Mike Tegroff suddenly finds himself dumped off at Matthews Military Academy, an ugly breeding ground of racism and intimidation.

Stone, Bruce. *Been Clever Forever*. 1988. New York: Harper (0-06-447013-X). Ages 14–18.

Tenth grader Stephen A. Douglass is a smart wisecracker and everyone expects a lot from him. It takes a run-in with a disturbed teacher to help him understand that the only expectations he needs to live up to are his own.

Vail, Rachel. *Ever After*. 1994. New York: Orchard/Richard Jackson (0-531-06838-2). Ages 11–14.

Although Molly has begun to chafe under her best friend Vicky's domineering attitude, she's too insecure to really rebel until she discovers that Vicky has betrayed her by reading her diary.

Wilkinson, Brenda. *Definitely Cool*. 1993. New York: Scholastic (0-590-46186-9). Ages 11–14.

Fitting in and making friends in her new junior high aren't the only worrisome issues for Roxanne, who lives in a Bronx housing project and is bused to school in upscale Riverdale. Race and economics are topics that concern her and her African American friends as well.

Wolff, Virginia Euwer. *Probably Still Nick Swansen*. 1988. New York: Holt (0-8050-0701-6). Ages 14–18.

Nick Swansen has minimal brain dysfunction. Although he isn't certain exactly what that is, he knows that's why he's in Special Ed Room 19. But even though he needs some extra help with lessons, he sees no reason why he can't take his pretty former classmate to the school prom.

Woodson, Jacqueline. *Maizon at Blue Hill*. 1992. New York: Delacorte (0-385-30796-9); Dell, paper (0-440-40899-7). Ages 11–14.

Black, smart, and confident, seventh-grader Maizon Singh leaves her beloved grandmother and happy life to take advantage of a boarding school scholarship. The school is challenging and the campus beautiful, but Maizon doesn't fit in—not with the white kids, who seem to fear her, or with the black ones, who tell her she shouldn't mix with whites.

Me: My Rights, My Friends, Myself

ESTABLISHING A REALISTIC SENSE of self is one of the most difficult developmental tasks of adolescence. Most teenagers have a hard time accepting the fact that it's not possible to be perfect; few realize how their struggle to affirm themselves affects their relationships with parents, friends, the opposite sex, and society as a whole. Although self-esteem and identity are common themes in realistic young adult fiction, only recently have nonfiction writers begun to deal with them in a self-help context. Now, terms such as *positive self-talk, assertiveness,* and *codependency,* and the theories associated with them, are trickling down into teenage books. Self-concept workbooks are being used in some schools, and books on everything from setting personal goals and making friends to exploring legal rights and changing the world are now readily available to independent readers. Because weight concerns are also tied to self-concept, books on the subject are included in the following roundup, though they might just as easily have been part of the section on health issues.

NONFICTION

Barry, Lynda. *Come Over, Come Over.* 1990. New York: HarperPerennial, paper (0-06-096504-5). Ages 15–18.

This book bears no resemblance to a young adult self-help manual. It's actually a collection of comics culled from the multi-talented Barry's syndicated strip, "Ernie Pook's Comeek." But it's much more than an entertaining miscellany of cartoons. Maybonne Mullen, a freckle-faced redhead who may well be Barry's alter ego, is the featured character. The strips chronicle her fourteenth year—from arguments with her mother and experiments with cigarettes, alcohol, and boys to a rapprochement with her estranged dad. Barry's quirky, sophisticated humor won't appeal to everyone, but the frank, poignant collection captures the frustrations, the hopes, and the pleasures of growing up female in a refreshing new way. Girls can identify with Maybonne and laugh at her at the same time. Barry's 1994 book, *It's So Magic* (HarperPerennial) is more concerned with Marlys, Maybonne's irrepressible grade-school sister, than with Maybonne, but it does include some relevant teen issues, among them the date rape of Maybonne's girlfriend.

Beckelman, Laurie. *Body Blues.* 1994. Morristown, N.J.: Silver Burdett/ Crestwood House (0-89686-842-7); paper (0-382-24743-4). Ages 11–14.

As do others in the Hot Line series, this book packs a lot into forty-eight pages. The subject here is body image, certainly one of the top concerns of the teen years. Unlike many books on the link between body image and self-esteem, this one is directed to boys as well as to girls, with boys appearing in photos and used in the examples. Beckelman briefly examines the cultural underpinnings of the beauty myth and the influence of genetic heritage, then supplies ten suggestions for helping teens overcome the influence of their "inner critic" and focus on their strengths. Whether teens will actually "ask others what they like about you . . . and what they think are your strengths" (suggestion 3) is questionable, but Beckelman is certainly right on the mark when she advises teens to celebrate themselves: "By valuing yourself as you are today, you can become a better you tomorrow."

Bode, Janet. *Beating the Odds: Stories of Unexpected Achievers.* 1991. New York: Watts (0-531-15230-8). Ages 12–18.

Eleven young adults who've overcome enormous odds tell how they feel about themselves and what they've accomplished in a collection of upbeat profiles that includes one cartoon story. Unfortunately the picture-story doesn't work very well. Sandwiched between personal narratives, it is

likely to be ignored. And while it deals with a boy's experience in an abusive home, it is far less affecting than the detailed, unpretentious first-person narratives surrounding it that are more dramatic and more poignant. Declaring that self-esteem is the "only drug" she needs, Keisha describes what it's like to live in a welfare hotel overrun with drug pushers; 18-year-old Pawnee, a teenage mother, talks about making her daughter proud of her; and Matthew, a college freshman who was imprisoned at the age of 16 for shooting someone, explains how he refocused his life. Bode alternates kids' words with commentary from adults—some professional counselors and teachers, some simply adults who've overcome difficult situations in their own lives. Their combined testimonies provide readers with a firm, but also realistic, sense of possibilities, which Bode reinforces with simple but important advice on how to begin to turn life around: "read, reach out, keep busy, keep trying."

"You need positive things in your life. You need to be able to say, 'I did that kid's workshop and, damn it went well.' You need things you can brag about inside yourself. . . . That's my drug, self-esteem."

—Keisha, 16, from *Beating the Odds*

Bode, Janet. *Trust & Betrayal: Real Life Stories of Friends and Enemies.* 1995. New York: Delacorte (0-385-32105-8). Ages 14–18.

Even though this book is more scattershot than some of the author's previous ones, it will still speak loudly to teenagers. Peer relationships, friendly and not, are its subject, with Bode using a collection of first-person accounts to determine subject boundaries. Teens here relay concerns seriously and frankly, and, as is usual in Bode's books, they come across as distinct, real kids, not always composed or very articulate. Topical issues—teen pregnancy, homosexuality, even sexual harassment—woven into the testimonies dilute the trust/betrayal theme to some extent, and Bode's attempt to incorporate some interview-style segments among the teens' narratives doesn't work very well. However, she still gives readers lots to think about, presenting the topic in a string of scenarios that sound extraordinarily real.

Carrel, Annette. *It's the Law! A Young Person's Guide to Our Legal System.* 1994. Volcano, Calif.: Volcano Press, paper (1-884244-01-7). Ages 15–18.

Unlike Hempleman's *Teen Legal Rights,* following, which is a comprehensive view of laws pertaining to young people, this provides teenagers with a view of the legal system itself. Carrel focuses on types of laws, how they are made and changed, and what happens when they're broken, including what occurs when a person is arrested and put on trial. She conveys all this in easy-to-grasp language, at the same time instilling readers with a respect for the legal system and a picture of jurisprudence as an enabling force in society. A selection of activities makes the book excellent for use in the classroom.

Dawson, Jill. *How Do I Look?* 1991. London, Eng.: Virago, paper (1-85381-222-6). Ages 15–18.

Though this book's British perspective will deter some American readers, its subject translates well into American experience. Setting the stage with the story of her own seven-year battle with eating disorders, Dawson presents a patchwork of excerpts from letters and interviews she conducted with an articulate multicultural selection of British women, ranging in age from 17 into their early 20s. Some angry and confused, some confident and happy, the young women reflect on a variety of contemporary feminist issues, among them, cultural ideals of female perfection, eating disorders as a misguided means of self-determination, and the use of clothing to make personal and political statements. Taken together, the testimonies reveal an intriguing slice of modern culture. Not a downbeat, strident book of behavioral guideposts, this is, instead, a sensitive, forthright consideration of important women's issues meant to provoke thought, not shape it.

"I'm not sure what I'm aiming for when I look in the mirror. Some days I'm happy with the way I look, others I'm not. I don't know if this is to do with my lipstick or my attitude. The sad part is that I've come to hate my body so much, I blame it for everything."

—Helen, 23, from *How Do I Look?*

Duvall, Lynn. *Respecting Our Differences: A Guide to Getting Along in a Changing World.* 1994. Minneapolis: Free Spirit, paper (0-915793-72-5). Ages 14–18.

Although neither as powerful nor as immediate as Kuklin's *Speaking Out,* following, this is far more practical in its approach to prejudice. In fact, the book is actually an activist's manual designed to promote cultural awareness and diversity. Neither preachy nor strident in its approach, it briefly alerts readers to important diversity issues—from theories about race and the idea of political correctness to the current immigration controversy. The book's organization is haphazard, but Duvall has loaded chapters with ideas and resources to pursue. Probing questions in "Time Out" sections can inspire independent thought or classroom discussion, and the scattering of anecdotes featuring young people working to overcome prejudice are a direct call for action. Duvall's agenda may be obvious, but so is her deep sense of commitment.

Gay, Kathlyn. *I Am Who I Am: Speaking Out about Multiracial Identity.* 1995. New York: Watts (0-531-11214-4). Ages 14–18.

Although Gay does not write traditional self-help material, her latest book will help teens channel their thoughts into action. Combining input from child development experts with carefully chosen scenarios and personal comments, she offers a positive yet realistic look at what it's like growing up with a mixed-race background. Her wide-angle perspective touches on cultural, historical, and political aspects of the subject—from current controversies surrounding transracial adoptions to racial pigeonholing. Gay obviously recognizes discrimination, but she puts it into balanced perspective by emphasizing that race is only part of what makes an individual "who I am." For teens who need support or want to become active in fighting prejudice, she includes a chapter explaining the work of several important organizations.

Heine, Arthur J. *Surviving after High School: Overcoming Life's Hurdles.* 1991. Virginia Beach, Va.: J-Mart Press (0-9628376-0-1); paper (0-9628376-1-X). Ages 16–up.

Directed to emancipated teens or high-school graduates ready to live independently, Heine's book is filled with practical advice about entering the "jungle called 'real life.'" With a dash of homespun philosophy, his text spells out how to become self-sufficient, including advice on everything from job hunting to buying a car and renting an apartment. Using reproductions of actual forms, Heine explains important facts about insurance, taxes, leases, and loan agreements, then supplies a few words about managing health concerns—some counsel about safe sex, plus tips on exercise and nutrition. Chapters conclude with space for jotting down notes.

Hempleman, Kathleen A. *Teen Legal Rights: A Guide for the '90s.* 1994. Westport, Conn.: Greenwood (0-313-28760-0). Ages 14–18.

Libraries may consign this book to the reference shelf because of its rather stiff price (nearly $40). A circulating copy might be warranted as well, for teens will find it a storehouse of valuable information. An attorney in private practice, Hempelman has done her homework, not only in laying out the legal specifics, but also in targeting concerns of prime interest to young adults.

Using a minimum of legal jargon and a question-answer approach, she explains and comments on a wide array of rights—from emancipation to matters of sexual privacy, personal appearance, and treatment in juvenile court. She also provides an excellent glossary, full notes, and further readings. Despite a scattering of black-and-white photos and the use of boldface type for the questions, the format of the book is dull. The content, however, is both exceptionally comprehensive and clearly expressed.

Hoose, Phillip. *It's Our World, Too! Stories of Young People Who Are Making a Difference.* 1993. Boston: Little, Brown (0-316-37241-2). Ages 11–15.

This is not a self-help book in the traditional sense, but because Hoose seeks to raise social consciousness and promote youthful idealism, his book may be of value in helping young people become involved in activities that can build their self-esteem. Following some historical perspective on the influence young people have had on their world, Hoose offers personal profiles of some contemporary young "movers and shakers" who are aiding the homeless; speaking out against gangs, racism, and sexism; and promoting peace. Final chapters set down specific ways enthusiasm for a cause can be channeled into positive actions. The oversized book is attractive enough to encourage browsers. Black-and-white photographs, sidebars, and pithy comments from teen activists will immediately grab reader attention, while the intensity, sincerity, and optimism expressed by the kids give readers a clear signal that they can change themselves by working to make changes in their world.

Johnson, Julie Tallard. *Celebrate You: Building Your Self Esteem.* 1991. Minneapolis: Lerner (0-8225-0046-9). Ages 12–15.

Johnson encourages teenagers to take pride in themselves in this upbeat 72-page guide that touches on both the practical and the spiritual. A quiz sets the stage for the simply written text that describes how negative thoughts and outside circumstances influence one's self-concept. Johnson explains the concept of "positive self-talk" and supplies a list of simple ways to boost the spirits: exercise, talk to a supportive friend, and meditate, among them. She also talks about making choices and accepting responsibility for them, an integral part of building self-esteem. Concise comments from teenagers appear throughout the text, and Johnson contributes personal perspective in a final chapter in which she speaks of her own childhood lack of confidence and of the strength she now derives from her belief in "a power greater than all the troubles and challenges you face." She doesn't proselytize, but her message is unmistakable. The author is a psychotherapist who works with teens.

Kohl, Candice. *The String on a Roast Won't Catch Fire in the Oven: An A–Z Encyclopedia of Common Sense for the Newly Independent Young Adult.* 1993. Littleton, Colo.: Gylantic, paper (1-880197-07-3). Ages 16–up.

Although a lot of what's here may seem like common sense to adults, emancipated teens or teens about to embark on life on their own at college, in an apartment, or in some other situation may be very grateful for Kohl's tips. She assumes young adults know little if anything about taking care of themselves. With the most obvious exception being joining a church, she has a word or two to say about nearly every aspect of independent life—from apartment hunting, budgeting, and shopping for insurance to mundane household chores. It's her motherly tone and her thorough coverage of the routine aspects of daily life that most distinguish her book from Heine's, mentioned previously. Of course, what Kohl suggests won't necessarily be the same as the wisdom proffered by an individual's own parents, but her book is a handy resource that answers questions teens usually don't think to ask before they actually leave—and may be too embarrassed to ask once they've packed their bags, said goodbye, and closed the door.

Kolodny, Nancy J. *When Food's a Foe: How to Confront and Conquer Eating Disorders*. Rev. ed. 1992. Boston: Little, Brown, paper (0-316-50181-6). Ages 14–18.

Questions and awareness activities are the heart of this book that revolves around the idea that sufferers of eating disorders can do much to help themselves if they admit their illness, find out about it, and take positive action to control it. Kolodny, head of a behavior-modification eating-disorders program in Connecticut, prefaces the practical part of her text with solid background on anorexia and bulimia and a thought-provoking analysis of the link between body image and self-esteem. Then, through combined use of charts, insightful questions, and straightforward discussion, she helps readers pinpoint self-destructive patterns and defuse the "negative triggers" that make food a destructive force in their lives. Her text is both positive and realistic. Kolodny never pretends getting well will be easy or that her suggestions will work for everyone. In fact, she includes an excellent chapter about avenues of extra help for teens who acknowledge they can't go it alone.

"My brother saw the movie *Ghostbusters* and told me that I was like Sigourney Weaver in the film. He said I'd been invaded by a powerful demon like she was supposed to have been, and that mine was anorexia."

—Larrayne, 16, from *When Food's a Foe*

Kronenwetter, Michael. *Under 18: Knowing Your Rights*. 1993. New York: Enslow (0-89490-434-5). Ages 14–18.

Following a chapter that puts children's rights and responsibilities into broad social and legal context, Kronenwetter takes a responsible look at laws pertaining to contemporary young people's lives at home and at school. Case studies show not only the kind of regulations currently in place to protect the young, but also the frequency with which these laws are overlooked or purposely violated. With due consideration for variations in interpretation by the states, Kronenwetter tackles many areas of concern to young adults, including the right to personal privacy, school dress codes, and classroom rights. The format is more conducive to report writing than personal-interest reading, but Kronenwetter's attention to detail and smooth writing style will capture curious readers anyway.

Kuklin, Susan. *Speaking Out: Teenagers Talk on Sex, Race and Identity*. 1993. New York: Putnam (0-399-22343-6); paper (0-399-22532-3). Ages 14–18.

Of all of Kuklin's interview-style books, this will have the greatest impact because it is set in one of the places teenagers identify with most—the school. A year's worth of observations of students and faculty at a Manhattan public high school with an ethnically diverse student population provided Kuklin with an eye-opening perspective on prejudice among today's young people and on the impact discrimination has on personal identity. Students and teachers speak openly about being teased because of a speech impediment or a learning disability or because of sexual orientation—but racial and ethnic prejudice are, by far, the main topics of discussion. What the comments reveal will either shock readers considerably or validate what they already know. In either case, Kuklin's revelations are compelling enough and genuine enough to persuade readers to focus on their own prejudices. Kuklin is a bit arbitrary in her mixing of personal testimony and biographical profiles, but that won't dilute the book's value as a tool for class discussion or as a stern reminder of the power of words and actions to hurt and to heal.

Landau, Elaine. *The Beauty Trap.* 1994. New York: Macmillan/New Discovery (0-02-751389-0). Ages 13–17.

This hasn't the intimate feel of Dawson's *How Do I Look?,* but in terms of helping young women understand how culture affects the evolution of self-concept and the status of women in society, this is better organized and more thorough. It is also intelligent and thought provoking. Forceful personal stories alternate with factual material to present a wide-ranging view of women confronted by the "beauty myth," from Barbie dolls and Miss America to breast implants and bulimia. Landau strays occasionally into more-general discussions of women's roles in society, but her book is largely an exposé of a contemporary problem that she feels can be solved only when women themselves unite. For readers interested in exploring the subject further, she includes a list of readings and names of activist organizations "concerned about the status of women."

Landau, Elaine. *Weight: A Teenage Concern.* 1991. New York: Dutton/Lodestar (0-525-67335-0). Ages 12–17.

The embarrassments and prejudices associated with being overweight reverberate through the comments of many of the teens who tell their stories here. Landau sets their accounts in perspective, adding information about what causes obesity, how fatness is related to anorexia nervosa and bulimia, what society thinks about "heavyweights," and the kinds of weight-loss methods available today. She goes several steps further than most teenage books on the subject by also including testimonies of teens who have come to terms with their extra-large size. She also takes a quick look at how organizations such as NAAFA, the National Association to Advance Fat Acceptance, promote self-pride and fight discrimination.

Landau, Elaine. *Your Legal Rights: From Custody Battles to School Searches, the Headline-making Cases that Affect Your Life.* 1995. New York: Walker (0-8027-8359-7). Ages 12–15.

Not as specific as Hempelman's *Teen Legal Rights* or as broad in scope as Carrel or Kronenwetter's books, *Your Legal Rights* will intrigue readers because of the preponderance of actual cases it describes. Celebrated and sensational ones (including a few considered to be landmarks) are recounted in an effort to heighten awareness about children's rights, predominantly with respect to child custody, abuse, and neglect. Certainly the stories give the subject flash, and Landau summarizes them smoothly with pivotal commentary as well as enough gritty detail to keep the pages turning. But because discussion of specific rights is very brief and largely relegated to a closing chapter, this is less successful in terms of telling teens about legal particulars than it is for its candid view of how things used to be for young people—and how they sometimes still are.

LeBow, Michael D. *Overweight Teenagers: Don't Bear the Burden Alone.* 1995. New York: Insight Books (0-306-45047-X). Ages 12–17.

The title is a turn-off, but this book, by the director of a Canadian obesity clinic, is one of the best of its kind to come out in the last few years. Although aimed at kids who are obese, not simply "pleasantly plump" or "heavy," its sensible guidelines speak to any weight-conscious teen. Because LeBow understands the stereotypes and the cycle of ridicule and self-hate that frequently accompany obesity, he ministers to the psyche as well as the appetite as he talks about everything from setting goals to keeping off the weight once it's gone. A chapter just for parents further shows his sensitivity. Teens will have to look elsewhere for actual meal plans (LeBow suggests they consult their physician), but some handy charts are appended. Teens who are serious about losing weight and want to do it safely will find this a good place to start.

LeShan, Eda. *What Makes You So Special?* 1992. New York: Dial (0-8037-1155-7). Ages 10–14.

Despite your desire to be "like everyone else," you are special, you are different. That's the message of this book, which explores the environmental and hereditary forces that mold individuality. LeShan's flowing, nontechnical narrative is filled with concrete examples that illustrate how home life, school experiences, peers, family background, and world events influence self-concept and help forge identity. As in many of her books for young people, LeShan draws incidents from her own life (she's now in her seventies) to furnish readers with historical perspective. Understanding but firm in her personal convictions, she functions not only as a narrator and commentator about kids' issues, but also as a compassionate, perceptive children's advocate. Her respect for individual differences and her love of life echo through the text.

LeShan, Eda. *When Kids Drive Kids Crazy.* 1990. New York: Dial (0-8037-0866-1). Ages 10–14.

"I remember very well how I felt when I was growing up and someone made fun of me, or a friend deserted me, or I felt very unpopular," recalls LeShan, who acknowledges how tough it is to be a kid, especially in today's complicated world. Writing in the same honest, sympathetic voice she has used in other books for young people, she mixes personal childhood memories with anecdotes about ordinary kids to establish the rationale underlying many hurtful, bewildering behaviors. Her scope is broad; she considers not only peer influence and the impact of physical and emotional maturation, but also confusing messages about sex and sex-role stereotypes that bombard today's young. A chapter entitled "Special Problems" sensitively discusses kids coping with physical disabilities or extraordinary outside pressures such as poverty, prejudice, or community violence. The idea that our personal relationships help shape us comes through loud and clear.

McCoy, Kathy. *Changes and Choices: A Junior High Survival Guide.* 1989. New York: Putnam/Perigee, paper (0-399-51566-6). Ages 11–15.

The coauthor of the *Teenage Body Book* and a columnist for *Seventeen* magazine addresses 12- to 15-year-olds about some of the challenges they face as they become physically and emotionally mature. Managing to be both sensible and upbeat, McCoy talks first about dealing with the emotional ups and downs that come with adolescence. Complaints about parents ("They favor my brother"; "They don't give me any privacy"; "They expect too much") fill a chapter on changing family relationships. Thorough discussions of friendships, school, and a variety of social situations follow, with McCoy explaining how to cope with such common concerns as first love, teacher trouble, and embarrassing physical changes. Tough topics—the use of recreational drugs and alcohol and premarital sex—are dealt with in a separate section.

McCoy is firm but not shrill in her disapproval of all three activities for this age group. The book's attractive cover photograph should make browsers eager to pick up the oversized paperback.

"I really like my best friend a lot. So why am I so nasty to her sometimes? If a teacher yells at me or me and my mom have a fight before school, I start taking my bad mood out on my friend. I'm scared of losing her and don't know how to stop this."

—Jessica, a student, from *Changes and Choices*

McCoy, Kathy, and Charles Wibbelsman. *Life Happens.* 1996. New York: Berkley/Perigee, paper (0-399-51987-4). Ages 14–18.

The authors of the *New Teenage Body Book* (1992) expand on the discussion of feelings and emotions they inaugurated in their earlier volume. They explore what they call "common crises" and suggest, in an expanded checklist form, ways to get past problems and move on with life. Most of the topics touched on—the death of a family member, teen pregnancy, the end of a romantic relationship, being homosexual, having an alcoholic parent—have been well covered in young adult literature, but this book is particularly successful because it reduces each subject to manageable proportions without oversimplifying and emphasizes the benefits of being open with feelings. One of the best chapters concerns everyday stressors—living up to parental expectations and balancing schoolwork with fun. There are also helpful, clear-cut sections explaining depression and describing what to expect from a mental-health specialist.

Maloney, Michael, and Rachel Kranz. *Straight Talk about Eating Disorders.* 1991. New York: Facts On File (0-06-021641-7); Dell, paper (0-440-21350-9). Ages 14–18.

A doctor and a free-lance writer inform readers about the three best-known eating disorders—anorexia nervosa, bulimia, and compulsive eating. They deal first with society's mixed messages about weight and body image and lay out the basic facts about eating patterns. It's their use of composite, cause-and-effect case studies that distinguish their book. Young adults will need to keep in mind that things are more complicated in real life than they are in these studies, but the intriguing scenarios depict the psychological underpinnings of the illnesses in a way that's bound to sharpen understanding and make it easier for teens to remember the factual information the book supplies.

Moe, Barbara. *Coping with Eating Disorders.* 1991. New York: Rosen (0-8239-1343-0). Ages 12–16.

Straight Talk about Eating Disorders, discussed previously, is more comprehensive as well as more specific about health consequences, but Moe covers some of the same ground in a more accessible way. Without probing deeply, she discusses the characteristics of each of the three major eating disorders—bulimia, anorexia, and compulsive eating—and examines the impact of the media on our weight-conscious culture and how eating disorders arise as a result of family dysfunction. Numerous authentic-sounding thumbnail profiles provide a strong sense of the dangers of destructive eating, and there's discussion of establishing sensible goals for teens ready to confront their illness. A solid selection of follow-up resources rounds out the book.

Nash, Renea D. *Coping as a Biracial/Biethnic Teen.* 1995. New York: Rosen (0-8239-1838-6). Ages 12–14.

Nash is encouraging without being chirpy as she identifies some common problems experienced by biracial individuals, tags the "stages" biracial children go through as they cement their identity, and discusses parental responsibilities in the process. It's all pretty slight, the photos are amateurish, and the book title is a bit misleading as there's very little discussion of biethnicity. Even so, Nash's attempt to get teens to communicate their concerns to their parents and her conclusion that identity is the sum of many parts will start at least some teens on the road to feeling better about themselves.

Parsley, Bonnie M. *The Choice Is Yours: A Teenager's Guide to Self-Discovery, Relationships, Values, and Spiritual Growth.* 1992. New York: Simon & Schuster, paper (0-671-75046-1). Ages 14–18.

There are plenty of books on sexuality, personal relationships, and identity that young adults can turn to, but Parsley's is one of the few that concentrates on the building blocks of humanity: our values. Her Christian identity surfaces in the final chapters (she's actually fairly critical of religious dogma), but her opinions on honesty, independence, kindness, and self-discipline are shared by individuals of many different faiths. In a quiet, serious voice that never scolds, she encourages young people to accept themselves as the first step in handling relationships with parents and peers, and she steers them gently but firmly away from addictive behaviors and premarital sex. This book provides a deeply committed message intended to help teens see beyond the mechanics of day-to-day survival to personal fulfillment and "a complete and total awareness" of who they are and where they fit in the larger scheme of life.

Post, Elizabeth L., and Joan M. Coles. *Emily Post's Teen Etiquette.* 1995. New York: HarperCollins, paper (0-06-273337-0). Ages 12–16.

Probably not on any teenager's must-read list, this book nevertheless contains a lot of information young adults need to know as well as a lot they will simply mock. It features much of the same sort of information the authors gathered together in their 1986 book *Emily Post Talks with Teens about Manners and Etiquette.* Chapters on table manners and communication are the most extensive, with the latter even featuring etiquette for using E-mail, call-waiting, and beepers. There are suggestions for keeping family relationships running smoothly and advice on conducting oneself on a date (the authors hedge a bit on the subject of sex) and with peers, with admonitions about giving in to peer pressure and using drugs or alcohol, smoking cigarettes, shoplifting, or having sex "for the wrong reasons." The voice is a little chirpy and lecturish, but the book shows readers that good manners aren't simply about how to behave.

Ré, Judith, and Meg F. Schneider. *Social Savvy: A Teenager's Guide to Feeling Confident in Any Situation.* 1991. New York: Simon & Schuster (0-671-69023-X); paper (0-671-74198-5). Ages 12–16.

Though this book won't prepare teens for every situation as its subtitle implies, it does contain lots of useful advice. Ré, who runs

weekend courses in social behavior for young adults, supplies the agreeable voice of the text, which proceeds from the premise that good manners are a sign of respect and consideration for others, not just a bunch of silly rules. Using quick-to-read scenarios depicting specific manners dilemmas, called "Miserable Moments," and their solutions, the authors discuss familiar etiquette quandaries such as making introductions and restaurant protocol as well as a few etiquette perplexities not routinely covered in this kind of book—dealing with friction among one's friends, for example, or negotiating a bigger allowance. The most rigid guidelines appear in the section on table manners. Unfortunately, a few of these rules (e.g., the etiquette for removing paper from a straw) cross the silliness line the authors seemed so anxious to avoid.

Schneider, Meg F. *Popularity Has Its Ups and Downs*. 1992. Englewood Cliffs, N.J.: Messner (0-671-72848-2), paper (0-671-72849-0). Ages 12–15.

This clear, congenial book tackles a subject of prime importance to teens without speaking down to them. Its pages are filled with positive, common-sense counsel that doesn't make light of teens' concerns but plainly reveals why being popular may not be all it's cracked up to be. According to Schneider, it's real friendship that counts, and she starts teens out in the right direction with sound advice on how to form true friendships and become more self-assured.

Septien, Al. *Everything You Need to Know about Codependency*. 1993. New York: Rosen (0-8239-1527-1). Ages 12–15.

Part of the Need to Know Library targeted at reluctant readers, this manages, in a mere 64 pages, a surprisingly inclusive summary of a self-help topic that's usually strictly the province of books for grownups. Using psycho-babble sparingly and keeping his youthful audience clearly in mind, Septien discusses dysfunctionality in the family and how skewed relationships affect an individual's behavior, emotional well-being, and self-image. As with others in the series, his book has plenty of attractive color photos featuring teenagers, and the spacious layout will encourage kids who normally don't like to read to browse through the material.

Silverstein, Alvin, and others. *So You Think You're Fat?* 1991. New York: HarperCollins (0-06-021642-5). Ages 12–18.

Compulsive eating, the least publicized of the principal food-abuse disorders, gets full attention in this direct but not overly formal presentation. Consideration of a lengthy list of health problems—from heart disease to depression—related to being overweight leads off, followed by well amplified discussions of psychological, cultural, and biological factors that contribute to obesity. The authors also take a look at the diet industry and supply a wealth of diet-related miscellany, covering everything from yo-yo dieting to exercise. A few dieter's tips are included, but this is a background book, not a practical weight-loss guide. It's the kind of book that needs to be read before the word "diet" even comes up for discussion.

Taylor-Gerdes, Elizabeth. *Straight Up: A Teenager's Guide to Taking Charge of Your Life*. 1994. Chicago: Lindsey Publishing (1-885242-00-X). Ages 12–17.

The picture of two African-American teenagers on the cover will draw an audience too often neglected in books on self-esteem for young adults. Taylor-Gerdes, an educator and motivational consultant who grew up in a Chicago ghetto, puts her background and talents to good use as she encourages black teens to lighten up (keep a positive attitude); open up (explore the world and other cultures); give it up (lend a hand to others); and live it up (create the life you want). She keeps her target audience well in mind as she acknowledges barriers to personal success, including racism, family dysfunction, and self-doubt. Though her text is occasionally clichéd and sometimes grammatically awkward, her words are unpretentious and uplifting as they explore the way positive thinking and accepting responsibility for one's own life can yield great results.

Testimony: Young African-Americans on Self-Discovery and Black Identity. Ed. by Natasha Tarpley. 1995. Boston, Mass.: Beacon (0-8070-0928-8). Ages 16–up.

In her introduction, Tarpley recalls her own less-than-happy college experience and makes clear her commitment to enlighten and inform young African-Americans about contemporary issues of importance to their self-image and role in contemporary society. Her book is a collection of essays and poetry, written largely by African-American college students, who speak with candor and wit on a wide range of subjects—among them, black identity, racism, gender roles, self-discovery, politics, and culture. Not self-help material in the usual sense, this book offers no prescriptions for action. It is, however, filled with food for thought about the evolution of self and self-esteem.

Wirths, Claudine G., and Mary Bowman-Kruhm. *Are You My Type? Or Why Aren't You More Like Me?* 1992. Palo Alto, Calif.: Consulting Psychologists Press, paper (0-89106-055-3). Ages 11–14.

Wirths has a degree in psychology; both she and Bowman-Kruhm have teaching credentials. The pair meld their specialties in a book that will totally fascinate some teens and totally confuse others. Writing in a mock-interview style, they introduce teens to the subject of temperament typing. Each of four chapters concentrates on one personality type—SP (likes action, makes decisions quickly), SJ (follows rules, needs to belong), NF (is upbeat, uses feeling rather than logic to make decisions), NJ (thinks things through, needs to be competent)—with plenty of situations from everyday life to show the positive and negative ways each type reacts. The authors fully realize that cramming everybody into four classes is greatly oversimplifying psychological theory. Their hope is that readers will accept the classifications as "useful guidelines . . . not personality profiles cast in stone." The final two chapters suggest ways teens can put their new knowledge about themselves and others to work in school and at home.

Wirths, Claudine G., and Mary Bowman-Kruhm. *Choosing Is Confusing: How to Make Good Choices, Not Bad Guesses.* 1994. Palo Alto, Calif.: Consulting Psychologists Press, paper (0-9106-068-5). Ages 11–14.

Loaded with opportunities to fill in the blanks, this book may be a librarian's nightmare. Still, it's worth a close look because the authors have entered territory largely uncharted in children's nonfiction. Through a lively question-answer dialog ostensibly carried on with an inquisitive group of middle-grade or possibly junior-high kids, the authors discuss choices—the different kinds, how and why people make them, the consequences, and how to make them in more mature ways. It's questionable whether kids will take the time to "picture possibilities" and write down pros and cons of choices as suggested, and there's no denying the authors' simplistic division of personality types (Sane-and-Sensible, People Person, Considering-and-Careful, and Free-and-Fearless). Still, thanks to a nonstuffy style and lots of examples reflecting young peoples' concerns, readers are likely to come away a little wiser about making decisions—in emergencies and in their daily lives.

FICTION

Bauer, Joan. *Squashed.* 1992. New York: Delacorte (0-38530-793-4); Dell, paper (0-440-21912-4). Ages 13–16.

Ellie Morgan, overweight and self-deprecating, struggles to best odious Cyril Pool by growing the biggest pumpkin in Iowa. Her endeavors catapult her into the limelight and forever change her opinion of herself.

Bennett, James. *Dakota Dream.* 1994. New York: Scholastic (0-590-46680-1). Ages 14–18.

Tired of being forced from one foster home to another, Floyd Rayfield accepts as prophecy a vision that comes to him in a dream and sets off to find himself and his destiny as a member of the Dakota Indian tribe.

Busselle, Rebecca. *Bathing Ugly.* 1989. New York: Watts/Orchard/Richard Jackson (0-531-05801-8); Dell, paper (0-0440-20921-8). Ages 11–14.

Smart, overweight Betsy quietly and determinedly diets only to discover that losing weight has little effect on her friendships—her enemies don't suddenly mellow, and girls who've befriended her don't care whether she's fat or thin.

Cole, Brock. *The Goats.* 1987. New York: Farrar (0-374-32678-9); paper (0-374-42575-2). Ages 12–15.

Stripped, then left on a remote island as part of a cruel summer-camp joke, Laura and Howie escape from the island and run away, discovering much about themselves as they struggle to survive.

Cooney, Caroline. *Driver's Ed.* 1994. New York: Delacorte (0-385-32087-7). Ages 14–18.

Raging hormones and the thrill of taking a risk prompt Remy and Morgan to rip off some street signs. An innocent young mother dies as a result of their escapade, and the two teens are left with a nightmarish burden of guilt that catapults them headlong into adulthood.

Cooper, Ilene. *Buddy Love: Now on Video.* 1995. New York: HarperCollins (0-06-024663-4). Ages 11–13.

When Buddy interviews family and friends on videotape, he learns that there's more to his world—and to him—than he thought.

Davis, Terry. *If Rock and Roll Were a Machine.* 1992. New York: Delacorte (0-385-30762-4); Dell, paper (0-440-21908-6). Ages 15–18.

Six years after a humiliating run-in with a fifth-grade teacher strips him of his self-respect, Bert Bowden begins to fight back—with the help of racquetball, a caring English teacher, and some sage words from the owner of the motorcycle shop where he buys his first Harley.

Garland, Sherry. *Shadow of the Dragon.* 1993. San Diego: Harcourt (0-15-273530-5); paper (0-15-273520-1). Ages 12–16.

The eldest son of parents who emigrated from Vietnam, Danny Vo feels torn between his native culture and his desire to be "American." The arrival of his cousin from overseas and his attraction to pretty Tiffany, whose brother is a rabidly prejudiced skinhead, help him focus his attention on what matters.

Going Where I'm Coming from: Memoirs of American Youth. Ed. by Anne Mazer. 1995. New York: Persea; dist. by Braziller (0-89255-206-9). Ages 15–18.

Naomi Shahib Nye, Gary Soto, and Susan Power are among the contributors to this collection of thoughtful, complex stories that put life experience and a young person's traditional search for identity into sharp multicultural perspective.

Hall, Barbara. *Fool's Hill.* 1992. New York: Bantam (0-553-08993-5). Ages 13–16.

Libby sees her opportunity to cut loose from life in her small Virginia hometown when Rosalyn and Linda arrive in their snappy Mustang convertible and take her under their wing.

Klass, Sheila Solomon. *Rhino.* 1993. New York: Scholastic (0-590-44250-3). Ages 13–16.

Annie has the family nose, large and with a noticeable bump, and that's a real problem for a 15-year-old girl who doesn't want to look different from everyone else.

Koertge, Ron. *Boy in the Moon.* 1990. Boston: Little, Brown (0-316-50102-6); Avon, paper, (0-380-71474-4). Ages 14–18.

A high-school senior, Nick worries about his acne, his physique, and his lack of sexual experience, especially now that he's becoming increasingly attracted to his longtime friend and classmate, Frieda.

Lipsyte, Robert. *One Fat Summer.* 1977. New York: HarperCollins (0-06-023896-8); Bantam, paper (0-553-25591-6). Ages 12–15.

Being overweight and having a father who demands a lot are difficult burdens for Bobby Marks—until one telling summer when he learns that being thin and tough isn't nearly as important as being compassionate and doing the right thing.

Lynch, Chris. *Iceman.* 1994. New York: HarperCollins (0-06-023341-9). Ages 14–18.

Angry at his unresponsive family and terrified of growing up, Eric slams out his frustration and suffering in the hockey rink, where he's known as Iceman "the animal," so out of control that even his teammates shun him.

Mazer, Norma Fox. *Missing Pieces.* 1995. New York: Morrow (0-688-13349-5). Ages 13–15.

Fourteen-year-old Jesse Wells doesn't think she can ever feel whole until she finds out about her father, who abandoned her and her mother years before.

Mori, Kyoko. *Shizuko's Daughter.* 1993. New York: Holt (0-8050-2557-X). Ages 14–16.

Left at age 12 with an aloof father and self-serving stepmother after her birth mother, Shizuko, commits suicide, Yuri finds solace in her artistic talent, a legacy she inherited from her troubled mother.

Myers, Walter Dean. *Fallen Angels.* 1988. New York: Scholastic (0-590-40942-5); paper (0-590-40943-3). Ages 15–18.

More to postpone a dead-end life in Harlem than because of political principles, 17-year-old Richie Perry enlists in the army. The friendships he makes among fellow soldiers in Vietnam change his life forever.

Newman, Leslia. *Fat Chance.* 1994. New York: Putnam (0-399-22760-1). Ages 14–16.

Judi's obsession with her weight drives her from sporadic attempts at dieting to fasting and finally to binging and purging, the consequences of which she sees firsthand when a bulimic classmate becomes seriously ill.

Paulsen, Gary. *The Island.* 1988. New York: Watts/Orchard/Richard Jackson (0-531-05749-6); Dell, paper (0-440-20632-4). Ages 14–16.

Despite pleas from his parents, who want him to come home, and visits from a nosy reporter and an idiotic psychiatrist, 15-year-old Wil Neuton still manages to puzzle out the essence of himself while he sits in self-imposed exile on an island near his home.

Prejudice. Ed. by Daphne Muse. 1995. New York: Hyperion (0-7868-0024-0). Ages 12–18.

A long-term advocate of young people's rights, Muse has assembled a stellar collection of short stories and excerpts from novels that explore self-esteem and discrimination. Chris Crutcher, Ntozake Shange,

Marie G. Lee, and Lynda Barry are among the writers whose works are included.

Rites of Passage: Stories about Growing Up by Black Writers from around the World. Ed. by Tonya Bolden. 1994. New York: Hyperion; dist. by Little, Brown (1-56282-688-3). Ages 14–18.

Bolden offers a moving collection of seventeen stories focusing on what it's like to grow up black, mainly in the U.S., but also in Africa, Australia, Britain, the Caribbean, and Central America. The book's main appeal will be to teens of African descent, but many of the pivotal events in the characters' lives have a universality that will speak to most young adults.

Roybal, Laura. *Billy*. 1994. New York: Houghton (0-395-67649-5). Ages 14–18.

Billy Melendez's life comes to a shocking halt when he discovers that he was kidnapped at age 10 by his father and is really someone named William James Campbell with a family in Iowa to whom he must return.

Staples, Suzanne Fisher. *Haveli*. 1993. New York: Knopf (0-679-84157-1). Ages 15–18.

The young Pakistani woman Shabanu, whose story was so eloquently told in *Shabanu: Daughter of the Wind* (1989), is now married with a child, Mumtaz, whom she needs to protect from the cruelties of others in her elderly husband's household. To do that, she must find a way to balance her personal feelings with the expectations of her traditional culture.

Strasser, Todd. *How I Changed My Life*. 1995. New York: Simon & Schuster (0-671-88415-8). Ages 14–18.

Shy Bo begins to work on her weight problem and make friends when she becomes involved in her high school's drama department and attractive Kyle Winthrop enters the picture.

Who Do You Think You Are? Stories of Friends and Enemies. Selected by Hazel Rochman and Darlene Z. McCampbell. 1993. Boston: Little, Brown (0-316-7535-5-6). Ages 14–18.

Fifteen great short stories—by Toni Cade Bambara, Richard Peck, Louise Erdrich, Tim O'Brien, and others—show the ways love and hurt entwine and how friends are made, lost, and sometimes kept for a lifetime.

Williams-Garcia, Rita. *Fast Talk on a Slow Track*. 1991. Dutton/Lodestar (0-525-67334-2); Bantam, paper (0-553-29594-2). Ages 14–18.

Smooth-talking and clever, Denzel Watson breezes through school and through life until he fails at Princeton's summer program for minority students. Then a streetwise dropout introduces him to a fast-track city life that makes middle-class Denzel question where he really belongs.

Woodson, Jacqueline. *Between Madison and Palmetto*. 1993. New York: Delacorte (0-385-30906-6). Ages 12–15.

After leaving her elite prep school, African-American Maizon returns to her Brooklyn neighborhood only to encounter a new set of problems: the father who abandoned her as a baby returns, and her best friend, Margaret, develops bulimia.

Safe Passage: At Home, At School, In the Community

ALTHOUGH FICTION IS still the most common form for dealing with topics such as rape, domestic violence, and gangs, nonfiction for teens about safety-related issues at home, at school, and in the community has become more common. Sexual harassment is probably the newest such issue to be tackled, but violence in the community has also become a matter of great interest to nonfiction writers, in large part because it is a concern among adolescents. Increasing numbers of young adults are the perpetrators or the victims of crimes; gangs and guns are now hot-button political issues; and support groups, security guards, metal detectors, and other antiviolence measures are often a routine part of the school experience. Urban kids are not the only ones at risk. According to the July 1995 newsletter prepared by the National Center for Education Statistics, gang activity in schools is not restricted to city institutions, nor is it strictly a problem faced by minority students: rural teens and rich, suburban white ones are getting mugged and shot—sometimes by their peers—in growing numbers. The last few years have seen a dramatic increase of books committed to stopping violence by depicting its terrible toll and by helping teenagers prepare themselves to act responsibly in a crisis situation. Some of the best ones are listed in this section.

NONFICTION

Benedict, Helen. *Safe, Strong, and Streetwise.* 1987. Boston: Joy Street Books/Little, Brown (0-316-08900-4); paper, (0-87113-100-5). Ages 12–18.

A rape crisis counselor discusses sexual assault and explains how teenagers can prepare for, protect against, and deal with it should it occur. Statements from victims add immediacy to the text, which emphasizes that "awareness and escape," not physical defense methods, are the most important factors in self-protection. Benedict goes farther than most authors who write about sexual assault by recognizing the concerns of male victims, and she provides sound guideposts for young people of both sexes who may be confused by sexually exploitive situations on dates, on the job, or at school. Sensitive, explicit, and practical, the book is dedicated to helping teenagers survive in a world where, Benedict feels, personal safety can no longer be taken for granted.

Bode, Janet, and Stan Mack. *Hard Time.* 1996. New York: Delacorte (0-385-32186-4). Ages 12–18.

Bode's twelfth book, her third with Mack, is perhaps her best since *Voices of Rape.* Unashamedly meant to raise the consciousness of readers, the multipart text explores violence in the lives of today's young adults—from what it's like in lockup to the ways violence pervades kids' everyday world. As in other books by this team, the uninterrupted words (including poetry) of teenagers from many walks of life, speaking singly or in groups, do the work. Gathered here are expertly edited, well-chosen comments from teens who are victims and perpetrators of crimes or have a relative in jail and from adults who work with offenders and troubled young people within the correctional system and the community. Adding to the intensity are responses from a questionnaire the authors distributed to 125 jailed youths and a scattering of current statistics on crime gleaned from the popular press. Mack, a reporter/cartoonist whose strips have appeared in *The Village Voice,* contributes some excellent cartoon sequences, terse and thought-provoking, which depict, sometimes even better than kids' actual words, the fear, the shocking lack of remorse, the heartache, and the hope. They help to make this truly riveting book a must read for young adults as well as for grownups who want a better understanding of how a growing segment of teenagers view their present and sometimes their future.

"Rich kids shoplift, poor kids mug. The difference is what happens if they get caught."

—Comment made at a suburban high-school writing workshop, from *Hard Time*

Bode, Janet. *Voices of Rape.* 1990. New York: Watts (0-531-15184-0); Dell, paper (0-440-21301-0). Ages 14–18.

A rapist, a police officer, a rape survivor, and a defense attorney are among the people who speak out on a sensitive subject that is rarely presented as candidly in books for young adults as it is here. Young people speak out frankly: "We're not just a two legged penis," insists one young man involved in a discussion Bode orchestrated in a ninth-grade classroom. Professionals are equally forthright. Dr. Judith Becker, director of a juvenile sex offender treatment program, voices strong concern about violence in contemporary society and talks openly about aberrant sexual behavior, addressing some of her comments directly to teenage boys; a nurse explains what attack victims experience in the hospital; a veteran police officer discusses procedures used by the sex crimes unit of a large metropolitan police department. Bode also includes some voices of an different sort: a boy who's convinced that what he did wasn't rape and a victim of date rape who admits she is still attracted to her attacker. Then the author takes the speaker's platform for herself, first addressing males, then females, then both on how to stop the crime. As an assault survivor and a rape crisis worker, Bode knows the issues, and she describes them extremely well.

"It wasn't sexual assault . . . we were just taking advantage of a girl who was there." —Kevin, 15, from *Voices of Rape*

Janet Bode Tackles Tough Subjects

An enthusiastic speaker and writer totally dedicated to her audience, Janet Bode routinely tackles tough, important issues. Rape is one of them, and Bode was one of the first to write about it for teenagers. In fact, her own survival of a vicious attack started her on a writing career that has lasted more than twenty years. "We use the expression 'I'm going to write a book about it,'" she says. "I did." It was a book for the adult trade market. But writing for adults, which she continues to do, was not enough. A former secondary school teacher, Bode felt a strong affinity for teenagers, and she believed she had something important to tell them. *Rape,* her first young adult book, was published in 1979. She calls *Voices of Rape,* published in 1990, its update. Actually, it is a great deal more than a new edition. It's a book about individuals, not about statistics, and how Bode wrote it is as fascinating as the book itself:

SZ: *How do you go about finding teenagers to interview, especially when you're going to ask questions about a subject like rape?*

JB: I ask a school's permission. Then after I speak to a group, I say, "If any of you students would ever be interested in having me interview you for one of my books, please put down your name and phone number and write a line about yourself." Lots of kids will do that. Librarians are another source. I impose on them. I explain who I am and what project I'm dealing with, and I ask if there's a student or students they feel would be good for me to interview.

I speak with many more people than I include in my books. I select the ones that I feel will best reflect a body of information or express a point of view. I felt it was important in *Voices of Rape,* for example, to include Kevin, who participated in the gang rape, and a young woman who went through a date rape because, I'm sad to say, they were representative and typical.

SZ: *Do your visits to schools generate ideas for new books as well as potential interview subjects?*

JB: Yes. Students are my best resource. I remember this teenage boy sitting back in the library, leaning back in his chair . . . I was sure he was going to fall over . . . but he raised his hand and said, "I hate my brothers and sisters. You ought to write a book on that." So I did. *[Truce: Ending the Sibling War]* The same thing led to *Different Worlds,* my book about interracial and-cross-cultural dating.

SZ: *How do you get teenagers to feel enough at ease to talk openly?*

JB: I think that one of the lucky talents I have is to get teenagers to open up honestly. Some interviews I do face to face. Often I do phone interviews because I talk to kids across the country. They know the rules ahead of time: I will change their name and the fine details of their identity to protect their privacy. There has to be some type of general conversation first. They don't immediately sit down and say, "Let me tell you about this terrible experience that happened to me." I may ask something like, "Describe the room where you're sitting right now." They can talk a little about that room, and sometimes I'll tell them I live in New York City, and I'm sitting at my desk, and I can look out the window and see the Empire State Building. They like that. It gives them a little definition of who I am.

What always impresses me is that teenagers take the interview very seriously. They clean up their language; there are not many swear words in what they tell me because they're being listened to. They know they have a chance to help other people who might have been in a similar situation. They really are quite wonderful.

SZ: *How do you manage to capture the individuality of the people you interview?*

JB: I work very hard to preserve the spirit of what people say. I take out some of the "likes" and "you knows." I do leave some in because it's important for me to use each teenager's words and idiomatic expressions. And I listen. A little bell goes off, a "wow, that's a great way to put that," or "that's so important," or "that really moved me," or "that speaks to other teenagers in a way they will really understand." At a certain level, it's just gut instinct.

SZ: *It must have been very hard for you, a rape survivor, to write* Voices of Rape.

JB: Yes. I thought it had been a long enough time. Time does make a difference, and I felt I had learned and grown from my experience. But *Voices of Rape* ended up being a difficult book to do. It brought back more memories than I wanted. I didn't want to have to start thinking about that stuff again; I didn't want to have to go to a police station or to start thinking in the way that I do when I write. I get totally involved in my topics. But I think that teenagers deserve the best books I can possibly write; they deserve the most interesting people I can possibly interview. That's why I interviewed a famous defense attorney named Barry Slotnick. He was the lawyer who handled the trial of Bernie Goetz, New York City's subway gunman. I thought Slotnick was an articulate, quotable man. If I were doing a book for adults, that's who I'd interview, so that's who I talked with for *Voices of Rape.*

SZ: *Slotnick talked about defending rapists in court. You probably didn't like what he had to say, but it certainly didn't show in your book.*

JB: You're right. I had to control myself; I wanted to jump across the room at him. When I described him in the book I wanted to use adjectives that weren't very nice.

SZ: *Do you think boys will read* Voices?

JB: Well, boys aren't the traditional audience for this kind of book. When I envision my audience I see many more 15-year-old girls than I do boys. But I think we *expect* that. I hope teenage males will pick it up. If a boy reads the chapter by Dr. Judith Becker, an expert on juvenile sex offenders, and sees that he's doing things that might lead to difficulties . . . it's the old teacher in me. If I can just change one person, my whole job is worthwhile.

SZ: *Your first book about rape for teenagers came out in 1979. Have attitudes changed over the decade between the publication of that book and* Voices?

JB: I think a few things have changed in ten years, but not enough. I believe much more can be done. I am a little concerned now that women are becoming subservient again in some ways, and that troubles me. I have seen improvement with the police. Now some police forces are required to take sensitivity training. That was something those of us who worked in the rape crisis centers only dreamed of happening. When you go into a hospital in a major city now, people are much more considerate than they were when I did the last book. Back then they'd often scream out, "Rape victim, come in," . . . just what you didn't want. Laws have changed, too. Today, the sexual history of the woman testifying on the stand cannot be examined. I think that is a tremendous improvement, even though, in some cases, attorneys still manage to bring it up.

SZ: Voices *is an extremely forthright book. Dr. Becker, for example, speaks very candidly about violent sexual behavior in teenage boys. Do you think* Voices *is going to become a target of the censors?*

JB: Judith Becker even asked about that when I spoke with her. It may. But I think knowledge is power, and only through listening and reading and beginning to think about information can we deal with topics like this. When I talk to kids, they agree that you don't solve problems by ignoring them or by not being willing to discuss them. You have to get the high-intensity light out. You have to look at them, discuss them. And you have to deal with them in order to become better and strong and end this horrible thing called rape. [*Voices* has been the target of censors.]

Chaiet, Donna. *Staying Safe on Public Transportation*. 1995. New York: Rosen (0-8239-1866-1). Ages 14–18.

This is one of the better titles in the new Get Prepared Library series for young women, with others dealing with safety at school, at work, on dates, etc. Written by the president of Prepare, Inc., an organization that conducts teen safety programs, it contains sensible tips for traveling safely aboard buses, trains, and taxis. Firm verbal response and common-sense advice about escaping dangerous situations are the focus here, not physical self-defense maneuvers. The cover photo is nice, but other pictures are so staged that they detract from the information. There's a good deal of padding within the series, and a plug for Chaiet's organization included in each book seems a waste of space. Still, the brief text is very accessible, and Chaiet's sensible tips for staying alert and thinking ahead will help young women be better prepared for whatever comes their way.

Cohen-Posey, Kate. *How to Handle Bullies, Teasers and Other Meanies: A Book That Takes the Nuisance out of Name Calling and Other Nonsense*. 1995. Highland City, Fla.: Rainbow Books (1-56825-029-0). Ages 10–13.

In one of the few books around that's really practical, a practicing Florida therapist gives kids some hope when they're being bullied. Her focus is on bullies who use words as weapons, not on the sort of person who threatens with physical violence. Using examples that sound fairly authentic, she explains a variety of verbal comebacks victims can use to turn the tables on name callers and nasty teasers. The illustrations are amateurish and juvenile, the antimeanness clubs the author talks about probably won't go over well, and it's optimistic to assume, as Cohen-Posey suggests, that a few verbal defeats will help a bully reform. Even so, fighting intimidation is such a common and formidable problem for this age group that Cohen-Posey's more practical advice will be welcomed, both as a means of helping kids develop a plan of action and for the support and shot of confidence it gives.

Goedecke, Christopher J., and Rosemarie Hausherr. *Smart Moves: A Kid's Guide to Self-Defense*. 1995. New York: Simon & Schuster (0-689-80294-3). Ages 12–14.

A martial-arts instructor and a veteran children's book author-photographer have put together a fine "sourcebook of safety and survival strategies." At the outset, they encourage kids to join a self-defense class and provide plenty of black-and-white photos of young people learning techniques properly with a martial-arts teacher. Because the authors also recognize the inevitability of kids' training on their own, they do their best to explain the risks and set clear practice guidelines. Descriptions of specific self-defense maneuvers—from blocking punches to escaping choke holds—are clear as well. Despite the focus on the physical, there's no mistaking the authors' attitude toward violence: they constantly reiterate that nonaggressive action should be the first choice. Their five-step plan for dealing with bullies is bound to draw some attention, but it's the book's final section that will really start young people thinking about personal safety. Eleven authentic scenarios, each one more menacing than the last, are depicted, along with suggestions for appropriate self-defense responses. This is all very serious stuff (in fact, it begs for classroom discussion). The authors know that, and they make sure their readers do, too, emphasizing over and over that self-defense isn't about invincibility, striking first, or retaliation—it's about not getting hurt and about staying alert, being smart, and acting wisely in a risky world.

Goldentyer, Debra. *Gangs*. 1994. Austin, Tex.: Steck-Vaughn (0-8114-3527-X). Ages 12–15.

This is certainly not a glamorous picture of gang life: crime, danger, and violence are the watchwords, not brotherhood and family. But Goldentyer is never so strident that she'll alienate her audience. Equally important is her recognition of the lure of gang association, something she tries to balance with facts about gang activity. Comments from former and present gang members tell part of the tale, with the author going on to explore the reasons teens join—from poverty and racism to lack of family support—and to answer common questions. She also suggests some ways teens can enter the fight against gangs in their neighborhoods.

Grosser, Vicky, and others. *Take a Firm Stand: The Young Woman's Guide to Self-Defense*. 1993. London, Eng.: Virago; dist. by Trafalgar Square, paper (1-85381-390-7). Ages 16–18.

Though this looks like a cheaply produced paperback, and the British orientation might scare off some American readers, it is actually a useful, timely title. Following several chapters that consider the when and why of self-defense, the authors use a combination of well-captioned black-and-white photographs (not particularly sharp) and text to introduce protective physical strategies, from how to fall safely and counter a stranglehold to ways to ward off an attack by someone with a weapon. As in Goedecke's book for a younger audience, mentioned previously, avoidance and escape are seen as the most desirable responses, and practice with a friend is encouraged, as is attending a self-defense class (or organizing one if there isn't one available). The book provides young women with the tools for making wise decisions when danger is involved.

Guernsey, JoAnn Bren. *Sexual Harassment: A Question of Power.* 1995. Minneapolis: Lerner (0-8225-2608-5). Ages 14–18.

An entry in the Frontline series, this timely, sensitive consideration begins with a historical perspective before opening into a broad review of harassment in the workplace, school, and daily life. Guernsey focuses mainly on women but doesn't neglect men as victims. She also presents a male perspective on the issue, which she ably demonstrates as being very complex. Her book is not as readable as Landau's anecdote-laden book, following, which contains more-practical advice on dealing with harassment. But Guernsey's treatment is the more discerning of the two: its carefully orchestrated combination of cases, opinions, and facts is written with a clarity and directness that will compel teens to really think about the subject.

Gutman, Bill. *Recreation Can Be Risky*. 1996. New York: Twenty-First Century Books (0-8050-4143-5). Ages 10–14.

———. *Hazards at Home*. 1996. New York: Twenty-First Century Books (0-8050-4143-5). Ages 10–14.

These two books in the new Focus on Safety series (upcoming titles will deal with issues such as stranger danger, bullies, and going to and from school) build on the idea that awareness is a big part of staying safe. In *Recreation,* Gutman alerts young people to the risks inherent in the team and individual sports they commonly play—from basketball and football to swimming and inline skating—and explains the way weather can factor into outdoor activity. He also introduces some basic first aid, including a note about contact with bleeding injuries. Explanations of the Heimlich maneuver and CPR are part of the first-aid section in *Hazards at Home,* but Gutman makes very clear the difficulty in performing them and the responsibilities involved. Separate chapters discuss safety measures to reduce the risk of falls, fires, accidents with household tools and appliances, and contact with toxic substances. In addition, Gutman explains how a handgun can be moved safely out of the reach of young children in an emergency. The writing is clear and crisp and the information sensible and appropriately cautious. With very little quality material like this available for the age group, these books should be welcomed.

Hinojosa, Maria. *Crews: Gang Members Talk to Maria Hinojosa*. 1995. San Diego: Harcourt (0-15-292873-1); paper (0-15-200283-9). Ages 15–18.

Prompted by a vicious subway stabbing, National Public Radio correspondent Hinojosa arranged to meet and talk with members of several New York City "crews." This book includes not only the transcript of the radio program that resulted but also Hinojosa's extended conversations with the young men and women gang members. Unedited for grammar and syntax, the interviews are filled with the rough, foulmouthed jargon of the streets (a glossary is appended), and the stories told paint shocking pictures of street violence, drugs, and guns, which are rationalized with shocking ease. But Hinojosa is a clever questioner, and her gentle probing reveals the vulnerability beneath the toughness of these kids, whose words can't fail to move the reader toward a better understanding of how gangs sacrifice the individual and cast their destructive spell.

Hodgson, Harriet. *Powerplays: How Teens Can Pull the Plug on Sexual Harassment*. 1993. Minneapolis: Deaconess, paper (0-925190-67-5). Ages 14–18.

Hodgson, who was a victim of sexual harassment while in junior high, is a little too long-winded and not entirely successful in her efforts to connect sexual harassment to sexual abuse. Even so, her book is still worth a look, as it is more focused on teens than the others listed in this chapter. Like Guernsey and Landau, Hodgson supplies a broad definition of harassment, explores some of the roadblocks to reporting it, and discusses the aftereffects. Her best chapters, however, are the practical ones, the ones that stir kids to action. These contain information about keeping records to prove a case and explain how to find official help and enlist parents as advocates. Hodgson also includes sample forms for recording and reporting harassment and an extensive bibliography for teens who want to know more about the subject and how people are fighting back.

Kosof, Anna. *Battered Women: Living with the Enemy*. 1995. New York: Watts (0-531-11203-9). Ages 14–18.

Personal stories are only part of this book, which attempts to do more than simply show the tragic aftermath of being battered. Kosof effectively delves into what lies at the bottom of abusive relationships, asking and answering basic questions about who abuses and why and, equally important, why many women are as afraid to leave as they are to stay. Unquestionably her sympathies lie with the victims, but she clearly demonstrates that abusive relationships are infinitely more complicated than most people realize. Not a self-help book in the traditional sense, but a fine book to inform and prompt discussion among young women.

Landau, Elaine. *Sexual Harassment.* 1993. New York: Walker (0-8027-08266-3). Ages 15–18.

While Landau responsibly admits that the definition of sexual harassment has not been totally agreed upon by the courts let alone by mainstream America, she relates numerous incidents in an effort to give readers the clearest possible sense of the behavior. Of particular interest to teenagers will be the chapter about harassment at school, which includes the stories of several young women who found school administrators hesitant to act on their behalf. The final section rounds up suggestions of specific things to try to stave off harassment before legal recourse is sought. A candid, cautiously optimistic book that won't sit on the shelf for long.

"Sexual harassment is actually not about sex—it's about power and its abuse."

—from *Sexual Harassment*

La Valle, John. *When You Are the Male Survivor of Rape or Sexual Assault.* 1995. New York: Rosen (0-8239-2084-4). Ages 16–18.

The language is straightforward and the examples (including descriptions of male rape) graphic in this entry in the Need to Know Library, but La Valle's accounts present a clear view of how victimizers manipulate children's emotions to achieve their own ends. Forms of abuse are the focus, but also included is information about abusers, aftereffects, pornography, and personal safety. Integration of general information with material specifically for boys is not always smooth, with La Valle sometimes awkwardly switching from third to second person, and there's a good deal of oversimplification. Sixty-four pages is not adequate to give the subject the consideration it deserves. Still, the concise, forthright approach has some advantages: the easy-to-read format, characteristic of the series, makes the material accessible, and the explicitness of the text will fill in blanks for teens who may not really understand male abuse despite protests that they already "know it all." Helen Benedict's *Safe, Strong, and Streetwise* (1987), addressed to both young men and women, is a less explicit, more encompassing alternative.

Levy, Barrie. *In Love and in Danger.* 1993. Seattle, Wash.; Seal Press, dist. by Publisher's Group West, paper (1-878067-26-5). Ages 15–18.

A California therapist explores the connection between power, dependency, and abuse in a support-information book built around candid, firsthand accounts from women who observed or were part of abusive relationships. Levy recognizes the difficulties of breaking the dependency cycle in the book but strongly counsels victims to take steps to end an abusive relationship, explaining what constitutes "addictive love" and how to begin the process of retaking control of one's life. Presented without professional jargon and larded with personal commentary from abuse victims, this is explicit and eye-opening.

Mather, Cynthia L., and Kristina Debye. *How Long Does It Hurt?: A Guide to Recovering from Incest and Sexual Abuse for Teenagers, Their Friends, and Their Families.* 1994. San Francisco: Jossey-Bass, paper (1-55542-674-3). Ages 14–18.

After carefully clarifying different kinds of incest (the making of inappropriate sexual comments to a child is included) and exploring the reasons why victims so often try to rationalize their experience, the authors concentrate on the aftermath of abuse, especially on what happens when the "secret" is out. The book takes readers step-by-step through the reporting process. The section about what happens in court (including what occurs when the verdict is "not guilty") is exceptionally good; there's even a diagram of what courtrooms usually look like. Also excellent is the section about forgiveness, which explores what it is and what it isn't. The illustrations are amateurish, but comments from teens of both genders, including the stories of three incest survivors, will make readers forget the silly graphics. That Mather, an abuse survivor, and Debye, coordinator of the Baltimore County Sexual Abuse Treatment Program, know what they're talking about is perfectly clear.

"I understand that it wasn't my fault.
I understand that if it wasn't me, he would have hurt someone else.
I understand that he's the one who made the choice to abuse. What I don't understand is why!"

—Ross, 14, abused by his coach, from *How Long Does It Hurt?*

Miller, Maryann. *Coping with Weapons and Violence in Your School and on Your Streets*. 1993. New York: Rosen (0-8239-1435-6). Ages 14–16.

Miller slights a couple of important areas in her discussion (family violence, for one), nothing is fully documented, and she relies so heavily on quotes to support her points that she dilutes her arguments. Still, she accomplishes much in terms of alerting young adults to the pervasiveness of violence in society and explains ways in which they can help to stem its rise. Her discussion ranges widely, if not deeply, from an exploration of aggression as a fundamental part of the human makeup to victims' rights, conflict resolution, and the controversy at the heart of attempts to stem increasing violence in the media. Of particular interest will be her chapter on gangs, which examines several different kinds, and a section in which teens express their opinions about issues such as the escalation of violence, gun control, and punishment.

Miller, Maryann. *Working Together against Gun Violence*. 1994. Minneapolis: Rosen (0-8239-1779-7). Ages 12–14.

A more focused book than *Coping with Weapons and Violence,* this spends less time on facts, statistics, and personal experiences than on getting kids to decide where they stand on the issues and how they can work to further their cause. As is characteristic of all books in the Library of Social Activism series, there's a brief review of the controversy, studded with questions to discuss aloud or think about independently. Miller also gives readers an idea of what some young people have already done to act on their commitments and describes, in brief, very practical ways readers can involve themselves—from research and surveys to petitions and lobbying.

Mufson, Susan, and Rachel Kranz. *Straight Talk about Child Abuse*. 1991. New York: Facts On File (0-8160-2376-X); Dell, paper (0-440-21349-5). Ages 12–18.

While the dust jacket shouts "textbook," this cooperative effort by a free-lance writer and a certified social worker will be as valuable to teenagers needing advice on how to cope with a problem at home as it will to those looking for report material. Part of the Straight Talk series, the book defines and discusses both physical and emotional abuse. It focuses, in particular, on abuse within the family and presents a clear idea of the consequences abuse leaves in its wake. Going further than most writers who deal with the subject for a teenage audience, Mufson and Kranz link child abuse to substance abuse and explain the complicated dynamics that make it possible for victims to love their abusers and blame themselves for what's not their fault. The authors are frank about what can happen when abuse is brought into the open—foster care, possibly family dissolution—but they strongly encourage teens to do what's necessary to alter the pattern. Profiles of teenage victims provide signposts for recognizing abusive situations.

Mufson, Susan, and Rachel Kranz. *Straight Talk about Date Rape.* 1993. New York: Facts On File (0-8160-2863-X). Ages 12–18.

Although men aren't entirely ignored in this book, the main focus here is on women as targets. After outlining the extent of the problem of rape in this country, Mufson and Kranz cut through myths and misapprehensions and provide a straightforward consideration of the subject. There's no stridency or accusatory language evident, and the authors supply some good-sense information on protecting oneself and coping after an assault. Unfortunately, the many statistics cited in the first part of the book are not fully documented and the bibliography is disappointing. Although not up to par with Mufson and Kranz's fine book about child abuse, this still contains a lot of information and insight young adults will find valuable.

Parrot, Andrea. *Coping with Date Rape & Acquaintance Rape.* 1988. New York: Rosen (0-8239-0784-8); paper (0-8239-0808-9). Ages 14–18.

Dr. Parrot, on the faculty of Cornell University, is a specialist in human sexuality and rape prevention. She contends that though an individual may make her- or himself vulnerable to attack (by drinking too much, for example), forced sex or sex performed because of threats is a criminal act that is not the fault of the victim. Explicit examples of date rape situations help her clarify the nature of the crime and define the legal, social, and emotional misconceptions and prejudices associated with it. Her discussion of popular myths, specific behaviors, and sex-role stereotypes contributing to the "date rape dynamic" focuses largely on women victims, but she also includes an excellent section on the special problems male victims face. The book's format is dull, but Parrot's forthright, earnest text puts to rest a number of widely held misconceptions. In addition, it presents a few sensible self-protection strategies and provides information on where to get help if rape occurs. Although this is an an older book, its one of the best in Rosen's Coping series and still one of the best on the subject.

Rench, Janice E. *Family Violence: How to Recognize and Survive It.* 1992. Minneapolis: Lerner (0-8225-0047-7). Ages 10–14.

Rench makes use of short, obvious but not melodramatic scenarios to introduce discussion about violence at home. Using a series of simple questions—"Why do my parents hurt me this way?" "What does a shelter look like?"—she takes some of the terrifying mystery out of the subject. Explanations, though brief, offer plenty of insight into what constitutes different kinds of abuse, who's at fault, and what needs to be done if family violence is occurring. A consciousness-raising section on elder abuse, a subject rarely introduced in books for young adults, is particularly noteworthy. There's also an occasional paper-and-pencil exercise to focus readers on the issues. A somber, truthful book, but not a frightening one, this will help young adults clarify their feelings and take appropriate steps, whether the family violence is directed at them or at someone they love.

Spies, Karen Bornemann. *Everything You Need to Know about Incest.* 1992. New York: Rosen (0-8239-1325-2). Ages 12–15.

Spies, who defines incest as a gross betrayal of trust that must be brought out into the open, differentiates, in simple terms, between several different types of touching—sexual, friendly, and nurturing—and several kinds of incestuous relationships before discussing incest's emotional and physical aftermath and how teenage victims can get help. The photographs are not well captioned and sometimes not well related to the accompanying text, but they're a good draw for browsers. Teens may also be lured by the book's length. Only sixty-four pages, the text is perfect for readers unable or unwilling to manage difficult language or a lot of details.

Stop the Violence: Overcoming Self-Destruction. Ed. by Nelson George. 1990. New York: Pantheon, paper (0-295-97367-6). Age 16–adult.

Rap music is a powerful medium for speaking to young people, particularly inner city youth, but it's often associated with crime and violence. Objections to what was perceived by rappers as unfair labeling resulted in the Stop the Violence movement, a coalition between rappers and the National Urban League dedicated to raising the collective conscience regarding urban, particularly black-on-black, crime. With a layout and an abundance of photos that make it look like a magazine, this book combines comments from rappers and song lyrics with essays by young adults to get the point across: stop the violence, now. Though the rap music may have changed over the years since this was published, the flashy format and timely subject will still draw readers.

"You can't reciprocate hate and violence with hate and violence. . . . An eye for an eye makes the whole world blind."

—Sonya, 19, from *Voices from the Future*

Voices from the Future: Our Children Tell Us about Violence in America. Ed. by Susan Goodwillie. New York: Crown (0-517-59494-3). Ages 16–adult.

With pictures by renowned photographer Mary Ellen Mark, this is a candid, forceful oral history. The narratives were gathered by journalists reporting for Children's Express, an award-winning Washington-based news service that uses material written and edited by children and teenagers. There's some strong stuff here, as victims and victimizers talk frankly about violence on the streets and in their homes, sometimes bragging, sometimes confrontational or dramatic, sometimes obviously desperate. Yet there are glimmers of humor and hope as well, which help temper but not diminish a portrait of alienated youth designed to raise the consciousness of both the individual and society.

Wormser, Richard. *Juveniles in Trouble.* 1994. Englewood Cliffs, N.J.: Messner (0-671-86775-X). Ages 14–18.

First-person narratives are a big part of Wormser's riveting examination of a disaffected generation, which alerts kids to the existence of Covenant House, an organization that works to help young people get their lives back on track. Runaways, single teenage mothers, prostitutes, thieves, and murderers are among those who tell their stories, with Wormser following them into shelters, jails, and courtrooms. In his conclusion, Wormser lays blame for much of what is happening to today's youth on the doorstep of the family, but whether teens agree with him or not, they'll find that this hard-hitting overview alerts kids to what awaits them on the streets and raises some disturbing questions about what society expects of the young today and what young people can expect in return.

"Banging ain't no parttime thing. It's a full time career. It's bein' down when nobody else down with you. It's getting caught and not tellin'. Killin' and not carin', dying without fear."

—Gang member, Sanyika Shakur, from *Juveniles in Trouble*

FICTION

Brown, Susan. *You're Dead, David Borelli.* 1995. New York: Simon & Schuster/Atheneum (0-689-31959-2). Ages 11–14.

It's bad for David when his mother dies, his father disappears, and he finds himself in a foster home very unlike the privileged household he came from. But it gets worse when he becomes the target of some vicious schoolyard bullies.

Coman, Carolyn. *What Jamie Saw.* 1995. Arden, N.C.: Front Street (1-886910-02-2). Ages 12–14.

Shocked awake in time to see his baby sister being thrown across the room by his stepfather, third-grader Jamie flees from home with his mother and his sister to begin an agonizing journey out of fear and into a new life. Told from Jamie's naive perspective, this subtle, powerful story will speak to kids much older than third grade.

Cormier, Robert. *We All Fall Down.* 1991. New York: Delacorte (0-385-30501-X); Dell, paper (0-440-21556-0). Ages 14–18.

Random violence committed by four middle-class teenagers out for excitement leaves a home in ruins, one of its occupants in a coma, and the lives of the violated family and at least one of the transgressors changed forever.

Crutcher, Chris. *Staying Fat for Sarah Byrnes.* 1993. New York: Greenwillow (0-688-11552-7). Ages 14–18.

Sarah desperately wants to escape from her abusive, dangerously unbalanced father, and fat Eric Calhoun, Sarah's loyal friend, is determined to help her. In so doing, he also helps himself.

Davis, Jenny. *Sex Education.* 1988. New York: Watts/Orchard/Richard Jackson (0-531-05756-9); Dell, paper (0-440-20483-6). Ages 14–18.

Abandoning the curriculum to teach a unit on sex education, a ninth-grade biology teacher begins with an unusual project: find someone to care about. Sixteen-year-old Livvie and classmate David Kindler choose fragile, pregnant Maggie Parker, Livvie's new neighbor, as the focus of their concern.

Deem, James M. *The 3 NBs of Julian Drew.* 1994. Boston: Houghton (0-395-69453-1). Ages 14–18.

Constantly belittled by his stepmother and father, always hungry, and forced to sleep locked in the garage at night, 15-year-old Julian lives only for the memory of his beloved, deceased mother, to whom he writes in coded notebooks that he hides from his family.

Grant, Cynthia. *Uncle Vampire.* 1993. New York: Atheneum (0-689-31852-9). Ages 14–17.

Caroline's uncle may not be a vampire like Bela Lugosi, but he's certainly a monster; he has so betrayed his niece that she's sunk into an elaborate, demented fantasy to ease her pain.

Haseley, Dennis. *Getting Him.* 1994. New York: Farrar (0-374-32536-7). Ages 12–15.

Blaming Harold, a nerdy, school-smart kid, for injuring his dog, Chief, Donald wants revenge, not by simple bullying or physical punishment, but by a more diabolical means.

Irwin, Hadley. *Abby, My Love.* 1985. New York: Atheneum/Margaret K. McElderry (0-689-50323-7); NAL, paper (0-451-14501-1). Ages 14–16.

Chip has known Abby since they were both children. But it's not until the pair is in high school that he finds out his clever, sensitive girlfriend has a terrible secret she's been hiding for years. A film vision of this title is also available from AGC Educational Media.

Krichner, Trudy. *Spite Fences.* 1994. New York: Delacorte (0-385-32088-4); Fawcett, paper (0-494-70442-0). Ages 14–18.

Physically and emotionally abused by her mother, 13-year-old Maggie finds a friend in an old black man, who becomes the target of vicious racist bullies in their small 1960 Georgia town.

Levitin, Sonia. *Adam's War.* 1994. New York: Dial (0-8037-1506-4). Ages 11–14.

Adam thinks the ready-built clubhouse he finds in the park is exactly what's needed to pull together the three boys in his club. Unfortunately, a nasty rival club has its eye on the place, and Adam is so determined not to give in that he turns to violence.

Lowery, Linda. *Laurie Tells.* 1994. Minneapolis: Carolrhoda (0-87614-790-2). Ages 11–13.

Laurie recognizes that she can no longer deal with being molested by her dad and reveals her pain and terror to her beloved Aunt Jan. With evocative paintings by Eric Karpinski, this haunting picture-book story is targeted at an age group for whom little on this subject is available.

Maclean, John. *Mac.* 1987. Boston: Houghton (0-395-43080-1); Avon, paper (0-380-70700-4). Ages 14–18.

A good friend, a competent student, and a generally nice guy, high-school sophomore Mac has grown up trusting and secure. Then he's assaulted by a doctor during a physical exam and his world turns upside down.

Mazer, Norma Fox. *Out of Control.* 1993. New York: Morrow (0-688-10208-5); Avon, paper (0-380-71347-0). Ages 14–18.

While an all-school activity is going on downstairs, high-school student Valerie is attacked by three male students on the third floor of her school. It takes all the courage she can muster to fight back after unsupportive school officials compound the horror by making her doubt herself.

Miklowitz, Gloria. *Past Forgiving.* 1995. New York: Simon & Schuster (0-671-88442-5). Ages 14–16.

Fifteen-year-old Alexandra counts herself lucky to have handsome Cliff as her boyfriend despite his terrible temper and his controlling behavior. She even tolerates his slapping her and his occasional verbal abuse, but she finally draws the line when he expects to be forgiven for raping her.

Myers, Walter Dean. *Scorpions.* 1988. New York: HarperCollins (0-06-024364-3); paper (0-06-447066-0). Ages 12–15.

Although his friend Tito tries to discourage him from becoming involved in his neighborhood gang, 12-year-old Jamal covets the promise of power enough to go to a gang meeting. He brings along his good friend Tito, and he brings along a gun.

Ruby, Lois. *Skin Deep.* 1994. New York: Scholastic (0-590-47699-8). Ages 14–18.

Dismal job prospects, lack of self-esteem, and family problems eventually drive high-school senior Dan Penner toward accepting the rhetoric of the local neo-Nazis—and his girlfriend Laurel Grady can't do anything about it.

Skinner, David. *The Wrecker.* 1995. New York: Simon & Schuster (0-671-79771-9). Ages 12–15.

Jeffrey is a bully, Theo is a smart eccentric, and Michael is a lonely new kid in school. When Theo asks Michael to help him turn the tables on Jeffrey, Michael agrees, not realizing the depth of Theo's hatred or the vastness of his scientific genius.

Talbot, Bryan. *The Tale of One Bad Rat.* 1995. Milwaukie, Ore: Dark Horse Comics, paper (1-56971-077-5). Ages 14–18.

In this full-color graphic novel, British teenager Helen runs away to escape her father's sexual abuse only to discover that leaving home is not enough to heal her spirit.

Tamar, Erica. *Fair Game.* 1993. San Diego: Harcourt (0-15-278537-X); paper (0-15-227065-5). Ages 16–18.

Laura Jean, Joe, and Cara tell about the brutal gang rape of a developmentally disabled teenager and how the incident affected each of their lives and the lives of the high-school jocks who were involved in the assault.

Thesman, Jean. *Summerspell.* 1995. New York: Simon & Schuster (0-671-50130-5). Ages 14–16.

When her brother-in-law Gerald's sexual advances finally cause her to run away, Jocelyn flees to Summerspell, where she spent happy summers with her grandparents. Demented Gerald discovers her whereabouts and follows.

Voigt, Cynthia. *When She Hollers.* 1994. New York: Scholastic (0-590-46714-X). Ages 15–18.

Driven to the breaking point by her father's sexual abuse, 17-year-old Tish first threatens to kill her dad with a butcher knife, then manages to tell her story to a lawyer, who helps her retake control of her life.

Wartski, Maureen. *Dark Silence.* 1994. New York: Ballantine, paper (0-449-70418-1). Ages 13–16.

With her mother recently dead and a new stepmother in her life, Randy Wilmot is so wrapped up in her own problems that she fails to recognize that her new friend Delia Abott isn't just shy: Delia is terrified—of her own father.

Weinstein, Nina. *No More Secrets.* 1991. Seattle, Wash.: Seal Press (1-878067-07-9); paper (1-878067-00-1). Ages 14–18.

Attacked at the age of 8 by a stranger who came to her room while her mother was elsewhere in the house, Mandy has never been able to admit she was actually raped. Now, at age 16, she finds the stress of the long-held secret more than she can bear.

White, Ruth. *Weeping Willow.* 1992. New York; Farrar (0-374-38255-7); paper (0-374-48280-2). Ages 13–16.

Tiny Lambert finally begins to flourish when she enters high school and discovers that she is not only a beautiful singer but also attractive enough to lure a boyfriend. Unfortunately, her physical blossoming has not gone unnoticed by her hill-country stepfather.

Woodson, Jacqueline. *I Hadn't Meant to Tell You This.* 1994. New York: Delacorte (0-385-32031-0). Ages 11–15.

No one understands why Marie likes Lena, the poor, white-trash new girl who doesn't fit in with Marie's middle-class African-American crowd. But their friendship is strong, and it gives Lena courage when she must take her little sister and flee from her father's sexual abuse.

Wellness: Being Sick, Staying Healthy

ONE OF THE most interesting developments in health-related materials for young people is the proliferation of books focusing on emotional and psychological issues. Topics such as stress, depression, and anorexia, until recently thought totally inappropriate for "impressionable" teenagers, are being written about and discussed more openly than ever before. But as with books on sexuality and sexually transmitted diseases, which are discussed in the chapter "Sex Stuff," their use still engenders controversy, the concern being whether teenagers will treat the advice in books as a substitute for the professional counseling they may really need. Although it's impossible to say how individuals will react to books (fiction, for example, may have greater impact than fact), most responsible treatments of health subjects make it plain to the reader that an author's suggestions are not the equivalent of a personal physician's care.

Teenage books about physical well-being and illness have also increased in number and kind. Only in the area of substance abuse is there a dearth of single titles, a surprising factor given the emphasis on drug education in the schools. Of course, where substance abuse is concerned, it's not easy to get teens to read books they know are intended to tell them what not to do. There are, however, a few on the subject that seem less like boring lectures. They are listed in this chapter, along with a selection of other titles on physical and psychological well-being that range from books on skin care to personal accounts of kids whose lives are full despite serious physical disabilities.

NONFICTION

Psychological Well-Being

Adderholdt-Elliott, Miriam. *Perfectionism: What's Bad about Being Too Good?* 1987. Minneapolis: Free Spirit, paper (0-915793-07-5). Ages 12–16.

An admitted perfectionist, Adderholdt-Elliott blends personal experience with research findings in an informative guide that clearly distinguishes the difference between obsessive perfectionism and the healthy pursuit of excellence. Using an informal style that makes the text easy to read, she explains the detrimental effects that the desire to be perfect has on mind, body, and relationships and explores alternate ways individuals can regain their perspective and still satisfy their desire to succeed. She also talks about finding professional help when it's necessary and discusses how young women can avoid falling victim to the burdens of rapidly changing role expectations. Cartoon drawings lighten the mood. Despite the 1987 copyright, this still contains some useful information and remains a one-of-a-kind book for teens.

Beckelman, Laurie. *Anger.* 1994. Morristown, N.J.: Silver Burdett/ Crestwood House (0-382-24744-2); paper (0-382-24744-2). Ages 12–15.

———. *Loneliness.* 1994. Morristown, N.J.: Silver Burdett/Crestwood House (0-382-24745-0); paper (0-382-24745-0). Ages 12–15.

———. *Stress.* 1994. Morristown, N.J.: Silver Burdett/Crestwood House (0-382-24746-9); paper (0-382-24746-9). Ages 12–15.

Beckelman carefully defines psychological jargon and keeps it to an acceptable minimum in these entries in the Hot Line series. She also packs a lot into the 48 pages that comprise each book. In *Anger,* she lends insight into everything from the roots of the emotion and the biological changes it prompts to the various ways people handle it. She eschews false comfort in *Loneliness* and delivers a share of good, common sense about finding help and getting on with life. *Stress* strikes a near equal balance between identifying stressors in teenagers' lives and suggesting techniques for dealing with them. The slightly enlarged type size and extra leading will attract reluctant readers, and the color photographs (though sometimes very staged) make the books seem relevant to teens, as will the scattering of young adults' personal stories. The combined glossary/index that rounds out each book is not entirely successful, but that shouldn't detract from the usefulness of these slim volumes, which validate three common emotions and explain how they can be channeled into positive action.

Carter, Sharon, and Lawrence Clayton. *Coping with Depression.* Rev. ed. 1992. New York: Rosen (0-8239-1488-7). Ages 12–16.

References to music and books familiar to today's teenagers make this discussion of depression in youth more approachable than many of the young adult titles available on the subject. The authors, a free-lance writer and a family therapist who works with adolescents, keep technical terms to a minimum as they explain the difference between the "blues" and clinical depression, explore the physiological underpinnings of the illness, and pinpoint some of the environmental triggers, such as stress or a death in the family, that are thought to provoke depression. Sample case histories humanize the discussion, and the authors include simple suggestions for handling the "downers": exercise, altering the wake/sleep cycle, and eliminating caffeine from the diet, among them. While honest about the stigma associated with therapy and emotional illness, the authors make it plain that professional intervention can help and urge teens to speak to an adult or seek counseling if their troubles begin to overwhelm them.

Dentemaro, Christine, and Rachel Kranz. *Straight Talk about Anger.*

1995. New York: Facts On File (0-8160-3079-0). Ages 14–18.

Although they cover some of the same territory as Beckelman, previously cited, Dentemaro and Kranz offer a far more thorough discussion of anger. The information is both lucidly presented and well organized, but in their attempt to be comprehensive, they deliver more about the subject than most readers will ever need or want to know. What's more, like others in the Straight Talk series, the book has a drab jacket and an unappealing format. What may save it from gathering dust on the shelf are the many examples of young adults responding to everyday life situations. Teens with a serious interest in psychology will be well served by the book; young adults less inclined toward in-depth analysis will be better off with Beckelman's more approachable Hot Line title.

"To express anger effectively, you need to understand what you're feeling and why."
—from *Straight Talk about Anger*

Dinner, Sherry H. *Nothing to Be Ashamed of: Growing Up with Mental Illness in Your Family.* 1989. New York: Lothrop (0-688-08482-6); Morrow, paper (0-688-08493-1). Ages 11–15.

Dinner offers support and reassurance to young people growing up in a family altered by mental illness. Though less detailed and directed to a younger audience than Greenberg's *Emotional Illness in Your Family,* discussed elsewhere in this chapter, Dinner's text covers some of the same important territory, including discussion of symptoms and treatments for such illnesses as schizophrenia, depression, Alzheimer's disease, and anorexia. A psychologist who has worked with children, Dinner acknowledges that, while facts help, understanding and acceptance of a condition may be difficult to achieve and that a change in family circumstances may actually be impossible. But she's convinced that coping strategies are useful and discusses how readers can become more positive in their outlook and more assertive as family members as well as where they can go to talk about their problems.

Dolan, Edward F. *Teenagers and Compulsive Gambling.* 1994. New York: Watts (0-531-11100-8). Ages 14–18.

Because of the densely packed pages, teens will probably steer clear of this except as a resource for reports. That's a shame because the book is an exceptionally well-organized, authoritative overview of the subject that explores the impact compulsive gambling has on the individual and on the family unit. About half the book is devoted to explaining the addict's typical downhill slide and three-phase recovery pattern, with Dolan adding immediacy by using the pronominal "you." Teens in need of outside help will find a description of the work of Gam-Anon and Gam-A-Teen, along with an address to write to for meeting locations. For young adults who "must gamble," Dolan suggests several common-sense reminders for playing wisely.

Greenberg, Harvey R. *Emotional Illness in Your Family: Helping Your Relative, Helping Yourself.* 1989. New York: Macmillan (0-02-736921-8). Ages 14–up.

A professor of clinical psychiatry talks about "living with other people's troubles" in a detailed book that combines medical facts with self-help guidance. To give readers a clearer understanding of various types of emotional illness, Greenberg includes a topically organized catalog of them—from anxiety-related complaints to eating disorders and illnesses that affect the elderly—explaining the symptoms and the usual medical treatment for each condition. Mindful of the dignity of the ill person as well as the needs of teenagers who live with them, he goes on to suggest age-appropriate ways young adults can assist without enabling, how they can deal with confused feelings they may have about their relative, and how they can be useful without losing perspective or becoming overwhelmed by responsibility or guilt. Filled with medical terms, the text is rather daunting and dry but organized for quick reference, and it strikes at the core of what being part of a family entails.

Haubrich-Caperson, Jane, and Doug Van Nispen. *Coping with Teen Gambling*. 1993. New York: Rosen (0-8239-1512-3). Ages 14–17.

The beginning is slow, and the book is repetitious at times as well as undeniably proscriptive. Yet, there's some solid information mixed in about the insidious means by which gambling has gained a foothold among the young as well as some guidelines to help teens recognize gambling addiction. The numerous personal accounts may entice readers. However, they are often so long and so message laden that readers won't miss much if they skip them and concentrate, instead, on more-focused sections that investigate the reasons teens gamble, what happens when betting spirals out of control, and how the addicted can fight the problem.

Maloney, Michael, and Rachel Kranz. *Straight Talk about Anxiety and Depression*. 1991. New York: Facts On File (0-8160-2434-0); Dell, paper (0-440-21472-6). Ages 14–18.

A responsible statement noting that "the advice and suggestions given in this book are not meant to replace professional medical and psychiatric care," prefaces this book, which is one of a handful that considers teenage stress from a real self-help perspective. Incorporating a revealing look at societal attitudes that can exacerbate anxiety-related illnesses, the authors identify common high-stress factors among teens, then clearly explain how such pressures evolve into anxiety and depression. Coping strategies suggested range from the simple and practical (exercise, read a book, clean your room) to well-detailed descriptions of sophisticated techniques such as visualization, positive self-talk, and relaxation. Biological depression is not explored nor is there much about medication, but the authors do contribute a thoughtful discussion about the kinds of professional care that are available. Like other books in the Straight Talk series, this won't attract the audience it deserves because of its drab format.

Porterfield, Kay Marie. *Straight Talk about Post-Traumatic Stress Disorder*. 1996. New York: Facts On File (0-8160-3258-0). Ages 14–18.

Although one of the weakest in a series that is usually excellent, this somewhat diffuse book nonetheless tackles a problem that may be affecting teens or members of their families. Porterfield alludes to the difficulties of diagnosing PTSD and admits that there seems no firm scientific reason why some individuals are stricken and others who live through the same stressful situation are not. She explains risk factors, symptoms, and treatments in some detail (there are separate chapters devoted to PTSD in young people), establishing continuity for the reader by focusing mainly on four people whose lives have been affected by PTSD—among them, a young man who was mugged and a girl whose home was destroyed by fire. A final chapter discusses getting help.

Physical Well-Being

Cheney, Glenn Alan. *Teens with Physical Disabilities: Real-Life Stories of Meeting the Challenges*. 1995. Springfield, N.J.: Enslow (0-89490-625-9). Ages 11–15.

Unlike Kreigsman's *Taking Charge,* discussed later in this section, this focuses more on feelings and teenagers' daily lives than on setting long-term goals and establishing commonalities. There's no soft pedaling when it comes to how the eight young adults introduced here feel or what they go through emotionally and physically to manage their days. The voices are often shrill, angry, and cynical as the talk ranges from wheelchairs to finding friends to worries about the future. And there are plenty of stark details about the various accidents or conditions that must be coped with, too. Yet, along with the gritty description and bitterness, there's also a sense of the determination that has helped these kids survive, a tenacity that can inspire any reader, disabled or not. The question-and-answer segments following each profile diminish the power of the narratives, with a few of the questions sounding downright silly: "How do kids with JRA (juvenile rheumatoid arthritis) feel about their condition?" At the same time, they bring together a few basic facts that may clear up misconceptions and reshape distorted attitudes.

"You gotta understand: Our lives suck. I mean anybody with a disability. It's a constant battle."

—Debbie Eisenberg, 18, from *Teens with Physical Disabilities*

Coffey, Wayne. *Straight Talk about Drinking: Teenagers Speak Out about Alcohol.* 1988. New York: NAL, paper (0-452-26061-2). Ages 12–17.

Coffey leaves no doubt about his views on alcohol, describing it as a substance that "pollutes" the body and destroys the mind. As the son of an alcoholic, he can testify firsthand to the damage it can cause. He incorporates his own experiences with comments from the medical director of a drug treatment center and some fifty teenagers who have been or are alcohol abusers or who live with an alcoholic family member. He includes facts about the physiological and psychological effects of alcohol as well as insight into why kids drink in the first place, and he explodes a host of common misconceptions about drinking: cold showers, for example, produce clean drunks, not sober people. Coffey discusses the dangers of drinking and driving in a separate section, and for teenagers concerned about a friend or parent who is addicted, he explains what "helping by not helping" means.

Dorfman, Elena. *The C-Word: Teenagers and Their Families Living with Cancer.* 1994. Portland, Ore.: NewSage Press, paper (0-939165-21-X). Ages 12–18.

Dorfman gives us sharp, candid, black-and-white shots that show kids with cancer at their best and worst—enjoying their family and friends, in pain, depressed, and without any hair. Such pictures are combined with

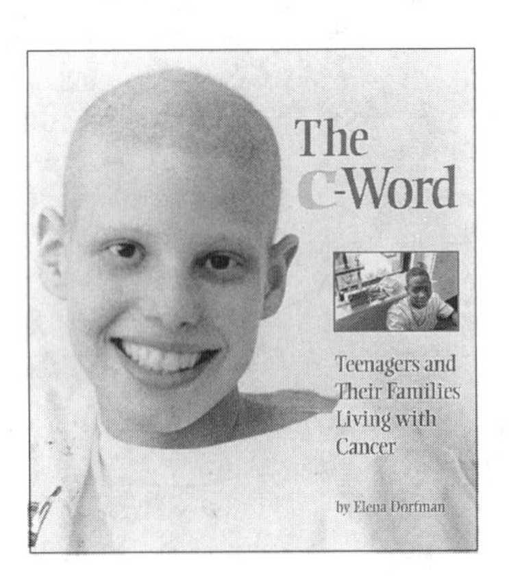

trenchant, revealing interviews Dorfman had with five young adults and their parents and sibs. A former cancer patient herself, Dorfman knows the emotions, the terms (there's an excellent glossary), and the kind of questions that need to be answered: What was the worst part of the treatment? Is there a positive side to having cancer? Does your family understand your illness? When you date, do you tell the girls you're sick? The result is a view of teens "fighting the brave fight," filled with experiences and words that will inspire others when their "own time to face death comes."

Goodheart, Barbara. *Diabetes*. 1990. New York: Watts (0-531-10882-1). Ages 12–15.

Goodheart's organization and approach make her book more likely to be chosen as curriculum support than as self-help material. Even so, her lucid overview can help diabetics and their family members as well as students attain a clearer picture of Type I and Type II diabetes. Her discussions of home and hospital testing and treatment incorporate information on how diet and exercise as well as insulin are used in diabetes management. Although Goodheart maintains that most diabetics who take proper care of themselves can live normal, productive lives, she is honest about the demanding nature of the illness, both on personal relationships and on one's daily routines. She makes the necessity of eating at regular intervals, exercising cautiously, and measuring blood-sugar levels abundantly clear.

If You Print This, Please Don't Use My Name. Ed. by Nancy Keltner. 1992. Davis, Calif.: Terra Nova Press, paper (0-944176-03-8). Ages 13–17.

A California advice column called "FYI" supplied the correspondence that makes up this book, which is one of those great items teens can pick up, put down, then return to again and again. Arranged into broad topical chapters, the letters (most are from teens, though a few are from parents), signed by a variety of "Just Luckys," "Undecideds," and "Feeling Guilty and Confuseds," express teens' concerns about many burdensome physical and emotional matters. Except for an occasional response submitted by the FYI editor, the queries have been answered by professionals—physicians, psychiatrists, and other specialists—whose credentials are supplied in an appendix. Their responses are informal, almost conversational in tone, yet still straight to the point. The book's graphics are amateurish, and its subject coverage is uneven; as is usual in this type of book, no topic is considered in much depth. But the FYI editor wisely includes end-of-chapter bibliographies (a mix of books for parents and teens) that will enable readers to investigate their concerns easily and more fully elsewhere.

Kaufman, Miriam. *Easy for You to Say: Q & As for Teens Living with Chronic Illness or Disability*. 1995. Ontario, Can.: Kay Porter Books; dist. by Publishers Group West, paper (1-55013-619-4). Ages 15–18.

Unlike Cheney's book, discussed previously in this section, this isn't a forum for angry feelings or a book that explains what having a disability is like. Nor does it deal with goal setting to the extent Kriegsman's *Taking Charge* does. Instead, this question-answer text, put together by a Canadian physician who works with adolescents, is aimed exclusively at teens who are disabled and includes information not usually presented in book form. There are a few fairly general chapters—on family dynamics, friendship, and recreation. The best sections, however, concern medical issues and sexuality. In these, teens ask specific, usually very personal questions about such things as drug interactions (several useful appendixes are included) and sexual behavior. Kaufman occasionally sounds too much like an all-wise counselor, but she's always frank and always careful to remind teens to act safely and responsibly, especially if they are considering sexual intimacy. Kaufman might have supplied stronger encouragement for teens to communicate with their doctors or parents, but that shouldn't compromise the value of this unusual book, which is filled with the sort of information disabled teens may desperately need but, in fact, are too embarrassed to ask for.

Kids Explore the Gifts of Children with Special Needs. Ed. by Westridge Young Writers Workshop. 1994. Santa Fe, N. Mex.: John Muir; dist.

by Norton, paper (1-56261-156-9). Ages 9–13.

This collection of inspiring profiles of disabled young people, the culmination of an elementary school writing project, is frank, enlightening, and candid about kids' curiosity regarding people who appear different from themselves. Ten youngsters, ranging roughly in age from 10 to 18, share bits and pieces of their lives with student scribes. The book does more than simply reveal the personal frustrations of managing with such conditions as hemophilia, dwarfism, or Down syndrome, and more than enlighten the unschooled about support groups, adaptive equipment, and therapies. It presents a message about personal achievement that can be taken to heart by any reader. With photos, student artwork, and some question-answer information about the disabilities introduced accompanying kids' own words, this is an honest, accepting look at the shaping of self-image and the fruits of self-determination.

Krementz, Jill. *How It Feels to Fight for Your Life*. 1989. Boston: Little, Brown (0-316-50364-9). Ages 10–15.

As she did in other volumes in her How It Feels series, Krementz ably preserves the individuality of the fourteen young people she interviewed for this affecting collective profile, which is illustrated with excellent black-and-white photographs that Krementz took herself. The children, who range in age from 7 to 16, articulately express how they cope with the fear and the pain associated with traumatic conditions such as cystic fibrosis, arthritis, and epilepsy. Their words are unpretentious and never sentimental. Their special strengths and personalities emerge distinctly through their accounts, as do the feelings and interests that bond them with most other children.

Krementz, Jill. *How It Feels to Live with a Physical Disability*. 1992. New York: Simon & Schuster (0-671-72371-5). Ages 10–15.

Similar in format to *How It Feels to Fight for Your Life*, this book introduces readers to a special group of twelve young people who face physical disabilities ranging from dwarfism to blindness to cerebral palsy. Each chapter contains a different story told from the child's perspective. As is usual in books in this series, black-and-white photographs cement the connection between readers and the young people profiled. The children speak frankly about the exigencies of their disabilities, but what comes across most clearly are not the challenges they face day to day but the emotional strength they've developed along the way. Of all Krementz's books in the How It Feels series, this is perhaps the most powerful. There's no self-pity in these kids' words. Instead, it's the pride they have in their achievements that rings out. Whether they tell of making a new friend, tying a shoe, or walking for the first time with an artificial leg, the stories are examples to us all.

Kriegsman, Kay Harris, and others. *Taking Charge: Teenagers Talk about Life and Physical Disabilities*. 1992. Bethesda, Md.: Woodbine House, paper (0-933149-46-8). Ages 14–18.

With the special needs of disabled teens in mind, the authors deal with a host of concerns common among adolescents—self-image, dating, sexuality, and getting along in a family and with friends. Responses to straightforward questions asked of fifteen disabled teenagers are the core of the book, which also touches on a few specialized issues, for example, coping when a wheelchair-accessible bathroom is not available or communicating when speaking clearly is a problem. There's a reassuring if rather general chapter on sexual intimacy that mentions an assortment of resources teens can investigate for specific answers as well as information spelling out some of the legal rights accorded by legislation such as the Americans with Disabilities Act. Written without a hint of pretentiousness or false comfort, this is an honest book that will help disabled young people view themselves and their goals with more assurance and clarity.

Krizmanic, Judy. *A Teen's Guide to Going Vegetarian*. 1994. New York: Viking (0-670-85114-0); Puffin, paper (0-14-036589-3). Ages 14–18.

Much more than a guide to modifying one's diet, this book takes pains to explain why vegetarianism is beneficial both to the individual and to the planet. Drawing on numerous resources, Krizmanic thoroughly investigates the reasons people choose not to eat meat, then encourages readers to become actively involved in vegetarianism by listing organizations and newsletters that deal with the subject from various perspectives. The last part of the book tackles vegetarianism pragmatically, discussing how to explain the switch to parents and friends, how to manage when eating out, and how to maintain good nutritional balance. There's even a small selection of recipes. This encouraging, consciousness-raising overview will provide dedicated vegetarians with additional facts and push the curious toward commitment.

Langone, John. *Tough Choices*. 1995. Boston: Little, Brown (0-316-51407-1). Ages 14–18.

Nobody who reads this can miss Langone's stand on using alcohol, drugs, and tobacco (he's the least charitable about tobacco, which he calls "the filthy weed"). Even so, the author is never so strident he'll turn off his audience. It helps that he's as upfront about contradictory medical evidence as he is about his own opinions. Langone covers the most familiar substances and important, timely issues related to their use—for example, the debate over legalization of drugs and concerns about crack babies. It's only in the final chapter, which discusses what can be done about drug abuse by an individual and by society, that he deals in any practical way with the idea of self-help, and then only briefly. Yet, because he treats the psychological reasons behind abuse more fully than do other authors on the subject, his discussion gives readers lots to think about with respect to their own lives and the lives of their significant others. Unfortunately, he hasn't documented his facts.

LeVert, Susanne. *Teens Face to Face with Chronic Illness*. 1993. New York: Messner (0-671-74540-9); paper (0-671-74541-7). Ages 14–18.

The words of young people with chronic conditions such as asthma, diabetes, cancer, and arthritis are the core of this book, much as they are of Krementz's *How It Feels to Fight for Your Life*. But instead of using a single chapter to reflect each child's perspective, LeVert smoothly integrates kids' comments throughout the text. Although this gives readers less sense of individual children, it allows LeVert to provide more background on each illness than Krementz is able to do. In fact, the first part of the book is an introduction to each of the illnesses covered in the text. Other chapters are solid, revealing discussions of the practical aspects of coping with chronic conditions and the way such illnesses affect daily activities, self-esteem, and personal relationships.

McMillan, Daniel. *Winning the Battle against Drugs: Rehabilitation Programs*. 1991. New York: Watts (0-531-11063-X). Ages 14–18.

In the strict sense, McMillan's book is not a self-help text. It doesn't attempt to promote self-esteem or prepare readers to cope practically with their struggle against drug abuse. What it does do is analyze the basic philosophies of drug rehabilitation by zeroing in on different types of treatment centers. McMillan reviews the programs at a comprehensive rehab endeavor that offers both inpatient and outreach service, an adolescent residential program, a Narcotics Anonymous outpatient group, and a methadone maintenance clinic. He also explores the success of various treatments and the controversy surrounding their use—in particular the use of methadone. There are no case studies or personal perspectives to humanize the text here, but the author's writing style is forceful, direct, and without jargon. Readers in search of general information about programs available, whether for themselves, a friend, or a family member, will discover much of value. McMillan's selective state-by-state listing of drug rehabilitation facilities will be of help as well.

Rosenberg, Maxine B. *On the Mend: Getting Away from Drugs.* 1991. New York: Bradbury (0-02-777914-9). Ages 14–18.

Although Rosenberg once again bases her text on personal interviews, this book differs from some of her previous books. Instead of devoting a chapter to each individual, she combines the stories here, running them together in sometimes confusing topical chapters that track the teens from their initial involvement with drugs through their crises, counseling, and struggles to stay "clean." Her subjects are not as diverse a group as she's chosen in the past: there are no adult perspectives, and the author admits to being "selective in both language and detail." But her book is a frankly spoken record, and the kids, who do most of the speaking (Rosenberg fills in some background), do eventually emerge as compelling distinct examples of the damage drugs can do. An afterword brings the individuals' stories up-to-date. Most, but not all, end successfully.

"In rehab a miracle happened. For the first time I started listening to people. When they talked about living I really tuned in. I wanted to live so badly."

—Cindy, from *On the Mend*

Ryan, Elizabeth. *Straight Talk about Drugs and Alcohol.* Rev. ed. 1995. New York: Facts On File (0-8160-3249-1). Ages 14–18.

Ryan is forceful but not preachy in this combination of fact and earnest advice. A look at the confusing messages young people receive from the media and from adults comes first. Then Ryan turns to statistics, including some published as recently as 1994. In separate chapters she details the negative impact alcohol and commonly abused hard drugs have on the body and on family relationships and offers guidelines to help young people determine if they actually have an addiction problem. Urging young people to get help if they need it, Ryan supplies an extensive list of facilities that treat teenage substance abusers and a list of print resources.

"If there's one message you should take away from this book, it's that there is always something you can do to make your life better, that you can make good choices that will work for you."

—from *Straight Talk about Drugs and Alcohol*

Salter, Charles A. *Looking Good, Eating Right: A Sensible Guide to Proper Nutrition and Weight Loss for Teens.* 1991. Brookfield, Conn.: Millbrook (1-56294-047-3). Ages 12–15.

Learning to eat right takes information as well as self-discipline. Salter provides the former while giving teens plenty of encouragement and excellent reasons to invoke the latter. He includes helpful insights into fads and eating disorders, though the majority of the book is devoted to outlining the basic principles of healthy eating and weight control, which he presents in a pleasant conversational tone. Chapters describe sensible, age-appropriate ways to lose weight, including brief exercise guidelines. A final section is devoted to answering common questions teenagers ask about dieting. For more-specific information on eating disorders teens can turn to books by

Landau, Maloney and Kranz, or Silverstein, described elsewhere in this section. Salter focuses more on eating "right" than eating "wrong."

Salter, Charles A. *Food Risks and Controversies: Minimizing the Dangers in Your Diet.* 1993. Brookfield, Conn.: Millbrook (1-56294-259-X). Ages 12–15.
———. *A Nutrition-Fitness Link: How Diet Can Help Your Body and Mind.* 1993. Brookfield, Conn.: Millbrook (1-56294-260-3). Ages 12–15.

Like Salter's other books in the Teen Nutrition series, these offer practical advice and answer common questions about foods and fitness. Athletes will be especially interested in the book about nutrition and fitness, which considers topics ranging from what to eat prior to playing sports to using vitamin supplements and carbohydrate loading. In *Food Risks and Controversies,* Salter, who is neither shrill nor menacing, makes full use of his background in research and his work as a practicing nutritionist as he discusses food additives, dehydration, and much more. Both books are attractively produced, with each containing charts and an annotated bibliography.

Salter, Charles A. *The Vegetarian Teen.* 1991. Brookfield, Conn.: Millbrook (1-56294-048-1). Ages 12–15.

"It is always wise to consult your doctor before changing your diet in a major way" begins an introduction to vegetarianism that is enthusiastic but also considerate of the nutritional needs of teenagers. Salter helps the curious decide whether a vegetarian diet is something they'd like to try and supplies enough background to get them started safely. A question-answer section spotlights common concerns teenagers have about the life style ("Should I tell dates I'm vegetarian?" "How can I be a vegetarian in the school cafeteria?" "How do I get my parents to go along with my vegetarianism?"), and a selection of simple-to-prepare recipes provides the incentive to begin experiments with new foods right away. Salter does cram a lot of information into this little book (barely ninety pages), but young adults serious about vegetarianism will need still more, especially about maintaining a nutritionally balanced diet. Unfortunately, Salter's list of further readings is too limited to be much help.

Silverstein, Alvin, and others. *Overcoming Acne: The How and Why of Healthy Skin Care.* 1990. New York: Morrow (0-688-08344-7). Ages 11–14.

Statistics point out that nearly 90 percent of young people between the ages of 12 and 17 have acne of one kind or another. That makes the subject of keen interest to teen readers. In straightforward fashion, Silverstein and his coauthors (his wife and son, in this case) examine what's known about the troublesome condition, explaining that while it cannot be cured, it can be treated. As in most of their many health-related books, the authors begin with basic physiology. They then describe how acne lesions develop, what causes them, and what can be done to manage them at home (with appropriate cautions about over-the-counter products) and with the help of a dermatologist.

Simon, Nissa. *Good Sports.* 1990. New York: HarperCollins/Crowell (0-690-04902-1). Ages 11–14.

Simon explains what exercise does for the body and for the mind in a helpful two-part guide that leads off with information about exercise physiology and aerobics, which she calls "the foundation for all sports." In her discussion of exercise basics she makes the importance of warm-ups and cool-downs clear and explains the kind of workout necessary to increase strength and endurance. In a section that relates nutrition to better performance, Simon suggests a simple carbohydrate diet and provides a sample menu. The book's second half focuses on sports injuries, describing some of the more common ones and explaining how factors such as steroid use or weather conditions can threaten well-being. The author stresses a sensible approach to exercise, whether a person's ultimate goal is improving physical fitness or boosting self-esteem.

Simpson, Carolyn, and Penelope Hall. *Rx: Reading and Following the Directions for All Kinds of Medications*. 1994. New York: Rosen (0-8239-1696-0). Ages 15–18.

Simpson and Hall, who is a board-certified internist, have written one of the more interesting and useful books in the Lifeskills Library, an easy-to-read series dedicated to introducing young adults to practical aspects of daily living, such as using classified ads, reading maps, and interviewing for a job. In this slim volume, the authors accept adolescence as the time when young people begin to assume responsibility for some of their own medical care: they often speak to the doctor without their parents and begin to buy and use medications without adult supervision. Although their book is certainly no substitute for advice from a doctor or parent, it does instruct teens in some important basics. Each chapter is launched by a pointed fictional scenario, with the main text introducing, in the broadest of terms, how various professions function in the health-care system and how to buy, store, and use over-the-counter medications. Photos are marginal at best.

Slap, Gail B., and Martha M. Jablow. *Teenage Health Care*. 1994. New York: Pocket, paper (0-671-75412-2). Ages 14–18.

Although written for parents, this book will also interest teenagers looking for a clear-cut, comprehensive view of issues related to their growth and development, health, and well-being. Special concerns of teens and pre-teens—for example, weight, eating disorders, or parental involvement in teenagers' health care—are addressed as are general medical issues such as infections, headaches, and bronchitis. For information on puberty, readers will be better off with Robie Harris's *It's Perfectly Normal* or one of Lynda Madaras's books, but sections on behavioral issues, such as drug abuse, teen pregnancy, depression, and learning disorders, are nicely done, with the authors providing both medical background and a distinct sense of the difficult challenges that come with such behaviors. The authors make it clear that their book is not intended as a substitute for professional care but rather "a forum for a sharing and open discussion" between parents and teens.

Taylor, Clark. *The House That Crack Built*. 1992. New York: Chronicle (0-8118-0133-0). Ages 11–15.

This has many of the characteristics of a picture book (less than forty pages; large, double-spread illustrations; verse based on a familiar children's rhyme), but it definitely isn't a book for the lap-sitting set. It's a warning to older children and teens about drug abuse: "This is the Street of a town in pain / that cries for the Drug known as cocaine." In cumulative verse that has the rhythmic flavor of rap, Taylor builds a stark picture of a society in which violence and drugs intertwine. Surreal illustrations, contributed by Jan Thompson Dicks, show the human misery and torment as they take readers from the mansion of the drug lord to the streets and the hungry baby, forgotten by its crack-addicted mother. It's a stunning presentation that will draw a large teenage audience despite the conspicuous "don't do it" message.

Vogel, Carole Garbuny. *Will I Get Breast Cancer? Questions & Answers for Teenage Girls*. 1995. Morristown, N.J.: Messner (0-671-88046-2); paper (0-671-88047-0). Ages 14–18.

Vogel, who's knowledgeable enough to know there's no real answer to her title question, still provides a lot of exceptionally useful information in this book, which is targeted at girls concerned about their own medical heritage and those with a loved one who has breast cancer. After setting down appropriate background about breast structure and development, Vogel answers a host of questions about diagnostic procedures, treatment options, nutrition, risk factors, and emotional stress, even including some very painful, embarrassing ones: "Can a woman who has had breast cancer still have sex?" "Am I a selfish person if I forget about my mom and have fun?" The facts are up-to-date, and the book features a selection of good, detailed drawings and black-and-white photographs to add impact and clarify the information. A closing chapter, "Losing the Battle," acknowledges the work of Dr. Elizabeth Kübler-Ross, and there's an extensive glossary to help readers better understand the medical terms they'll surely hear should cancer strike. This fine book never pretends and never patronizes.

Weiss, Jonathan H. *Breathe Easy: Young People's Guide to Asthma.* 1994. New York: Magination Press, paper (0-945354-62-2). Ages 10–14.

Comprehensive without being overloaded with detail, casual in tone without being flip or losing focus, this is one of the most accessible guides to self-care for asthma sufferers available to young people. Weiss, who talks directly to his readers, pulls no punches in his description of what an asthma attack is. Even so, he manages to be encouraging in his descriptions of how the condition can be managed. Chapters explain ways to identify and avoid personal triggers, handle prescribed medication, and deal with an attack when it occurs. Weiss even devotes a section to deep breathing and relaxation techniques. The diagrams are amateurish, but that's a small criticism for a book that is in keeping with the current medical trend toward arming asthma sufferers with appropriate information to help them help themselves.

FICTION

Anderson, Rachel. *Black Water.* 1995. New York: Holt (0-8050-3847-7). Ages 14–17.

Albert is an epileptic, but in the Victorian England in which he's growing up, he's a freak—to himself and to nearly everyone else except his beloved mother and an eccentric writer and artist by the name of Edward Lear.

Anderson, Rachel. *The Bus People.* 1992. New York: Holt (0-8050-2297-X). Ages 15–18.

This stark, affecting collection of vignettes brings to life a group of physically and mentally disabled young people who ride "Bertram's Bus" to school every day and levels sharp criticism at people who lack kindness and understanding where disabilities are concerned.

Bennett, James. *I Can Hear the Mourning Dove.* 1990. Boston: Houghton (0-395-53623-5); Scholastic, paper (0-590-45691-1). Ages 15–18.

Sixteen-year-old Gracie, who has suffered several serious bouts of depression, wakes up in the psychiatric unit yet again. This time it takes an angry, defiant fellow patient to convince her that she's still capable of getting better and getting out.

Brooks, Bruce. *No Kidding.* 1989. New York: Harper (0-06-020722-1); paper (0-06-447051-2). Ages 13–16.

Guardian of his younger brother, 14-year-old Sam is the consummate byproduct of a twenty-first century where rampant alcoholism has caused the collapse of traditional society and children are educated to become the custodians of their families and their futures.

Cadnum, Michael. *Calling Home.* 1991. New York: Viking (0-670-83566-8); Puffin, paper, (0-14-034569-8). Ages 14–18.

Peter, who is horrified when he kills his best friend in a drunken brawl, tries to hide his secret by slipping into alcoholic oblivion.

Caseley, Judith. *My Father, the Nutcase.* 1992. New York: Knopf (0-679-833-94-3). Ages 14–18.

Fifteen-year-old Zoe ricochets from anger to pain to compassion as she watches her father, who is deeply depressed, change from a supportive, caring parent into a zombie.

Childress, Alice. *A Hero Ain't Nothin' but a Sandwich.* 1973. New York: Avon, paper (0-380-00132-2). Ages 14–16.

Benjie Johnson, 13 years old, is a heroin addict. He thinks he can break his habit whenever he wants, but when he's forced to try, he discovers it's not as easy as he thought it would be.

Crutcher, Chris. *Crazy Horse Electric Game.* 1987. New York: Greenwillow (0-688-06683-6); Dell, paper (0-440-20094-6). Ages 14–18.

When an injury in a water-skiing accident leaves star athlete Willie Weaver with an awkward, lurching step and slow speech, he copes by running away.

Erlich, Amy. *The Dark Card.* 1991. New York: Viking (0-670-83733-4); Puffin, paper (0-14-036332-7). Ages 15–18.

Consumed by pain and guilt after her mother's death, 17-year-old Laura Samuels finds solace in a nearby gambling casino, which lures her with the promise of excitement and the chance to be somebody else—somebody daring and anonymous, somebody who's happy.

Feuer, Elizabeth. *Paper Doll.* 1990. New York: Farrar (0-374-35736-6). Ages 15–18.

Teenager Leslie, a gifted violinist who lost her legs in a car accident, meets smart, sensitive Jeff, who has cerebral palsy. Their loving, sexual relationship helps Leslie discover courage as well as pleasure.

Fox, Paula. *The Moonlight Man.* 1986. New York: Bradbury (0-02-735480-6); Dell, paper (0-440-20079-2). Ages 14–18.

When Catherine finally gets an opportunity to spend time alone with her father after her parents' divorce, she discovers that the man she's always idealized is dashing, intelligent, and charming—but only when he's sober.

Frank, Lucy K. *I Am an Artichoke.* 1995. New York: Holiday (0-8234-1150-8). Ages 12–14.

Sarah, 15, is looking forward to a summer as a mother's helper—until she discovers that her 12-year-old charge is anorexic and the girl's mother refuses to believe or do anything about it.

Franklin, Kristine L. *Eclipse.* 1995. Boston: Candlewick (1-56402-544-6). Ages 12–15.

For Trina Stenkawsky the pride of earning a coveted school prize, starting her period, and attending her first school dance is tempered by her father's increasingly strange and scary behavior and her mother's preoccupation with the late-in-life child she is expecting.

Fraustino, Lisa Rowe. *Ash.* 1995. New York: Orchard (0-531-06889-7). Ages 15–18.

In a poignant diary, 15-year-old Wes writes about his older brother, Ash, once adored, smart, and tough, now a virtual stranger who talks to himself, hurls vicious insults, and thinks nothing of bashing his head against a door.

Getz, David. *Thin Air*. 1990. New York: Holt (0-8050-1379-2); Harper, paper (0-06-440422-6). Ages 11–14.

Jacob Katz suffers from crippling asthma that causes his parents to hover over him and his brother to pity him. More than anything else he wants to be in a regular sixth-grade classroom and have the kids treat him like a person who sometimes gets sick, not a person who'll never be well.

Greenberg, Joanne. *I Never Promised You a Rose Garden*. 1964. New York: NAL, paper (0-451-16031-2). Ages 14–up.

Committed to a mental institution when she's diagnosed as psychotic, teenager Deborah Blau describes her difficult road to recovery and the compassionate psychiatrist who helped her.

Jensen, Kathryn. *Pocket Change*. 1989. New York: Macmillan (0-02-747731-2); paper (0-590-43419-5). Ages 14–18.

Sixteen-year-old Josie Monroe is alarmed and puzzled by her beloved father's increasingly violent behavior. Unwilling to pretend nothing is amiss, she secretly investigates and concludes that her dad's experiences in Vietnam may be causing his problems now.

Johnson, Angela. *Humming Whispers*. 1995. New York: Orchard/Richard Jackson (0-531-06898-6). Ages 14–18.

Sophy is talented and well-centered and is devoted to her older sister, Nicole. But Nicole was diagnosed with schizophrenia at Sophy's age, and Sophy now wonders if she, too, will someday lose her mind.

Koertge, Ron. *Tiger, Tiger, Burning Bright*. 1994. New York: Orchard/Melanie Kroupa (0-531-06840-4). Ages 12–15.

Jesse is concerned about his grandfather. Once Jesse's wise and patient teacher, Pappy is now easily distracted and dangerously forgetful, so much so that Jesse fears his mother will put Pappy in a retirement home.

LeMieux, A. C. *The TV Guide Counselor*. 1993. New York: Morrow (0-688-124202-X); Avon, paper (0-380-72050-7). Ages 14–18.

Even his newly discovered interest in photography and a supportive girlfriend aren't enough to stop 17-year-old Michael's depression after his parents divorce.

Metzger, Lois. *Barry's Sister*. 1992. New York: Atheneum (0-689-31521-X); Puffin, paper (0-14-036484-6). Ages 12–14.

Ellen, who's 14, tells the story of her family's struggle to adjust to a new baby, Barry, who was born with cerebral palsy. The story continues in *Ellen's Case* (1995, Simon & Schuster), which focuses on Ellen's feelings about a malpractice suit her parents are filing in Barry's behalf.

Meyer, Carolyn. *Killing the Kudu*. 1990. New York: Macmillan/Margaret K. McElderry (0-689-50508-6). Ages 15–18.

Helped by his cousin Scott and a beautiful nurse, a paraplegic teenager breaks away from his overprotective mother and finds both love and independence.

Miklowitz, Gloria. *Anything to Win*. 1989. New York: Delacorte (0-385-29750-5); Dell, paper (0-440-20732-0). Ages 14–18.

Cam Potter has a chance at a big college scholarship if he puts on 30 pounds. Ignoring health warnings, he starts on steroids to bulk up quickly. It takes rejection by his girlfriend and the death of a longtime steroid user he knows well to shake him out of his destructive pattern.

Naylor, Phyllis Reynolds. *The Keeper.* 1986. New York: Atheneum (0-689-31204-0). Ages 12–15.

Both Nick Karpinsky and his mother realize that Nick's father is mentally ill. But Mr. Karpinsky refuses to seek help, and Nick and his mom, powerless to force him to go to a doctor, must cope as best they can.

O'Neal, Zibby. *Language of Goldfish.* 1980. New York: Viking (0-670-41785-8); Penguin, paper (0-14-034540-X). Ages 12–15.

Middle child in a newly affluent, happy family, 13-year-old Carrie finds herself less and less able to relate to her family or make new friends at her new school. Her unhappiness and depression deepen to the point that she no longer wants to live.

Philbrick, Rodman. *Freak the Mighty.* 1993. Scholastic/Blue Sky (0-590-47412-X); paper (0-590-47413-8). Ages 14–16.

With an ungainly body, a learning disability, and the stigma of being the son of a killer, Maxwell Kane despairs of ever having friends. Then along comes brilliant Kevin, born with a birth defect that's stunted his growth but not his capacity to have fun or to teach Max how to have confidence in himself.

Rodowsky, Colby. *Hannah in Between.* 1994. New York: Farrar (0-374-32837-4). Ages 12–14.

Hannah knows her mother is drinking too much. She's found bottles Mom hides around the house and has seen Mom make a fool of herself in front of strangers. What she doesn't know is what to do about it.

Rubin, Susan Goldman. *Emily Good as Gold.* 1993. San Diego: Harcourt (0-15-276632-4); paper (0-15-276633-2). Ages 11–14.

To her loving parents, Emily has always been Emily Gold, "good as gold," their developmentally disabled child, who would never grow up. But at 13, Emily has indeed begun to grow up, and she's angry, confused, and frustrated because she can't accomplish everything she wants.

Ruby, Lois. *Miriam's Well.* 1993. Scholastic (0-590-44937-0). Ages 13–18.

Miriam Pellham has bone cancer and knows that her religion prohibits medical intervention, but increasing pain and her growing attachment to Adam Bergen, who is Jewish, test her religious commitment. In the meantime, the courts become involved.

Shepard, Elizabeth. *H.* 1995. New York: Viking (0-670-85927-3). Ages 16–adult.

As a series of letters from his parents, his psychiatrist, his camp counselor, and 12-year-old Benjamin himself reveal, Ben lives in a world all his own, governed by his relationship with a stuffed toy letter, *H,* which he tries to carry wherever he goes.

Shreve, Susan. *The Gift of the Girl Who Couldn't Hear.* 1991. New York: Morrow (0-688-18318-9); paper (0-688-11694-9). Ages 11–14.

Moody and insecure, 13-year-old Eliza forgoes a chance to sing in the class musical only to find out that her best friend, Lucy, who has been deaf since birth, wants to try out. Lucy communicates orally, but she needs Eliza to teach her how to sing.

Slepian, Jan. *The Alfred Summer.* 1980. New York: Macmillan (0-02-782920-0). Ages 11–14.

An outsider because of his cerebral palsy, Lester finds a friend in Alfred, the "retarded kid from the house at the corner," in tomboy Clarie, and in Myron, whose boat-building project brings the kids together and helps each develop a positive sense of self-worth.

Strasser, Todd. *The Accident.* 1988. New York: Delacorte (0-440-50061-3); Dell, paper (0-440-20635-9). Ages 12–16.

Even though jocks don't usually mix with burnouts, Matt Thompson and Chris Walsh, who spends most of his time hung over or in trouble, are still friends of a sort. So when Chris is posthumously blamed for the drunk-driving accident that caused his death and the death of three others, Matt feels responsible for making certain that what everyone is saying about Chris is actually true.

Thiele, Colin. *Jodie's Journey.* 1990. New York: HarperCollins (0-06-026132-3). Ages 11–13.

Eleven-year-old Jodie is convinced that the pain in her joints is from rigorous practice on her beloved horse, Monarch. The doctor, however, diagnoses rheumatoid arthritis.

Ure, Jean. *See You Thursday.* 1983. New York: Delacorte (0-385-29303-8). Ages 13–18.

In a warm, tender romance, bossy 16-year-old Marianne and 24-year-old Abe, who won't let his blindness overwhelm his life, bring out the best in each other.

Voigt, Cynthia. *Izzy, Willy-Nilly.* 1986. New York: Atheneum (0-689-31202-4); Fawcett, paper (0-449-70214-6). Ages 14–16.

When a drunk-driving accident results in the tragic amputation of her leg, 15-year-old Izzy Lingard struggles to accept what's happened to her body, to her feelings, and to her relationships with her family and friends. The challenge makes her strong.

Werlin, Nancy. *Are You Alone on Purpose?* 1994. Boston: Houghton (0-395-67350-X). Ages 11–15.

Alison and Harry couldn't be more different, and they dislike each other immediately. But when an accident confines Harry to a wheelchair, Alison decides he needs a friend.

Wood, Jane Rae. *When Pigs Fly.* 1995. New York: Putnam (0-399-22911-6). Ages 11–14.

A project for her family living class has 13-year-old Buddy involved in caring for a hard-boiled-egg "baby." That's not as problematic for Buddy as for some kids, because Buddy is so used to watching out for her younger sister, Rennie, who has Down syndrome.

Sex Stuff

CONFRONTED BY BLATANT media exploitation of sex on the one hand and warnings about AIDS and pregnancy on the other, today's teens are caught in a dilemma no previous generation has had to face. Learning to evaluate all they see and hear about sex and to use the information wisely and responsibly is no easy task. Books can help, and there now exists a greater variety of quality material on the subject than ever before, with titles from presses representing widely divergent perspectives. There are books meant to be shared with parents, easy-to-read paperbacks for teens whose reading skills are poor, question-and-answer quick-reference guides for browsing, and books designed to reinforce a particular moral point of view. The selections that follow include some of the best of the various types of books available, along with some intriguing perspectives from author-teacher Lynda Madaras, who discusses sex education and the role of parents and books in the learning process.

Books and Sex: Some Perspectives from Lynda Madaras

Lecturer, teacher, teen advocate, and outspoken author of books for both teens and adults, Madaras has taught sex education to students ranging in age from 9 to 18. Her popular What's Happening to My Body books about puberty (one for boys, one for girls) have each sold more than 200,000 copies and have appeared on numerous lists, including the American Library Association's Best Books for Young Adults roundup. Her latest books, companion volumes coauthored with her daughter Area and published in 1993, are entitled *My Body, My Self* and *My Feelings, My Self.* Updated revisions of two earlier workbook titles, they allow girls to become more comfortable with the physical and emotional changes they're undergoing by using a combination of information and "freewriting," quizzes, checklists, and exercises.

SZ: *How did you come to write the What's Happening to My Body books?*

LM: My daughter Area was beginning to go through some physical changes that she felt really good about. Then I saw a shift in attitude. Suddenly, she didn't want to grow up and get breasts or do any of that sort of thing. There were also changes going on in our relationship. I realized that even though Area had known details about sex from the time she was a toddler, I had not talked to her about menstruation in the same way I talked to her about other aspects of sexuality. I wanted to find a book that would communicate what I wanted to say to her. Actually, I wasn't too picky in those days. If a book didn't make sex sound like a disease and it wasn't full of hideously sexist things, it would have passed my muster. But I couldn't find one, so I wrote one.

SZ: *Were you teaching while you wrote your books?*

LM: What actually happened was that the head mistress of Area's school called me up and said "We have spring fever—will you come down and talk to the kids?" Of course, as soon as I walked in the classroom and said the words *penis* and *vagina* the kids just totally disintegrated. That's why I evolved the technique of coloring Xerox pictures. I talk about that in the books. I hand out pictures of the genital organs in my classes, and I have the kids color something in red, something in blue, and so on. I'm tempted every once in a while not to use pictures with the high-school kids. But I've found that they allow people to do some legitimate giggling and help them deal with nervousness. I also write slang terms that kids use on the blackboard. I do that to help give kids a clearer idea of which word is appropriate in which setting—which word you can use with your mom, which you can use with the doctor, which you can use on the playground, or which might offend whom.

SZ: *You gave your daughter and Dane Saavedra, the son of a neighbor, author credit. How involved in the books were they?*

LM: Well, Dane just read the manuscript of the book for boys, but Area actively functioned as an editor. I'd write a chapter, and she'd read it from a kid's point of view. The books are really built up around the kinds of questions I get from kids. I think every question anyone has ever asked me is somehow covered. Of course, occasionally I'll get a new one. In the book for girls I mention one particular question from a girl who came up to me after class. She wanted to know whether a girl's breasts could burst—you know, like a balloon. It happens that developing breasts are sometimes sore, and people often make comments like "Wow, you're really busting out all over." This girl was really afraid breasts could burst. I think it's very easy for us as adults to forget how we thought about things when we were children. I'll also get deliberately lewd questions, the kind that include a lot of swear words or dirty words just to test me. But I often find these questions are sincere, too.

SZ: *I suppose you learn a lot from your students.*

LM: Well, I certainly get a different perspective, and I'm constantly reminded of how piecemeal the sexual information we give kids is.

SZ: *Do you use your books in your classes?*

LM: I follow the plan of the books, but I don't use them when I'm teaching. They are used as textbooks in a lot of schools, though. I really wrote them for parents and children to read together or to read separately and discuss. I think it's really important that parents and kids communicate about sex. When I was growing up it was the "just say no" approach. Actually, nobody even said "just say no." They never talked about sex. They wanted to protect kids from sexual experiences that might be harmful to them. But kids today are growing up in a very different world. They are bombarded by sexual messages in a way that no other generation in the history of the planet has been. We use sex to sell everything from toothpaste to dog food. The implicit message is that the goal of teen life is to have sex. Yet, teenagers get very little sexual information. What they get is usually not from their parents or from their synagogues or churches or their teachers at school. Mostly, it's from TV or from their peers, a source the kids themselves don't really trust. Obviously, the ideal situation is for parents and kids to communicate, and when parents and kids interact, having a book helps. Books make it easier for many parents to introduce the topic.

SZ: *What do you feel are the hallmarks of a good sex education book for preteens?*

LM: A lot of factual information about what happens to you. I get thousands of letters from kids who like the idea of the stages of development that I use in my books. For kids, having stages is like having a map—this territory has been charted. And illustrations. Kids always want to know how things work.

SZ: *You integrate a lot of comments from kids into your books, don't you?*

LM: Yes. I don't know if that's necessary, but it's certainly the part kids like the best. They all think they're the only ones who ever thought a particular way, so having someone else talk about the same feelings is very reassuring.

SZ: *At what age should kids start reading and learning about sex?*

LM: It's generally accepted in my field that if a child has gotten to be 5 and hasn't asked the "where do babies come from?" question, parents should introduce the subject. Different age groups have different interests. With toddlers, the big issue is gender identity. Adults and older children know that you're born a boy or you're born a girl and you pretty much stay that way. That's not intuitively obvious to little kids. As for older children, there's a lot of anxiety about penis size. I would say that next to the "Am I normal?" queries I get in letters, that is the major concern among boys. A boy looks at his father and looks at himself. It isn't necessarily obvious to that kid that when he grows up, his whole body grows. And it shouldn't be.

SZ: *If you were to write a general sex education book for older teens who've gone through puberty, say ages 16, 17, and 18, what would you include that's different from the material you included in your books for preteens?*

LM: I'd include discussion of sexual decision making. And the book should talk about love. Kids really want to know about love. I think any book for older kids would have to address feelings and emotional issues. It also has to tell kids the truth and talk about skills for saying "no" and negotiating your sexual life.

SZ: *How about sexually transmitted diseases? I know you included some information on them in your books about puberty, but aren't they more of a factor for older kids?*

LM: Oh, absolutely. Actually, I only added information on STDs to my puberty books with great reluctance. In the wake of the teen pregnancy epidemic and AIDS, people decided that we'd better start sex education earlier. I'm sure there's something to be said for starting prevention programs early, but too often what happens is that sex education addresses the agendas of nervous adults instead of the agendas of kids. Though it varies by community, less than 2 percent of sixth graders are sexually active. For a lot of them, a discussion of sexual decision making makes about as much sense as telling them what to pack to wear to the moon. What kids are really concerned about at that age are things like "How come my penis curves to the left?" I find that if you address kids' agendas they develop an immense gratitude. I sometimes think that if I told my kids to paint their feet blue, they would. They're just so grateful when someone tells them about all the stuff they are worried about. Also, if you address their concerns, they believe you care about them. Then they are more willing to listen when you talk about sexual morality or healthy rules for conducting a sexual life.

SZ: *Your books are explicit. Have they had censorship problems?*

LM: Yes, they've made the banned books list. Whenever a banning situation comes to my attention, I always respond personally with an open letter to the community. I've also actually gone to places and talked with the people involved. My experience has been that people get crazy and make claims that are overblown. They really hang themselves with their own rope. In every community where I've been personally involved in a banning situation, the book has been unbanned. I've also found that the vast majority of parents are really grateful for this kind of a book. I should say something here. Thank God for librarians. The Committee on Intellectual Freedom has done incredible work standing up to the book-banning mentality. I often use the fact that the American Library Association has selected the books as "best" books. Their imprimatur has meant a lot to me, not only because I'm personally honored by it but also because it carries a lot of weight in a banning situation.

NONFICTION

Puberty

Baer, Judy. *Dear Judy, Did You Ever Like a Boy (Who Didn't Like You?).* 1993. Minneapolis: Bethany House, (1-55661-431-5). Ages 10–14.

Baer counts on her great popularity as an author of Christian fiction for girls to attract readers to this nonfiction advice book. As Judy Blume did in *Letters to Judy: What Your Kids Wish They Could Tell You* (1986), Baer draws her topics from the hundreds of letters she has received. However, unlike Blume, whose book is really for parents, Baer aims her counsel squarely at middle-school/junior-high girls, who often identify strongly with the characters in Baer's Cedar River Daydreams problem novels. Making friends, dealing with boys and dating, and the role of faith in personal relationships are the author's prime concerns. Verses from the Scripture are integrated into the discussion, traditional Christian values are emphasized, and there's clear opposition to sex outside of marriage and to smoking. Nothing is considered in much depth, yet Baer's motherly tone is pleasant, her counsel firm without being judgmental, and her heartfelt message—taking pride in one's faith and in oneself will make concerns about sex and growing up easier to bear—is conveyed with strength and optimism.

Bell, Alison, and Lisa Rooney. *Your Body, Yourself: A Guide to Your Changing Body.* 1993. Los Angeles: Lowell House, paper (1-56565-045-X). Ages 11–14.

By a free-lance writer and a Connecticut pediatrician, this book isn't as thorough as Madaras's or Harris's books, which are described later in this chapter, but it stands up well as an approachable introduction to female sexuality. The authoritative yet genial tone of the text will put girls just beginning to think about their changing bodies at ease, as will the authors' choice not to overload their readers with information. Consequently, some things are glossed over or left out: there's nothing about masturbation or homosexuality and only very basic descriptions of intercourse and pregnancy. As far as pubertal change is concerned, the text will be quite helpful, with especially useful sections on breast self-examination (illustrated), skin care, and sanitary protection. There's also a chapter on nutrition and an illustrated explanation of the sexual organs, male and female. The authors become a little preachy when they lay out the dangers of drug abuse and cigarette smoking, but the message is certainly difficult to argue with, and their concern is evident in every word.

Bourgeois, Paulette, and Martin Wolfish. *Changes in You and Me: A Book about Puberty, Mostly for Boys*. 1994. Kansas City, Mo.: Andrews and McMeel (0-8362-2814-6). Ages 11–14.

———. *Changes in You and Me: A Book about Puberty, Mostly for Girls*. 1994. Kansas City, Mo.: Andrews and McMeel (0-8362-2815-4). Ages 11–14.

Like *Your Body, Yourself* (for girls), above these companion books for middle-grade/junior-high kids are good introductions and are written in a friendly tone that's reassuring as well as earnest. It's their attractive design, which includes an oversize format and lively cartoon-style drawings, that gives them an edge. The discussions are honest and forthright as far as they go, and there are several areas in which they will be particularly helpful: each book contains a useful chapter about puberty in the opposite sex; the book for boys includes information about shaving and jock straps; and the book for girls contains an unusually complete explanation about tampons and their use. But there are also some informational gaps. Abortion is not discussed in either book (though it is briefly defined in the glossary), and there are only three or four sentences about birth control, with readers directed to Planned Parenthood or a medical professional if they want information. Also, the transparent overlays each book contains are gimmicky, and the books' diagrams are not very precise. The jacket photos, however, are joyous, and the authors' comforting responses to basic questions make the texts great for adolescents who do want the facts—but not all at once. Each book has a great glossary that includes a number of slang terms (balls, etc.) kids may be familiar with but don't really understand.

Cole, Joanna. *Asking about Sex and Growing Up: A Question-and-Answer Book for Boys and Girls*. 1988. New York: Morrow (0-688-06927-4). Ages 10–13.

Although the pen-and-ink cartoon sketches (there are also several anatomical drawings) will attract mostly upper-elementary kids, older children will not find Cole's question-answer text patronizing in the least. In fact, its simple, forthright approach to common questions about puberty, sex, reproduction, and related matters is suitable for anyone who wants a quick, clear summary of an important part of life. Questions, printed in enlarged, boldfaced type, run the gamut from "Why do girls and women have their periods?" and "What is a wet dream?" to "Can homosexuals be parents?" and "How does a person get AIDS?" There's certainly less detail about any one concern here than in the Changes in You and Me books, discussed previously, but there's slightly more breadth in coverage, with Cole succinctly tackling in nonjudgmental fashion a surprisingly wide range of issues—from pregnancy, masturbation, crushes, and puberty to birth control and AIDS. Although this is a relatively old book, it is still worth keeping on the shelf.

Glassman, Bruce. *Everything You Need to Know about Growing Up Male*. 1991. New York: Rosen (0-8239-1224-8). Ages 12–16.

The companion book for girls in the Need to Know Library series is poorly organized and incomplete, but this book for boys is a straightforward, clearly written summary that is neatly packaged into sixty-four easy-to-read pages and illustrated with teen-appealing photographs. Its scope is surprisingly wide: Glassman deals with facts as well as feelings related to puberty, even touching briefly on the subject of male stereotypes. Noteworthy are a chapter on personal care that discusses shaving, pimples, and mouth hygiene; an explanation of how to use condoms; and a question-and-answer section about problems.

Harris, Robie. *It's Perfectly Normal: A Book about Changing Bodies, Growing Up, Sex, and Sexual Health*. 1994. Boston: Candlewick (1-56402-199-8); paper (1-56402-159-9). Ages 11–14.

This caring, contentious, and well-crafted book will certainly attract young teens and be a fine school- and home-library resource, but its forthright approach will raise a few eyebrows. For one thing, the colorful, gently humorous cartoon artwork, by Michael Emberley, is more candid than is usual for the book's target audience: for example, a double-page spread of nude figures is used to demonstrate the different shapes and sizes people come in; one picture shows a girl examining her genitals by looking in a mirror; another discreetly depicts a boy masturbating as he sits on his bed. Second, Harris's text is every bit as direct as Emberley's art. It encompasses all the "age appropriate" information (facts about puberty and the structure of the reproductive system, etc.) but also a good deal more—from terms people use when talking about sex to straightforward information about intercourse, abortion, sexual abuse, and issues of responsibility and respect. Teens won't find the answers to their questions as easily here as they will in Cole's question-and-answer book, discussed previously, but they'll find a more informative, attractive package that will help them understand and feel comfortable with what's happening to their bodies and accept the idea that sexuality comprises many things, not just one. A good precursor to Madaras's less approachable but more substantial books about puberty.

"Sex is about a lot of things—bodies, growing up, families, love, caring, curiosity, feelings, respect. . . . That's why there is more than one answer to the question, what is sex?"

—from *It's Perfectly Normal*

Madaras, Lynda, and Dane Saavedra. *The What's Happening to My Body? Book for Boys: A Growing Up Guide for Parents and Sons*. Rev. ed. 1988. New York: Newmarket (1-55704-002-8); paper (0-937858-99-4). Ages 11–15.

Madaras, Lynda, and Area Madaras. *The What's Happening to My Body? Book for Girls: A Growing Up Guide for Parents and Daughters*.

Rev. ed. 1988. New York: Newmarket (1-55704-001-X); paper (0-937858-98-6). Ages 11–15.

These two books are perfect vehicles for parent-preteen sharing. Madaras addresses the lack of material on puberty for boys in her first book, written with input from 15-year-old Saavedra, the son of a friend. Her book for girls was written with her daughter. Both volumes provide in-depth information on all aspects of puberty. Grounded in Madaras's experience as a California sex-education instructor, the explicit, authoritative texts include questions and comments from students in Madaras's classes as lead-ins for discussion of a variety of topics, among them the stages of puberty, intercourse, birth control methods, and romantic feelings. A section on sexually transmitted diseases provides more information on the subject than is usual in books for the age group. The books also include discussion of sex-related health concerns (for example, jock itch and testicular cancer), and each features a chapter about puberty in the opposite sex. The dense-looking formats will put off lots of kids, but these books are among the most thorough on the subject of puberty available for the age group, despite their 1988 date. Their introductions for parents are Madaras's way of challenging adults to involve themselves in their children's sexual education.

"I have girlfriends who think if you get into heavy petting and all that with a boy, it's stupid or artificial or something not to go all the way and have sex with him. They say sex isn't such a big deal."

—from *What's Happening to My Body? Book for Boys*

Marzollo, Jean. *Getting Your Period.* 1989. New York: Dial (0-8037-0355-4); Puffin, paper (0-14-031693-6). Ages 11–15.

Marzollo takes some of the mystery out of puberty in a reassuring book that makes it plain "there is no perfectly 'normal' way to have your period. Instead there are lots of normal ways." Using a combination of straightforward description and commonly asked questions, she explains just a bit about what happens to the body during puberty before focusing on what to expect when menstruation begins. She includes illustrated, well-detailed information about different types of sanitary protection as well as common-sense advice about accepting menstruation as a part of life and managing the practical difficulties it entails. Though the book's main audience will be adolescents 11 and 12 years old, its sophisticated cover and unpatronizing tone will make it attractive even to older junior-high girls who've yet to get their periods.

Rue, Nancy N. *Everything You Need to Know about Getting Your Period.* 1995. New York: Rosen (0-8239-1870-X). Ages 11–14.

After a rocky start that introduces reproductive anatomy and terms, Rue manages to turn this entry in the Need to Know Library series for reluctant readers into a helpful book. Avoiding the pampering tone often used in books on this subject, she straightforwardly tackles some of the common and most worrisome questions girls have about their periods, among them, "What do I do if I stain my clothes?" "What about odor?" "I tried using tampons but they're painful. Am I doing something wrong?" Tampon insertion and use are fully explained, and there's an especially good chapter about menstruation myths. Entitled "Old Wives' Tales—and the Right Stuff," it's set up as an authentic-sounding slumber party gab session in which a host of common misconceptions are presented, then debunked. Bourgeois and Wolfish's *Changes in You and Me* and Madaras's *What's Happening to My Body? Book for Girls* give much fuller pictures of what's going on, but this is fine for the basic scoop.

Beyond Basics

Abner, Allison, and Linda Villarosa. *Finding Our Way: The Teen Girls' Survival Guide*. 1996. New York: HarperPerennial, paper (0-06-095114-1). Ages 15–18.

Written by a free-lance journalist and the executive editor of *Essence* magazine, both African-Americans, this is one of the best general-information books for young women to come out in a long time. The tone is light but not flip, and expected subjects are here—body image, puberty, sexual development, birth control, relationships with friends and family, and nutrition. So is information on trendy topics, such as tattoos and plastic surgery, and discussion of issues of rising concern among teens, such as personal safety. The text is enlivened by judicious use of teen comments and letters, and there's an obvious attempt to encompass multicultural differences. The chapter on body image, for example, notes differences in the "ideal" body type as accepted by African-Americans and whites. The authors manage to be upfront about their opinions: the stance on abortion is prochoice, and the chapter on birth control, which is both specific and very up to date, includes a critical assessment of the Norplant product and notes its enforced use among women "who are poor and/or black." Lack of specific documentation is sometimes problematic, and some of the suggested readings are woefully out of date (others are quite new), but such problems are more than balanced by the quality and quantity of information included and the extensive listings of support groups and organizations that accompany each chapter.

Bode, Janet. *Different Worlds: Interracial and Cross-Cultural Dating*. 1989. New York: Watts (0-531-10663-2). Ages 12–18.

Concentrating on five teenage couples, Bode investigates a complicated social issue, concluding that despite "the stars in your eyes," interracial or interethnic relationships are rarely easy to sustain. Drawing heavily on personal interviews, she explores the reactions of parents and friends to teen interdating and looks at the insidious nature of prejudice, which, she writes, can turn "you and your partner into a trio." Experts lend insight into society's views on the subject, the reasons some teenagers are attracted to individuals of a different race or background, and how young adults can deal realistically with the pressures they'll almost surely face. This is one of the first and still one of the best books on the subject.

"When I was a kid, I thought one day Prince Charming would come into my life. We'd fall madly in love. All my problems would go away. We'd live happily ever after. Sure. I woke up. I stopped looking. Prince who?"
—Ofelia, from *Heartbreak and Roses*

Bode, Janet, and Stan Mack. *Heartbreak and Roses: Real Life Stories of Troubled Love*. 1994. New York: Delacorte (0-385-32068-X). Ages 14–18.

Love may be a prime concern of teenagers and the stuff of countless young adult novels, but it's rarely the subject of teen nonfiction. Bode and Mack challenge that, but instead of exploring what love is, they focus on what it isn't. Here, they've included twelve real-life accounts that deal with abusive, obsessive, and selfish love. With the exception of two stories that are presented in cartoon form, the accounts are related in teens' own words, which evince the spontaneity and awkwardness of confidences exchanged with close friends. The teens speak frankly about sexual intimacy as well as about the pain and anger resulting from love gone wrong, and as in real life, the stories often have no satisfying closure. There is no authorial commentary to help readers put the accounts into perspective, but it's hard to miss the point behind what these kids have to tell.

Fenwick, Elizabeth and Richard Walker. *How Sex Works: A Clear, Comprehensive Guide for Teenagers to Emotional, Physical, and Sexual Maturity*. 1994. New York: Dorling Kindersley (1-56458-505-0); paper (0-7894-0634-9). Ages 14–17.

Plenty of attractive headshots of young adults give this book great appeal, though the book's large format and prominently displayed title may deter teens embarrassed about wanting to learn about sex. The text, which is buttressed with sidebars and question-and-answer boxes, succinctly and frankly introduces a wide array of concerns—from pubertal changes to relationships to discussion of oral sex. Some things are given surprisingly short shrift. What's said about "sexual preference," for example, is supportive of difference but slight in terms of informational content. The illustrations showing insertion of birth control devices, including the female condom, are one of the book's best features. There are also many other illustrations (two drawings show positions for sexual intercourse), including colorful diagrams, informative charts, and photographs. McCoy and Wibbelsman's book, following, is still the best bet for teens wanting comprehensive coverage, but this one is a nicely appointed overview.

Juhn, Greg. *Understanding the Pill*. 1995. Binghamton, N.Y.: Pharmaceutical Products Press (1-56004-851-3); paper (1-56024-908-0). Ages 16–up.

Although this is not a book specifically written for teenagers, it certainly is one that can help them if they are thinking about using oral contraceptives. The book's concise, no-nonsense approach is a plus when it comes to teen readers, and Juhn does a good job of identifying and introducing the medical facts—how the pill was developed, how it works, how to use it, side effects, and various types. The author also spends a good deal of time comparing and contrasting "the pill" with other modern methods of birth control. Numerous figures and tables make information more accessible, and each chapter ends with a list of additional resources. This is certainly not something to replace advice from a health professional, a parent, or a counselor, but it will be very useful to teenagers who want to be fully informed.

Landau, Elaine. *Interracial Dating and Marriage*. 1993. Englewood Cliffs, N.J.: Messner (0-671-75258-8); paper (0-671-75261-8). Ages 13–16.

Landau begins with a strong historical overview of American attitudes toward interracial relationships, concentrating largely on the experiences of African- and Asian-Americans. She follows with a series of heavily edited personal perspectives from ten teenagers and five adults. Although Landau's editorial intervention results in a lack of sponteneity, the accounts still reveal some surprising and important things—one young woman, for example, addresses "a shortage of desirable, educated black men." There's also much talk about old-fashioned romance, the kind where kids talk "until four in the morning . . . and she puts her head on my shoulder." The comments from adults are less likely to attract teens than the words of their peers, even though the adults' perspectives are not only insightful but also raise issues about culture and race that teens "in love" may not routinely consider. This isn't as compelling or readable as Bode's *Different Worlds,* but it does introduce some important and more-contemporary issues.

Lauersen, Niels H., and Eileen Stukane. *You're in Charge: A Teenage Girl's Guide to Sex and Her Body.* 1993. New York: Berkley, paper (0-399-57830-4). Ages 15–18.

Lauersen, an OB/GYN, seems to be the voice of this coauthored text, which sounds a little patronizing at times. Still, the breadth of coverage—from issues of puberty to sexual responsibility to healthful living—makes the frank overview worthy of more than a cursory glance. The authors counsel teens not to take a casual attitude toward sexual intimacy and come down sternly on smoking and alcohol abuse. Information on abortion takes into consideration recent changes in the laws, with the section on birth control methods also generally up to date. The stages of sexual arousal are treated with more attention than is usual in books for teens, but it's the chapter on menstruation that's the book's best feature. The extensive, highly informative discussion considers not only the cycle itself, but also such related topics as PMS and endometriosis, areas in which Lauersen is a specialist. Unfortunately, there's nothing in the book to help young women with questions about lesbianism, and neither footnotes nor further readings are included. Even so, young women will be enticed by the attractive paperback cover and will find information about many of their concerns.

McCoy, Kathy, and Charles Wibbelsman. *The New Teenage Body Book.* 1992. New York: Putnam/Perigee, paper (0-399-51725-X). Ages 14–18.

Frank questions make effective, informal lead-ins to the high-interest discussion topics included in this wide-ranging book about adolescence. Writing to teens of both genders, the authors combine responsive counsel with common sense and information about a wide variety of physical and emotional issues. Queries run the gamut from "How do you make love?" and "Will I be a virgin if I use tampons?" to "Is it selfish to say 'No' to sex?" and "How old do you have to be to worry about cholesterol?" The authors come out strongly against the use of alcohol, tobacco, and recreational drugs and take a cautionary view of premarital sex, acknowledging that the decision to become physically intimate is a highly personal one. For teens who choose to become involved, they include solid information on contraception and sexually transmitted diseases, as well as guidelines for safer sex practices. The book has fairly recent information on STDs and birth control, with descriptions of both the Norplant system and vaginal contraceptive film. Illustrations are scattered through the book.

Being Homosexual

Cohen, Susan, and Daniel Cohen. *When Someone You Know Is Gay.* 1989. New York: Dell, paper (0-440-21298-7). Ages 14–18.

The experiences and comments of teenagers supply a compelling human element here, but the Cohens's informally voiced, broad-minded perspectives are just as pivotal to this frank look at gay and lesbian life. Included is information about coming out, sex, homosexual parenting, and how AIDS has affected the gay community, along with highlights of gay history "from Plato to Stonewall" and a controversial chapter, incorporating biblical references, that investigates how mainstream religions view homosexuals today. The authors address typical misconceptions in an early section presented in a question-and-answer form: "Is it a sin?" "Do gay men hate women?" "If I'm the friend of somebody who's gay, won't they think I'm gay too?" A later chapter features lengthy, candid interviews with a drag queen, a transvestite, and a transsexual, which clarify different behaviors that are often confused. The text is addressed to nongays who seek a better understanding of a different way of life, but the broad-minded book also contains plenty of value to teens who are or think they may be homosexual.

"I came out to myself in ninth grade when I was fourteen. So what? I knew I was attracted to boys instead of girls, but what did I really know about being gay? Nothing!"

—Michael, from *When Someone You Know Is Gay*

Hyde, Margaret O., and Elizabeth Forsyth. *Know about Gays and Lesbians*. 1994. New York: Millbrook (1-56294-298-0). Ages 14–18.

This book occasionally reads like a term paper, with quotes and statistics sometimes awkwardly plugged in, and the book's brevity (only ninety-six pages) leads to some oversimplification. However, there's historical, biological, and cultural information here, some of which isn't available in other books for teens. Injecting an occasional anecdote, the authors attack stereotypes, survey history, examine cultural responses and current controversies (gays in the military, etc.), and review contemporary religious attitudes toward being gay. Readers will find the tone is understanding and sympathetic, but there's little that's cheerful in the discussion of what it's like to grow up gay these days and not much in the way of emotional support. Gay teens should look to Pollack and Schwartz's *Journey Out,* following, for that.

Pollack, Rachel, and Cheryl Schwartz. *The Journey Out: A Guide for and about Lesbian, Gay, and Bisexual Teens*. 1995. New York: Viking (0-670-85845-5); Puffin, paper (0-14-037254-7). Ages 14–18.

Unlike Sutton's book, reviewed later in this section, which uses personal testimony to communicate what it's like to be gay, this uses a traditional approach. In fact, with chapters on sexual orientation, gay history, stereotypes, and love, the book is a good lead-in to *Hearing Us Out*. The uncrowded format makes the text look approachable, and the tone is never strident, even when the authors are at their most serious—as in their refutation of Biblical literalists, in their discussion of "surviving in a homophobic world," or in their suggestions for coming out to parents. The authors take a scientifically controversial stance, noting a "probable" genetic basis for homosexuality, and in covering so much material, they sometimes give a subject short shrift, as in the chapter on health. But there are some unusual features to balance things out, among them an attempt to acknowledge a few of the special concerns of bisexuals and a chapter devoted to terms. Perhaps the book's greatest achievement, however, is its identification of a gay community that offers teens not only support but also opportunities to become active in fighting harassment and working to secure basic human rights for all. There are no footnotes, but the authors include a bibliography and a reading list, with several 1995 titles.

"Deep down in my heart, I want to be able to go to church—to know that God still loves me. After all, God loved me before I came out. Why can't He love me today?"

—Kevin, 17, from *The Journey Out*

Rench, Janice E. *Understanding Sexual Identity: A Book for Gay Teens and Their Friends*. 1990. Minneapolis: Lerner (0-8225-0044-2). Ages 12–15.

Rench provides reassurance as she reaches out to teenagers who know they are gay or who simply want some general information on the subject. Fictional scenarios head the chapters, which are presented in question-and-answer form. Topics range widely—from homophobia and AIDS to gay parents and religious attitudes toward homosexuality. Concise and forthright most of the time, Rench's answers are occasionally evasive or oversimplified. For example, to the question, "What do gay couples do together?" Rench responds, "All human beings do a variation of the same things for and to each other in a sexual relationship." Though that may be true, it probably isn't what most teens expect as an answer to the question. Those who want more-definitive information can turn to Pollack and Schwartz's *The Journey Out,* the Cohens' *When Someone You Know Is Gay,* or McCoy and Wibbelsman's *The New Teenage Body Book.* Reluctant readers and young teens will probably be the main audience here.

Sutton, Roger. *Hearing Us Out: Voices from the Gay and Lesbian Community.* 1994. Boston: Little, Brown (0-316-82326-0). Ages 15–18.

Sutton displays an expert editorial hand in this collection of personal profiles in which fifteen people reflect on their experiences growing up gay or lesbian. Written as first-person narratives, the profiles—a drag queen, a minister, and a student, among them—reflect widely divergent experiences, personal circumstances, and viewpoints. A few of the individuals included are teenagers, but Sutton has purposely selected mostly adults, noting in his introduction that "I thought it was important to show teenage gays and lesbians . . . that life goes on past junior-high humiliation and high-school ostracism." His book does just that, providing teenagers who are or think they may be gay or lesbian with support and a sense of community. At the same time, it functions as an informative, sensitive, personalized exploration of homosexuality that will enlighten readers who aren't gay but who may know someone who is. The book is realistic yet ultimately more positive and better focused than Heron's *Two Teenagers in Twenty,* following.

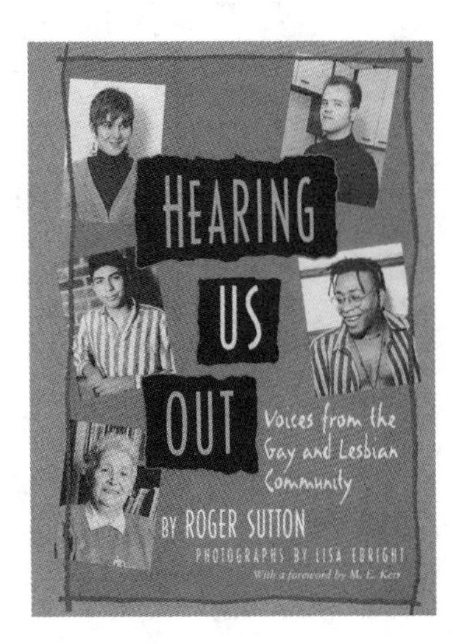

"I thought it was important to show teenage gays and lesbians . . . that life goes on beyong junior-high humiliation and high-school ostracism."

—from *Hearing Us Out*

Two Teenagers in Twenty: Writings by Gay and Lesbian Youth. Ed. by Ann Heron. 1994. Boston: Alyson (1-55583-229-6). Ages 15–18.

This update of Heron's 1983 *One Teenager in Ten* retains more than twenty of that book's personal narratives and adds some nineteen more. The original testimonies have lost none of their intensity, with newly added ones occasionally attending to recent issues such as AIDS. The emphasis is on sexuality, not sex, with a majority of the reflections about coming out—to oneself and to others. Unfortunately, because Heron includes so many profiles, she doesn't achieve much sense of individuality. And although she leads off with the words of a young person whose coming out was met with support and understanding, her introductory remarks and many of the teens' accounts she presents focus on the down side of growing up gay—the anxiety, loneliness, and sorrow. Despite that, however, gay and lesbian teens looking for some sense of their contemporaries will find this gives them much to think about.

"What benefit does it bring to know Gay Is Good when your peers think Homosexual Is Horrible?"

—Bill, 16, from *Two Teenagers in Twenty*

Sexually Transmitted Diseases

Blake, Jeanne. *Risky Times: How to Be AIDS-Smart and Stay Healthy.* 1990. New York: Workman, paper (0-89480-655-4). Ages 14–18.

A Massachusetts-based medical reporter focuses on risky behaviors, not risk groups, in this compassionate, eye-catching paperback designed to present sexually active teenagers with information about AIDS. Concentrating on transmission factors, treatment and testing, and the use of condoms, Blake delivers information in clear, straightforward terms young adults will understand as well as appreciate. However, it's the plainspoken words of other individuals whom Blake gathered together—concerned young adults, AIDS sufferers, and celebrities such as Martin Short, Cher, and Matthew Broderick—that go furthest toward convincing teenagers to "stop thinking they are immortal and start thinking about being safe." Black-and-white photographs individualize the speakers and give the text browser appeal. A video and parents guide are also available. All three can be purchased in Spanish.

"We all think about death at certain times, but I swear I never thought I'd have to think about it right after my 18th birthday. Being a teenager is hellish anyway. Drop AIDS into the picture and it becomes all the more confusing."

—David, 18, from *Risky Times*

Broadman, Michael, and others. *Straight Talk about Sexually Transmitted Diseases*. 1993. New York: Facts On File (0-8160-2864-8). Ages 14–18.

Part of the generally well-organized, informative Straight Talk series, this book names and describes a variety of sexually transmitted diseases and explains how they are treated, focusing in depth on some of the most common ones. The information is presented in understandable language, and there's no strident sermonizing. There is, however, a forceful discussion of the moral responsibility of disclosing illness to a sexual partner, which includes some reasonable suggestions on how to broach the topic. The dense format and the dreary dust jacket may not appeal to teens who have a personal interest in the subject, but students looking for report material will find a lot.

Daugirdas, J.T. *STD: Sexually Transmitted Diseases*. 3d. ed. 1992. Hinsdale, Ill.: MedText (0-9629279-1-0). Ages 14–18.

This fact-filled text focuses on six of the most common sexually transmitted diseases, among them AIDS and syphilis. Drawings, diagrams, and photos help the information go down more easily, and the language is understandable. There's no attempt to personalize and no soft peddling when it comes to the facts: information about symptoms and testing procedures is very specific, and Daugirdas includes an excellent section explaining the importance of partner notification, a topic often glossed over in sex-education materials. Teens will see right through the "case reports" that round out the text, which are little more than undisguised lessons about the unanticipated consequences of risky sexual behavior, and more complete information on AIDS is available in books like Johnson's *What You Can Do to Avoid AIDS* or Blake's *Risky Times.* But this is a solid, no-nonsense resource that provides basics briskly and directly.

Ford, Michael Thomas. *100 Questions and Answers about AIDS: A Guide for Young People*. 1992. New York: Macmillan/New Discovery (0-02-735424-5); Morrow, paper (0-688-12697-9). Ages 14–18.

Although it lacks the drama of *It Happened to Nancy,* discussed later in this section, this unpretentious book tackles AIDS in a question-answer format that makes information discovery easy and quick. The questions are cleverly designed to clarify background about AIDS, distinguish misinformation, present facts, and guide readers toward safer behaviors. Particularly distinctive are explanations of dental dams, anal sex, and the drawbacks associated with AZT, all of which Ford covers with more frankness and attention than is usual in material for teenagers. Ford also notes the rise in tuberculosis among HIV-positive individuals, a trend just recently being explored by the popular press. Adding a human element are plainspoken interviews with four HIV-positive people, including Dawn Marcal, whose story has appeared in several books on AIDS. Ford's own opinions occasionally come into play, as when he scolds the Center for Disease Control for not going far enough with data collection, but his feelings only serve to illustrate his commitment to the fight against the disease. While more cross-references would have been helpful, Ford has still done an outstanding job of succinctly telling what needs to be told.

Ford, Michael Thomas. *The Voices of AIDS*. 1995. New York: Morrow (0-688-05322-X); paper, (0-688-05323-8). Ages 15–18.

In a selection of frank, nicely edited traditional interviews (as opposed to the narrative-style ones writers such as Janet Bode are known for), Ford introduces 12 people who are determined to make a contribution to the fight against AIDS. Although some are HIV-positive, their concerns, brought out through Ford's careful questioning, go beyond the way AIDS has altered their own lives to encompass issues related to homophobia, AIDS education, and self-esteem. A music promoter talks about the way his organization, the Red Hot Organization, earns money to fight the condition; a former prostitute tells about her past and about her current job counseling Chicago prostitutes about HIV/AIDS; and a young gay man, who learned he was HIV-positive during his teens, tells why AIDS education in school didn't work for him and describes what he is now doing to "put a face to HIV." The voices of dedicated people committed to action ring loudly and clearly.

It Happened to Nancy. Ed. by Beatrice Sparks. 1994. New York: Avon/Flare, paper (0-380-77315-5). Ages 14–18.

As was the case with *Go Ask Alice,* also edited by Sparks, this book isn't clearly factual, despite its classification in the social sciences. Also like *Alice,* this is a teenager's diary, a format popular among young adult readers. It also concerns a hot-button, teenage health issue, in this case AIDS. Fourteen-year-old Nancy becomes HIV-positive after being raped by the young man she once thought she loved. Her diary entries coalesce into a poignant, often graphic account of her tragic slide from innocence to death. The intent of the book is never in doubt, but the story doesn't seem to be overpowered by the obvious message. In fact, Nancy (editor Sparks?) doesn't include some of the most-basic information about the virus and leaves some important questions unanswered. To resolve this, and possibly to make the book more than an anecdotal record, Sparks adds some of the "missing" information about AIDS and about rape in an afterword. Only Sparks really knows whether the book is fact or fiction. Teens probably won't care; it's likely to attract their attention either way.

Johnson, Earvin "Magic." *What You Can Do to Avoid AIDS*. 1992. New York: Times Books, paper (0-8129-2063-5). Ages 15–adult.

"If you don't know what you're doing about sex . . . don't do it. Wait." That's an important part of the message of a book that's aimed at teenagers but begins with words for parents. The popular basketball star, who was diagnosed with HIV in 1991, is the voice of this explicit text, which focuses on sexual activity as a means of spreading the disease. Johnson manages to stress caution without preaching as he deals forthrightly with subjects ranging from sexual responsibility to the specifics of using a condom and the increased risks facing runaway teens. He covers several other sexually transmitted diseases and drug and alcohol abuse in the same forthright manner. Boldface headings add emphasis, short bursts of text make information retrieval easy and quick, and the paperback format will fit nicely into pocket or purse. Johnson's book is one of the most complete and specific books about AIDS for teens to date. A cassette is also available.

Kittredge, Mary. *Teens with AIDS Speak Out*. 1991. Englewood Cliffs, N.J.: Messner (0-671-74542-5); paper (0-671-74543-3). Ages 15–18.

The book title tells only part of the story. Yes, Kittredge interviewed a number of young people who have AIDS, but their stories don't appear in lengthy profiles or in interview format as the title of this book implies. Instead, they are revealed through quotes, carefully and smoothly interwoven through seven distinctive chapters. The history of the virus, for example, is related in tandem with a profile of Dawn Marcal (also mentioned in Magic Johnson's book), who passed HIV to her unborn child. Such profiles humanize the subject while helping readers to see more easily the effects of discrimination and misinformation. Other chapters focus on transmission, treatment, and prevention, including information about making oral sex less risky, something rarely dealt with in books for teens. Most of what Kittredge discusses is broached in Johnson's book, but Kittredge's language and treatment are a bit more formal and not as detailed.

Madaras, Lynda. *Lynda Madaras Talks to Teens about AIDS: An Essential Guide for Parents, Teachers, and Young People*. Rev. ed. 1993. New York: Newmarket, paper (1-55704-180-6). Ages 14–18.

Readers won't find much about the discovery, symptoms, or treatment of AIDS here. Instead, Madaras concentrates on risky behaviors and the ways people can protect themselves from contracting the virus. Though she acknowledges that sex is going to be part of many teens' lives, Madaras is really an advocate of sexual abstinence for teenagers. To help kids deal with sexual pressure without the threat of HIV exposure, she suggests alternatives to intercourse that allow intimacy without compromising safety and offers advice on how to stick to a decision to remain celibate. For young adults who are sexually active, she presents a thorough discussion of condoms, including illustrated instructions for their use. Her information on intravenous drug transmission is equally detailed, with diagrammed instructions on how to sterilize needles with bleach. Madaras is authoritative and explicit here; she also demonstrates great concern for the young. A foreword for parents and teachers encourages them to become part of the AIDS education process.

FICTION

Am I Blue? Ed. by Marion Dane Bauer. 1994. New York: HarperCollins (0-06-024253-1); paper, (0-06-440587-7). Ages 14–18.

This varied collection of short stories, by sixteen familiar authors of young adult books, recognizes the physical and emotional pull of being gay or lesbian and goes beyond struggles and stereotypes to show characters who are credible, proud, and affectionate.

Arrick, Fran. *What You Don't Know Can Hurt You*. 1992. New York: Bantam (0-553-07471-7); Dell, paper (0-440-21894-2). Ages 14–17.

Debra Geddes is powerless to help her sister, Ellen, whose world falls apart when she discovers that the blood she has donated proves she is HIV-positive.

Block, Francesca Lia. *Baby Be-Bop*. 1995. HarperCollins/Joanna Cotler (0-06-024879-3). Ages 15–18.

L.A. high-school student Dirk knows that he is gay, but he's not sure how to tell his best friend, Pup. Although this is a prequel to Block's popular books about Weetzie Bat, it stands nicely on its own.

Blume, Judy. *Are You There, God? It's Me Margaret*. 1970. New York: Bradbury (0-02-710990-9); Dell, paper (0-440-40419-3). Ages 11–14.

When 12-year-old Margaret worries, she talks to God. It seems she's been worrying a lot lately—about her family, about people she knows, and about getting her first period.

Byars, Betsy. *The Burning Questions of Bingo Brown*. 1988. New York: Penguin, paper (0-14-032479-8). Ages 11–14.

Though sixth-grader Bingo Brown isn't sure what love actually is, he is certain he "fell in love three times during English class."

Clements, Bruce. *Tom Loves Anna Loves Tom*. 1992. New York: Farrar (0-374-37673-5); paper (0-374-47962-3). Ages 14–16.

Tom falls in love with Anna the first time he sees her. Anna loves Tom, too, but she has a secret that makes her more cautious than Tom in giving her affection.

Davis, Deborah. *My Brother Has AIDS*. 1994. New York: Atheneum (0-689-31922-3). Ages 12–15.

Lacy's busy, carefree life in middle school comes nearly to a halt when her mother announces that her older brother, Jack, has AIDS and must return home to be cared for.

Donavan, Stacy. *Dive*. 1994. New York: Dutton (0-525-45154-4). Ages 16–18.

Her father has been diagnosed with a fatal disease, her brother abuses drugs, and her mother is an alcoholic. The best thing in 15-year-old Virginia's life seems to be Jane, with whom she falls in love.

Fox, Paula. *Eagle Kite*. 1994. New York: Orchard/Richard Jackson (0-531-06892-7). Ages 12–16.

Liam is not supposed to know that his father is gay: he's supposed to think Philip Cormac contracted AIDS from a blood transfusion. Now his father is dying, and Liam, who has to face the truth, is angry, grief stricken, and ashamed.

Garden, Nancy. *Annie on My Mind.* 1982. New York: Farrar (0-399-21046-6); paper (0-374-40413-5). Ages 15–18.

High-school students Annie and Liza meet at New York City's Metropolitan Museum of Art. It isn't long before they discover they're falling in love.

Hamilton, Morse. *Yellow Blue Bus Means I Love You.* 1994. New York: Greenwillow (0-688-12800-9). Ages 15–18.

When high test scores secure Russian emigrant Timur Vorobyov a place in an elite prep school, the last thing he expects is that he'll fall in love with an American girl.

Hamilton, Virginia. *A Little Love.* 1984. New York: Putnam (0-399-21046-6). Ages 15–18.

Sheema feels slow and fat and insecure even though her boyfriend Forrest loves her and finds her desirable. It takes a trip with Forrest to find the father who left her at birth to complete her rites of passage.

Hobbs, Valerie. *How Far Would You Have Gotten if I Hadn't Called You Back?* 1995. New York: Orchard (0-531-09480-4). Ages 15–18.

In a vivid coming-of-age novel set in the 1950s, Bron Lewis grapples with her father's attempted suicide and with her attraction to two very different guys, one of whom is a sexy local "bad" boy.

Kerr, M. E. *Deliver Us from Evie.* 1994. New York: HarperCollins (0-06-02447-55). Ages 14–18.

Eighteen-year-old Evie has always known she's a lesbian, but when she falls in love with the pretty, preppy daughter of the local banker, who loves her back, Evie's parents and her brother, Parr, have to face the fact that "it's not just a phase."

Kerr, M. E. *Night Kites.* 1986. New York: Harper (0-06-023253-6); paper (0-06-447035-0). Ages 15–18.

In the midst of an affair with a kookie, sexy classmate, Erick learns that his older brother Pete has AIDS and is coming home to die.

Klein, Norma. *Just Friends.* 1990. New York: Knopf (0-679-80213-4). Ages 15–18.

Though Isabel doesn't realize it at first, she's in love with Stuart, who's been her New York City neighbor and friend since they were both small. When Stuart has an affair with Iz's pretty friend, jealous Isabel decides it's time she has her first sexual experience.

Koertge, Ron. *The Arizona Kid.* 1988. Boston: Little, Brown (0-316-50101-8); Avon, paper (0-380-70776-4). Ages 15–18.

Insecure, height-conscious Billy doesn't know what to expect when he arrives in Arizona for the summer. For the most part, he's pleased with what he finds: his gay uncle Wes is funny and caring; he likes his coworker Lew; and he has his first sexual experience with pretty Cara Mae.

Mullins, Hillary. *The Cat Came Back.* 1993. Seattle, Wash: Naiad Press (1-56280-040-X). Ages 14–18.

Naive Stevie tells in diary form how she falls in love with her prep-school classmate Andrea and discovers that Andrea loves her back.

Nelson, Theresa. *Earthshine.* 1994. New York: Orchard/Richard Jackson (0-531-06867-8). Ages 12–15.

Twelve-year-old "Slim" whose beloved, gay father, Mack, is dying, finds an understanding friend in 11-year-old Isaiah, whose pregnant mother is also battling AIDS.

Porte, Barbara Ann. *Something Terrible Happened*. 1994. New York: Orchard/Richard Jackson (0-531-08719-0). Ages 12–16.

When her vibrant mother contracts AIDS, 12-year-old, mixed-race Gillian is forced to exchange the nurturing protection of her mother and grandmother for the hospitality of her dead father's "plainwhite" relatives, whom she doesn't even know.

Vail, Rachel. *Wonder*. 1991. New York: Watts/Orchard/Richard Jackson (0-531-05964-2); Puffin, paper (0-14-036167-7). Ages 11–14.

Taunted by girls who used to be her friends (they dub her "Wonder" on the first day of school because her dress looks like a Wonder bread wrapper), and uncomfortable with her new adolescent body, seventh-grader Jessica salvages her pride by pretending not to care about anyone. Then along comes Conor O'Malley.

Velasquez, Gloria. *Tommy Stands Alone*. 1995. Houston, Tex.: Arte Publico/Piñata (1-55885-146-1). Ages 14–16.

Humiliated by boys who discover he's gay after reading a note they find in his pocket, Tom turns to alcohol, then to attempted suicide to numb his pain. Intervention from a caring Mexican American therapist helps him find his way back to happiness.

Walker, Kate. *Peter*. 1993. Boston, MA: Houghton (0-395-64722-3). Ages 14–18.

A yearning for intimacy and pressure from a macho gang push Peter toward sexual activity, but, though there's a girl he likes, he's really more interested in David, his older brother's gay friend.

One Plus One Makes Three: Marriage, Pregnancy, and Parenting

MORE THAN ONE million girls under the age of 18 become pregnant each year, but although many books on parenting and pregnancy exist, only a few focus on the concerns of teenagers. Morning Glory Press has emerged as a clear, dedicated leader in the publication of books on teen pregnancy, parenting, and marriage, with an array of titles that deal in nonjudgmental fashion with practical, emotional, and physical issues. Several of its books are listed in this chapter along with young adult titles from other publishers and a few unusual adult books that teenagers will find of particular value.

NONFICTION

Marriage

Ayer, Eleanor H. *Everything You Need to Know about Teen Marriage.* 1991. New York: Rosen (0-8239-1221-3). Ages 12–16.

Like Glassman's *Growing Up Male,* listed in a previous chapter, this book is part of the Need to Know Library series directed to reluctant readers. It uses a modified question-answer approach, shot through with the comments of young adults, to present a simplified view of what marriage involves—dirty socks and diapers as well as passion, trust, and caring. Ayer sees marriage as a risky proposition, and she weights her words accordingly ("When you have an argument with your date, isn't it nice to go home?"). But she isn't overtly preachy, and she does not ignore the fact that some teen marriages do work. She includes the remarks of teens who are happily married right alongside the words of those who've found getting hitched was a big mistake. Appealing color photographs featuring teens will attract browsers, as will the book's spacious format. While Ayer falls a good deal short of discussing "everything you need to know," she does introduce quite a lot in under one hundred pages.

Lindsay, Jeanne Warren. *Caring, Commitment & Change: How to Build a Relationship that Lasts.* 1995. Buena Park, Calif.: Morning Glory (0-930934-92-X); paper (0-930934-93-8). Ages 15–18.

———. *Coping with Reality: Dealing with Money, In-Laws, Babies and Other Details of Daily Life.* 1995. Buena Park, Calif.: Morning Glory (0-930934-87-3); paper (0-930934-86-5). Ages 15–18.

Marketed under the umbrella series title Teenage Couples, this two-book set rehashes and expands on some of the subjects broached in the Teen Parenting books listed elsewhere in this chapter. Cross references make it obvious that Lindsay hopes the books will be used in tandem. *Coping with Reality* is the most helpful of the pair, containing all sorts of clear-headed counsel on the day-to-day aspects of being part of a couple. One of its best chapters concerns life with in-laws. Others deal with budgeting, parenting styles, and pregnancy. *Caring* is more focused on personal issues than practical ones. Although it begins on a preachy note, it eventually settles down to present two especially good chapters—one concerning constructive arguing; the other, a discussion of the part that sexual intimacy plays in a total relationship. Also considered are conflicting expectations about sex within a marriage, a topic rarely mentioned in books for teens. The operative word in the books is "partnership," with Lindsay doing a first-rate job of showing how to lay the groundwork for a trusting, sharing one.

Pregnancy

Aitkens, Maggi. *Kerry, A Teenage Mother.* 1994. Minneapolis: Lerner (0-8225-2556-9). Ages 12–16.

Although Aitkens occasionally puts a damper on the drama of real life by shifting focus from 19-year-old Kerry to general information about teen mothers, her photo essay still accomplishes most of what's intended. Candid black-and-white photographs show Kerry and her mixed-race, 15-month-old daughter, Vanessa, in conflict and in cuddling embrace, while the text describes Kerry's endeavors to combine her role as mother on welfare with her responsibilities as a student trying for a better life.

A forceful picture of the difficulties faced by teen mothers emerges, but Aikens also allows for hope. The love between mother and child is obvious in both pictures and words, and there's a strong sense that Kerry and Vanessa will succeed: "No matter what happens to you in life, you can still become the person and have the life you really want if you're willing to work hard." The abundance of photographs and the open format make this an especially good book for reluctant readers.

"You think they're cute, huggable, lovable babies that wear little itty-bitty baby shoes and T-shirts. What you don't know is they take a lot of money . . . and it's a full-time job.

—Kerry, from
Kerry, A Teenage Mother

Bode, Janet. *Kids Still Having Kids: People Talk about Teen Pregnancy.* 1992. New York: Watts (0-531-11132-6). Ages 14–18.

Although Bode contributes a few facts (usually in boxed insets), her book is really about feelings and attitudes. It is also much broader in scope than the subtitle indicates, touching not only on pregnancy but also on related issues such as abortion, adoption, teen sex, and foster care, the latter a subject rarely introduced in books of this kind. Nothing is covered in much depth, and the cartoon story that's included provides little other than some visual variety. Kuklin's book, *What Do I Do Now?,* which is also composed of interviews with teens and adults, will have a greater impact, but it's obvious Bode knows the concerns of the audience she writes for, and readers will appreciate her honesty and integrity.

"I don't know a thing about being a mother. It's hard to believe that I am one. I'd always planned to go to college to be a lawyer. Now I am learning about law—paternity law."

—Nicolette, 16, from
Kids Still Having Kids

Kuklin, Susan. *What Do I Do Now?: Talking about Teenage Pregnancy.* 1991. New York: Putnam (0-399-21843-2); paper (0-399-22043-7). Ages 14–18.

Filled with sharp details about the girls and their circumstances, Kuklin's gritty book presents a close-up view of what it's like to be a pregnant teenager today. The author, who selected interviewees from among visitors to several New York-area agencies (a Planned Parenthood affiliate, a clinic licensed to perform abortions, and an adoption agency), followed more than a dozen girls from different racial and economic backgrounds into their homes, into their counseling sessions, and even into examining rooms. Merging the girls' comments with perspectives from health professionals, parents, and her own research, Kuklin has produced an affecting collective portrait. Some situations are shocking: a mother's

giving up her bedroom to her daughter and the girl's boyfriend; a girl's threatening the father of her baby with a butcher knife. Some are politically sensitive: staff members talking about right-to-life pickets protesting in the street outside an abortion clinic. But Kuklin avoids passing judgment or politicizing. This is a book about and for city kids; the small-town girl's dilemma isn't really addressed here. Nor does Kuklin give teenage fathers enough attention. Yet what's here is unforgettable: it's more than enough to cause at least some teens to think twice before putting themselves at risk for parenthood.

"When you think you might be pregnant it's one thing. When someone tells you your test is positive, that's a whole new ball game."

—Arlene, from *What Do I Do Now?*

Lindsay, Jeanne Warren. *Pregnant Too Soon: Adoption Is an Option*. Rev. ed. 1987. Buena Park, Calif.: Morning Glory (0-930934-26-1); paper (0-930934-25-3). Ages 12–18.

"Adoption is chosen by less than 5 percent of all single teenage mothers in the United States," begins Lindsay, who feels strongly that a dearth of information on the subject stops young parents from considering adoption as an acceptable alternative to teen parenting. Here, she attempts to fill in some of the background. Coordinator of a California teen-mother program and author of a number of books about and for pregnant teens, Lindsay relies heavily on first-person testimony from parents in her program to get her message across. Young mothers readily share feelings about their decision to choose adoption and their varied experiences with agencies and adoptive parents. Woven throughout is information on adoption mechanics, foster-care placements, adoptive parental screening, rights of the birth mother, and more—little of which normally appears in teen pregnancy materials. Although now somewhat dated, this is one of the few books for teens on an important choice.

Lindsay, Jeanne Warren, and Jean Brunelli. *Teens Parenting—Your Pregnancy and Newborn Journey: How to Take Care of Yourself and Your Newborn if You're a Pregnant Teen*. 1991. Buena Park, Calif.: Morning Glory (0-930934-51-2); paper (0-930934-50-4). Ages 12–18.

There are many more-comprehensive books on this subject in the adult section of the library, but Lindsay and Brunelli's book is notable because it's written just for teens. The authors demonstrate their teen orientation not only with quotes they've collected from prospective and actual teenage parents but also with chapters addressing such topics as three-generation households. Part of the four-book Teens Parenting series, this is a wide-ranging sourcebook that

touches on everything from prenatal care, labor, and delivery to a newborn's first days. Brief information on adoption is provided, as is an understanding look at the responsibilities facing expectant teen fathers. Unfortunately, the subject coverage is uneven. For example, the authors include a supportive discussion about breastfeeding but little about feeding with a bottle, and although the section on birth control mentions the new contraceptive implants, it supplies only the briefest information about birth control as a whole. The black-and-white photographs of young parents and their babies are a great feature, as is the authors' friendly, nonjudgmental tone.

Martin, Margaret. *The Illustrated Book of Pregnancy and Childbirth*. 1991. New York: Facts On File (0-8160-2570-3); paper (0-8160-2917-2). Ages 15–18.

If explicit photographs of birth and fetal development are unacceptable as a means of illustration, here's a book that gets the information across without using them. It's black-white-and-pink illustrations are not particularly attractive, but they are plentiful, enlightening, and well labeled. They are also a fine complement to the direct, well-ordered text written by the founder of the Pregnancy and Natural Childbirth Education Center in Los Angeles. Martin begins by supplying some basic anatomical information, then follows the progress of baby and mother through the first week after birth. The book's open format, with special terms in boldface type and enlarged, spaciously set text, is reminiscent of a children's picture book, but there's nothing patronizing or oversimplified in the text itself, which clearly re-creates what happens every step of the way.

Parenting

Ayer, Eleanor H. *Everything You Need to Know about Teen Fatherhood*. 1993. New York: Rosen (0-8239-1532-8). Ages 12–15.

Another volume in the Need to Know Library, a series of books aimed at teens who don't read well or don't enjoy reading, this considers, without preaching or scolding, the consequences of sexual intimacy and the emotional and practical commitment involved in becoming a father. Ayer encourages young men to take an active part in their children's lives, while making very clear the demands of fatherhood. Short, attractively illustrated chapters briefly suggest alternatives to parenting, discuss economic considerations, and present basic facts about pregnancy and childbirth, and a scattering of personal comments makes the material more approachable.

Gravelle, Karen, and Leslie Peterson. *Teenage Fathers*. 1992. New York: Messner (0-671-72850-4); paper (0-671-72851-2). Ages 14–18.

This is probably the best of the few books written for teenage fathers. Thirteen young men, who were between the ages of 12 and 18 when they became dads for the first time, describe their situations and feelings, with the authors contributing qualifying and interpretative comments. Ethnic origins are not obvious in every case, but Gravelle and Peterson have taken care to round up a diverse group of young men with widely differing opinions about fatherhood: Carlos, father of many, refuses responsibility for birth control and for the children he's fathered ("if the girl gets pregnant, then they [the children] are hers"), while Brian, a young house husband, loves his daughters and enjoys caring for them. Despite the different attitudes, recurring themes do appear. For example, many of the young men refer to economic pressures and to the male role models they had during their own growing-up years. Their words, which ring with disillusionment, fear, anger, and occasionally real joy, coalesce into a dramatic, eye-opening portrait of what teen fathers face and how they're handling it.

"I enjoy my son! Especially when I put my face in his stomach and watch him laugh. Oh man, that's fun!"

—John, from *Teenage Fathers*

Jessel, Camilla. *From Birth to Three.* 1991. New York: Dell, paper (0-385-30310-6). Ages 14–adult.

"How soon will my baby roll over?" "When will my baby begin to talk?" "How soon will I see my baby smile?" To answer these and other common queries, Jessel offers a remarkable album of photographs, all of baby Lee, whose development she's captured in full-color, candid pictures from the moment of his birth through his third year. Accompanied by informative captions, the photos record landmarks in Lee's physical and emotional growth and in the evolution of his speech, his socialization, and his learning and play patterns. Sidebars, color-keyed to each chapter, provide a background context for Lee's development that serves, in turn, as a flexible model of the changes most parents eventually will see in their babies. The text explores a baby's development in only the most general terms, but it is still a comforting look at the principal stages of child growth and a charming celebration of children.

Kitzinger, Sheila. *Breastfeeding Your Baby.* 1989. New York: Knopf, paper (0-679-72433-8). Ages 14–adult.

Published for an adult audience but accessible to new mothers of a variety of ages, this attractively and abundantly illustrated book answers a pressing need for materials on the subject of breastfeeding. Photographs, many in full color, accompany Kitzinger's authoritative guidance on breast care and nursing basics, which she augments with reassurance and insight into infant development and the evolving relationship between parent and child. Kitzinger is the author of several other child-care and development books that may also be of interest to teenage parents.

Lang, Paul, and Susan S. Lang. *Teen Fathers.* 1995. New York: Watts (0-531-11216-0). Ages 14–17.

Unlike Gravelle and Peterson's intimate perspective, *Teenage Fathers,* mentioned previously, and Lindsay's *Teen Dads,* this is a fact book that won't help young men develop better parenting skills, make them more diligent about birth control, or convince them to abstain from premarital sex. It will, however, clearly show them why teenage males often abdicate their parental responsibilities and how society's negative stereotype of the young father works against them even when they truly want to be good parents. The Langs draw widely on outside sources to support their conclusions, incorporating information gleaned from studies on such diverse but related factors as race, politics, and three-generation households. At times the text reads like a classroom lecture, but if teen dads can stick it out, they'll find the book an eye-opening view of how society sees them and how they seem to see themselves.

Lindsay, Jeanne Warren. *Teen Dads: Rights, Responsibilities and Joys.* 1993. Buena Park, Calif: Morning Glory (0-930934-77-6); paper (0-930934-78-4). Ages 14–18.

This book fits neatly into Morning Glory's Teens Parenting series, though it actually was not published as part of the group. There's no intimidation or rebuke in the text, which introduces young men to various aspects of parenting—things dads should know about but are usually considered more in mom's domain (breastfeeding and prenatal care, for example) as well as special problems for young fathers, such as maintaining ties when baby and dad live apart. Nothing is covered in much depth, but Lindsay's encouraging tone and the inclusion of comments from teen dads will make young men feel part of the fatherhood fold. Look to Gravelle and Peterson's *Teenage Fathers,* previously mentioned, for the really penetrating insights. This book will be useful for the practical issues it explores.

Lindsay, Jeanne Warren. *Teens Parenting—The Challenge of Toddlers: Parenting Your Child from One to Three.* 1991. Buena Park, Calif.: Morning Glory (0-930934-59-8); paper (0-930934-58-X). Ages 12–18.

In the final volume in the four-part Teens Parenting series, Lindsay once again manages to be both reassuring and truthful when it comes to the challenges facing young parents. Using a friendly tone that calls up visions of an experienced friend or concerned counselor, she picks up where *Teens Parenting: Your Baby's First Year,* described in a following citation, leaves off. Subjects touched upon range from sleep problems and temper tantrums to the importance of parent-child interaction. The loosely organized, topical chapters are really little more than catchalls of general advice and information, often presented without documentation. More-comprehensive materials on the subject can be found in the adult section of the library. But to her credit, Lindsay hits on all the basics, and she includes a whole chapter for teen dads, encouraging them to become involved parents. In addition, she conveys a strong sense of how children affect their parents' lives, strengthening her portrait with the words of young people who speak openly about the satisfaction of parenting as well as its difficult side. By and large, this is a genial, supportive overview that takes kids who have kids seriously.

Lindsay, Jeanne Warren. *Teens Parenting—Your Baby's First Year.* 1991. Buena Park, Calif.: Morning Glory (0-930934-53-9); paper (0-930934-52-0). Ages 12–18.

If readers can forgive the somewhat hit-or-miss approach and the annoyingly frequent references to other books in the Teens Parenting series, they'll find that this manual for new teen parents answers many common questions about baby-care basics. Written in a pleasantly informal style enhanced by comments from young moms and dads, the text is a mixture of practical advice and background on infant health and development. As is usual in Lindsay's parenting books, the practical (in this case, discussions of diapers, immunizations, food, child-proofing a home, and age-appropriate toys) is accompanied by consideration of teens' particular interests—managing money, establishing paternity, and returning to school. Lindsay supplies more encouragement than she does answers, but she never attempts to fool her audience into thinking she's covering it all.

Lindsay, Jeanne Warren, and Sally McCullough. *Teens Parenting—Discipline from Birth to Three: How to Prevent and Deal with Discipline Problems with Babies and Toddlers.* 1991. Buena Park, Calif.: Morning Glory (0-930934-55-5); paper (0-930934-54-7). Ages 12–18.

Another title in the four-book Teens Parenting series, this is organized in a loosely chronological fashion and highlights common dilemmas affecting the parents of children newly born to age three. The authors steer caretakers away from spanking and shouting, offering alternative strategies for dealing with normal behavioral changes as well as more problematic ones, such as thumb sucking and tantrums. As in the other series titles, comments from teenagers are an important part of the book, and the special problems experienced by teen parents (for example, the difficulty of asserting authority when grandparent caretakers disagree about discipline) are a priority. Black-and-white photographs add authenticity to the personal comments.

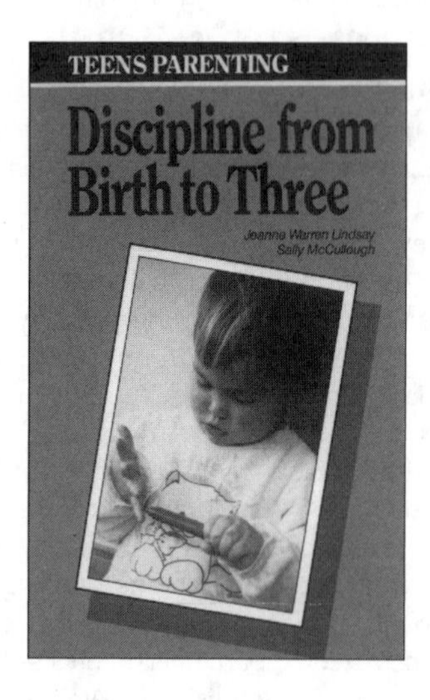

Marzollo, Jean. *Fathers & Babies: How Babies Grow and What They Need from You, from Birth to 18 Months.* 1993. New York: HarperPerennial, paper (0-06-096908-3). Ages 15–adult.

———. *Fathers & Toddlers: How Toddlers Grow and What They Need from You, from 18 Months to Three Years of Age.* 1994. New York: HarperPerennial, paper (0-06-096907-5). Ages 15–adult.

Large, comical line drawings on nearly every page give these simply written baby-care books, actually written for adults, an appealing informality that teenage fathers will like. The information, presented in concise, neat blocks that encourage browsing, attends to both specific and general parenting concerns—from game playing to storing toys to dealing with tantrums. Although these books cannot be considered substitutes for a comprehensive child-care manual, their humorous approach is refreshing, and they contain enough fathering philosophy and day-to-day child-care advice to make teen dads feel more comfortable with their caregiver role.

Simpson, Carolyn. *Living with Your Baby and Your Parents under One Roof.* 1996. New York: Rosen (0-8239-2150-6). Ages 14–18.

Because Morning Glory Press's multivolume Teens Parenting series is really the only other source for material about living in a three-generation household, this compact, sixty-four-page book (in the Need to Know Library series) should be welcome. Simpson targets key issues for teen parents living at home, addressing concerns such as personal space, household and child-care responsibilities, and goal setting. She also includes a chapter guiding young adults in the management of their sexual lives. One of the best features of the book is the acknowledgment that single teen dads can raise thriving children, especially if they have the right kind of support system. Simpson plainly shows that parenting is not easy, but she doesn't judge and she doesn't preach.

FICTION

Christiansen, C. B. *I See the Moon.* 1994. New York: Atheneum (0-689-31928-2). Ages 11–14.

Not yet really aware that love is more than the romantic flirtations she's talked about with her friends, 12-year-old Bitte is shocked to discover that her unmarried sister, who is 15, has decided to give up the baby she is carrying for adoption.

Cole, Sheila. *What Kind of Love? Diary of a Pregnant Teen.* 1995. New York: Lothrop (0-688-12848-3). Ages 14–16.

Fifteen-year-old Valerie is certain that her loving boyfriend will marry her now that a baby is on the way, but she doesn't count on family intervention that sends him away to school and leaves her to cope alone.

Doherty, Berlie. *Dear Nobody.* 1992. New York: Orchard (0-531-05461-6); Morrow, paper (0-688-12764-9). Ages 14–18.

Preparing to leave for college, Chris receives a packet of letters from his former girlfriend, Helen. As he reads them, he realizes they were not written to him, but to the baby Helen is carrying—a child he fathered but didn't know existed.

Kaye, Geraldine. *Someone Else's Baby.* 1992. New York: Hyperion (1-56282-149-0). Ages 14–16.

Pregnant after being raped by a stranger at a party, Teresa, a middle child with little self-esteem, acquiesces to family pressure to put her child up for adoption. As her pregnancy proceeds, however, she begins to waiver, gradually investing in her unborn child the unconditional love she was denied during her own growing up.

Klein, Norma. *No More Saturday Nights.* 1988. New York: Knopf (0-394-81944-6); Fawcett, paper (0-449-70304-5). Ages 15–18.

When he becomes an unwed father at the end of his senior year in high school and wins custody of his child, Tim Weber feels he has no choice but to take the baby with him to college in the fall.

Maguire, Jesse. *On the Edge.* 1991. New York: Ballantine, paper (0-8041-0447-6). Ages 15–18.

Eighteen-year-old Caroline discovers she's come out "on the wrong side of the birth control safety-rate statistics," and she has to make a choice between having her baby or having an abortion.

Myers, Walter Dean. *Sweet Illusion.* 1987. New York: Teachers & Writers Collaborative (0-915924-14-5); paper (0-915924-15-3). Ages 16–18.

In a book of fiction that reads like fact, a series of first-person narratives explore how inner-city teens—mostly minority young men and women—grapple with decisions about pregnancy and deal with the problems of parenting.

Reynolds, Marilyn. *Detour for Emmy.* 1993. Buena Park, Calif.: Morning Glory (0-930934-75-X); paper, (0-930934-76-8). Ages 15–18.

A talented singer, a soccer star, and a fine student, Emmy has managed to rise above the problems of her dysfunctional family. Then she becomes pregnant and is forced to face difficulties of her own making, including the burden of caring for her child while getting her life back on track.

Reynolds, Marilyn. *Too Soon for Jeff.* 1994. Buena Park, Calif.: Morning Glory (0-930934-90-3); paper (0-930934-91-1). Ages 15–18.

Jeff Browing sees a bright future ahead in college until his girlfriend Christy discloses she's pregnant. Although he's determined to turn his back on the problem and get on with his life, he discovers, to his own amazement, that he can't.

Rodowsky, Colby. *Lucy Peale.* 1994. New York: Farrar (0-374-36381-1); paper (0-374-44659-8). Ages 15–18.

Choosing to run away rather than be shamed into confessing her pregnancy in front of her father's fundamentalist congregation, Lucy finds help from a kindly college dropout who agrees to take her into his home, baby-on-the-way and all.

Rylant, Cynthia. *A Kindness*. 1988. New York: Watts/Orchard/Richard Jackson (0-531-05767-4); Dell, paper (0-440-20579-4). Ages 14–18.

Chip has always had an especially close relationship with his single-parent mother, Anne. Then Anne becomes pregnant, decides to raise the baby, and refuses to tell Chip who the father is.

Waddell, Martin. *Tango's Baby*. 1995. Candlewick (1-56402-615-9). Ages 15–18.

Tango is gentle and caring and tries his best to support 15-year-old Crystal and their baby. But he has no job, the couple can't get a council house from the local British government, and the police are after him. When Crystal loses faith and runs off with the baby, Tango determines to get his son back.

Willey, Margaret. *If Not for You*. 1988. New York: Harper (0-06-026494-2); paper (0-06-447015-6). Ages 13–16.

Bonnie thinks popular, pretty high-school senior Linda Mason's elopement with Ray Pastrovich is a bid for independence as well as just about the most romantic thing she can imagine—until she becomes the couple's baby-sitter and sees firsthand the difference between romance and real love.

Williams-Garcia, Rita. *Like Sisters on the Homefront*. 1995. New York: Dutton/Lodestar (0-525-67465-9). Ages 14–18.

Sent to stay with her mother's Georgia relatives after an abortion, 14-year-old Gayle, already the mother of a child, shocks her protected cousin with her street talk and her irreverence as she tries to find a place for herself and for her young son.

Wolff, Virginia Euwer. *Make Lemonade*. 1993. New York: Holt (0-8050-2228-7); Scholastic, paper (0-590-481-41-X). Ages 14–18.

To earn money for college, a word that bears such weight in her home "you have to walk around it in the rooms like furniture," 14-year-old LaVaughn goes to work for 17-year-old Jolly, a proud young mother with two small children who is desperately trying to pull herself out of poverty.

Woodson, Jacqueline. *The Dear One*. 1991. New York: Delacorte (0-385-30416-1); Dell, paper (0-440-21420-3). Ages 12–15.

Still reeling from several family tragedies, including her parents' divorce and her grandmother's death, 12-year-old Feni is angered when her mother disrupts life even further by allowing the 15-year-old pregnant daughter of a friend to come live with them in their home in an upscale African-American community.

Wurmfeld, Hope Herman. *Baby Blues*. 1992. New York: Viking (0-670-84151-X); Puffin, paper (0-14-034870-0). Ages 14–18.

Small-town girl Annie sadly and tenderly recalls her flirtation with Jimmy and thinks about the baby they made, who Annie decides she must give up for adoption.

Death: Romance and Reality

THE DEATH OF a loved one is universally recognized as one of the most stressful occurrences in a person's life, and teenagers, struggling with the changes of sexual maturation and finding their place in the adult community, are especially vulnerable to its emotional aftermath. Not only does death cause great upheaval in the family situation and personal relationships, it also forces young adults to face the scary thought of their own mortality—possibly for the first time. This chapter comprises books that explore teenagers' feelings about dying—titles that consider how they confront the loss of a loved one as well as how they view the prospect of their own dying. That adolescents are frequently unable to see beyond culturally entrenched romantic images of death is made painfully clear through their own words.

NONFICTION

Bode, Janet. *Death Is Hard to Live with: Teenagers and How They Cope with Death*. 1993. New York: Delacorte (0-385-31041-2); Dell, paper (0-440-21929-9). Ages 14–18.

One of the first to recognize the value of the personal interview for presenting sensitive subjects to young adults, Bode also knows the attraction of the sound bite. In this wrenchingly honest book, she uses both techniques. Poignant personal stories from teens coupled with input from a forensic specialist, a funeral director, a therapist, a minister, and others blend into a sweeping exploration that covers familiar territory (romantic notions about death and changes in family relationships) as well as some new issues—for example, auto-erotic death. But this is not as smoothly put together as Grollman's book, discussed later in this section, which also depends on brevity to attract readers in emotional crisis. Bode's interviews are sometimes artificially split into chunks or awkwardly interrupted by boxed insets. What balances things out are Bode's keen understanding of the issues important to her audience and her talent for drawing them into the open.

DiGiulio, Robert, and Rachel Kranz. *Straight Talk about Death and Dying*. 1995. New York: Facts On File (0-8160-3078-2). Ages 14–18.

Kranz, author of several books in the Straight Talk series, has teamed with a specialist in human development and family relations to produce this comprehensive book, which contains more for teens who must come to terms with their own impending death than do most books about dying. There are no personal interviews, but the text is neither pedantic nor difficult to read as it explains the stages of grief as they particularly affect young people and offers sensible advice on how teens can better deal with their painful, confusing feelings. Specific concerns ("Do I go to the funeral?" "Whom do I tell?" "How do I behave at school?") are treated in a practical and sensitive manner, with the authors including a separate chapter discussing where to find help when grieving becomes so overwhelming it interferes with daily life. Teens will come away from the book understanding that mourning is hard but very necessary work. A lengthy selection of further readings is appended.

"After all, how can you accept your death if you feel you haven't even had your life yet?"

—from *Straight Talk about Death and Dying*

Fry, Virginia Lynn. *Part of Me Died, Too: Stories of Creative Survival among Bereaved Children and Teenagers*. 1995. New York: Dutton (0-525-45068-8). Ages 11–14.

Candid descriptions of emotional pain make this book difficult to read, but Fry, a bereavement counselor, wants to do more than tell harrowing stories: she wants to help young people use their creative talents to get beyond their pain. Toward that end, she concludes each of the eleven real-life accounts with a selection of self-help activities that challenge kids to write, sew, or draw something that expresses their feelings. The stories themselves encompass a wide variety of situations. In one, a little boy deals with the death of a pet; in another, a girl recounts the horrific murder-suicide of her parents. The audience for this book is not, however, as clear cut as the emotions presented: the stories may be too harrowing for some older middle schoolers to whom many of the self-help activities seem directed, and the suggestions for additional readings aren't always age appropriate. Still, Fry does manage to capture the cruel legacy of loss while reassuring readers that with time and work their pain will ease. Original artwork by kids decorates the pages.

Gravelle, Karen, and Charles Haskins. *Teenagers Face to Face with Bereavement.* 1989. Englewood Cliffs, N.J.: Messner (0-671-65856-5); paper (0-671-65975-8). Ages 12–18.

Gravelle, a former psychotherapist, and Haskins, an Episcopal priest and pastoral counselor, supply the context for the moving testimonies of seventeen young people ranging in age from 10 to 18 at the time of their loss. The teenagers mourn friends, parents, brothers, and sisters and unpretentiously communicate their feelings in chapters that distinguish the stages of grief as they particularly affect the young—how it feels to return to school after the funeral, how friends help, and how roles change in a family after a parent's death. Denial, confusion, guilt, and other painful emotions reverberate through the text, but by gathering and sharing these emotions, the authors give shape to personal loss in a way that will help teens left behind feel less isolated in their grief.

"The day we had the memorial service . . . I realized she wasn't on vacation, she was gone!"
—Erica, from *Teenagers Face to Face with Bereavement*

Grollman, Earl A. *Straight Talk about Death for Teenagers: How to Cope with Losing Someone You Love.* 1993. Boston: Beacon; dist. by Farrar (0-8070-2500-3); paper (0-8070-2501-1). Ages 14–18.

A frequent contributor to *USA Today,* Grollman is also a prolific author of books designed to help people cope with personal trauma. Here, he validates the painful feelings teenagers experience following the death of a loved one, conveying a sense of the grieving as well as the importance of getting on with life. Occasionally, Grollman approaches his subject from an unusual angle: for example, he touches briefly on how the circumstances surrounding a person's death (accident, suicide, AIDS, etc.) color the survivor's feelings. But what sets his book apart from many others on the subject is the format in which the message is presented: short bursts of text appear on pages left otherwise largely blank. Grollman doesn't discuss anything deeply, but the unusual way his message is presented may attract teens who find their feelings simply too painful to explore more fully. It provides comfort in manageable terms.

Hermes, Patricia. *A Time to Listen: Preventing Youth Suicide.* 1987. San Diego: Harcourt (0-15-288196-4). Ages 13–18.

Although Hermes does include facts about suicide and advice on what to do should a reader suspect a friend or loved one of being in suicidal crisis, she is most concerned with defining the emotions surrounding the tragedy. Through informal interviews with suicide survivors, bereaved parents, a therapist, and a group of teenagers concerned about the suicide of a peer, she sheds light on the social and personal implications of the act. Her question-and-answer technique is awkward at times, but the voices of her subjects break through, as does a sense of the internal and external pressures teenagers face every day. This is an older title, but one that still has a lot to contribute.

"We see death every day on television—and we think, oh, he got shot, well, he'll be back the next day. And even the songs on the radio. There's one of them that starts off, 'Sometimes you're better off dead, there's a gun in your hand and it's pointed at your head.' "

—Richard Klein, suicide survivor, from *A Time to Listen*

Krementz, Jill. *How It Feels When a Parent Dies*. 1981. New York: Knopf, paper (0-394-75854-4). Ages 11–15.

Published more than a decade ago and the prototype for the author's How It Feels series, this was one of the first children's books to recognize a young person's need to express and discuss his or her feelings about a parent's death. Eighteen young people, coping with a mother's or father's death by suicide, accident, or illness, told Krementz their stories, and their heartfelt admissions are every bit as powerful and affecting now as they were all those years ago. Authentic in tone, the recollections express the confusion, anger, and guilt kids feel when tragedy strikes. They also reveal a variety of thought-provoking beliefs about what happens when a person dies. Although filled with painful details, these are ultimately accounts of triumph, and what they reveal about survival may help both children and adults better face difficult times. Black-and-white photographs, including at least one portrait of each young person, bring the documentary to life.

Kuklin, Susan. *After a Suicide: Young People Speak Up*. 1994. New York: Putnam (0-399-22605-2); paper (0-399-22801-2). Ages 14–18.

Kuklin turns right to the emotional issues involved in suicide, focusing not only on individuals whose attempts to kill themselves fail but also on friends and family left behind after a suicide. With artless candor, people who lost loved ones explain the ways death has changed their lives. Careful not to make the suicide seem simple, the author purposely includes the words of two people who courted death (one was a substance abuser, the other was uncomfortable with his sexual orientation) and presents a sample of a conversation on a suicide hot line. Kuklin's editorial intervention is subtle yet purposeful: she's left in not only the raw sentiment of the people she spoke with but also their harsh language. What her exploration ultimately reveals is a rocky but not impassable road to recovery.

Leder, Jane Mersky. *Dead Serious: A Book for Teenagers about Teenage Suicide*. 1987. New York: Atheneum (0-689-31262-8); Avon, paper (0-380-70661-X). Ages 13–18.

"Kids who threaten suicide aren't interested in ending their lives. They're interested in ending their pain," writes Leder, who frankly discusses the causes, the fallacies and facts, and the warning signs of suicide among teens as well as the ramifications of the act on surviving family and friends. Avoiding stuffy textbook jargon, she speaks directly to her readers, infusing her text with interviews, case studies, and lengthy scenarios, some including dialogue, to make her subject more relevant and compelling. She stresses that adult intervention is a necessity during a suicidal crisis, but she also recognizes that friends can play an important role in identifying a teenager at risk. Addressing individuals who are concerned about someone they know, she explains how to spot signs of trouble and become better listeners and more supportive friends, even when that means betraying a confidence by contacting a parent or a teacher or calling a suicide hot line.

"It's not surprising that the teen years are often filled with fear, loneliness, and insecurity. What is surprising is the fact that teenagers today seem less able or less willing to cope with the same changes and expectations their parents faced not so long ago."
—from *Dead Serious*

Nelson, Richard E., and Judith C. Galas. *The Power to Prevent Suicide: A Guide for Teens Helping Teens*. 1994. Minneapolis: Free Spirit, paper (0-915793-70-9). Ages 14–18.

Like most books about teen suicide, this one discusses risk factors, why teens kill themselves, and danger signals. It's different, however, in one important way. While most others advise young people to turn over to an adult the responsibility of helping someone in crisis, this one doesn't stop with telling. It encourages teens to take a helping role because, "You may be able to do a better job of reaching your friends than many of the adults around." That's a controversial stance, but Galas, a free-lance writer, and Nelson, an associate professor of counseling psychology, make a good case for keeping kids involved, even while telling them bluntly how difficult it is to help someone who needs so much support. In fact, part of the book is an activist's manual of sorts, explaining not only how to become a good listener but also how to assess a crisis situation and act swiftly and appropriately. The last section addresses readers who may be facing a suicidal crisis of their own.

FICTION

Bauer, Marion Dane. *Face to Face*. New York: Clarion (0-395-55440-3); Dell, paper (0-440-40971-5). Ages 11–14.

Unhappy at home and troubled at school, 13-year-old Michael thinks a summer of white-water rafting with the father he hasn't seen in eight years will turn his life around.

Brooks, Martha. *Two Moons in August*. 1992. Boston: Little, Brown (0-316-10979-7); Scholastic, paper (0-590-45923-6). Ages 13–18.

Even though her mother had been sick with TB for most of Sidonie's life, her death was a shock that struck the family hard. In grief, they have drawn apart, and Sidonie turns to attractive newcomer Kieran, who, it turns out, has problems of his own.

Coman, Carolyn. *Tell Me Everything*. 1993. New York: Farrar (0-374-37-390-6). Ages 11–14.

Told that her mother died while trying to save a lost young boy, Roz is left with anger, nightmares, and the burning question of why her mother would have left her for a stranger.

Conly, Jane Leslie. *Crazy Lady*. 1993. New York: HarperCollins/Laura Geringer (0-06-021357-4); paper (0-06-440571-0). Ages 11–14.

Still grieving for his mother, from whom he got his confidence, awkward Vernon Dibbs is drawn to Maxine Flooter, the neighborhood alcoholic and eccentric "crazy" lady, who deeply loves her severely disabled son, Ronald.

Draper, Sharon. *Tears of a Tiger.* 1994. New York: Atheneum (0-689-31878-2). Ages 14–16.

Neither his parents nor his doctor anticipate the tragic consequences when Andy spirals into depression following the death of his good friend Robert, who died in an alcohol-related automobile accident in which Andy was involved.

Ferris, Jean. *Signs of Life.* 1995. New York: Farrar (0-374-36909-7). Ages 12–15.

Neither Hannah nor her parents seem able to get over the death of Hannah's twin, Molly. A trip to France seems like a good idea—and it is, particularly for Hannah, whose dreams and relationship with a Gypsy juggler help her bring her grief to the surface.

Grant, Cynthia D. *Shadow Man.* 1992. New York: Atheneum (0-689-31772-7). Ages 13–18.

The news of the tragic death of well-liked 18-year-old Gabe McCloud causes the people who knew him to reflect about the kind of person that he was.

Hahn, Mary Downing. *The Wind Blows Backward.* 1993. New York: Clarion (0-395-62975-6); Avon, paper (0-380-77530-1). Ages 14–18.

Now in high school, Lauren has thought herself long over middle-school love Spencer Adams. But when he approaches her, memories of things they once shared come flooding back—but they are colored by a changed Spencer's troubled past and very troubled mind.

Hamilton, Virginia. *Cousins.* 1990. New York: Putnam/Philomel (0-399-22164-6). Ages 11–14.

Eleven-year-old Cammy hates her goody-goody cousin who makes fun of Cammy's beloved Gram. But when Cammy wishes Patty Ann dead and the wish actually comes true, Cammy's sorrow and guilt are almost too much to bear.

Hurwin, Davida Wills. *A Time for Dancing.* 1995. Boston: Little, Brown (0-316-38351-1). Ages 14–18.

Samantha and Juliana have been close since childhood, but when "Jules" is diagnosed with cancer, their friendship is tested. The girls must face the real possibility that they are not inseparable.

Johnson, Angela. *Toning the Sweep.* 1994. New York: Orchard/Richard Jackson (0-531-05476-4); Scholastic, paper (0-590-48142-8). Ages 14–18.

Emily has never gotten on well with her mother. She's always been much closer to her grandmother Ola, who has lived in the desert since Grandaddy died. Now things are changing: Ola is dying.

Lynch, Chris. *Shadow Boxer.* 1993. New York: HarperCollins (0-06-023027-4); paper (0-06-447112-8). Ages 12–15.

George, 14, and his troubled younger brother, Monty, are more rivals than friends, but both live in the shadow of their deceased father, who was a boxer.

McDaniel, Lurlene. *Don't Die, My Love.* 1995. New York: Bantam, paper (0-553-56715-2). Ages 14–17.

A couple since grade-school days, Julie and Luke have enjoyed a fairy tale relationship in true romantic style. Then fate steps in: Luke is diagnosed with a kind of cancer for which there is no cure.

Mahon, K. L. *Just One Tear.* 1994. New York: Lothrop (0-688-13519-6). Ages 11–15.

In a diary, a 13-year-old boy tries to come to grips with the death of his father, who was fatally shot right in front of him.

Peck, Richard. *Remembering the Good Times*. 1985. New York: Delacorte (0-385-29396-8); Dell, paper (0-440-97339-2). Ages 14–18.

Buck, Kate, and Travis have been friends since junior high, even though their home lives and backgrounds are very different. When Travis kills himself, Buck remembers the good times the three had together. He also realizes how little he really understood his friend.

Rylant, Cynthia. *Missing May*. 1992. New York: Orchard/Richard Jackson (0-06-020292-0); Dell, paper (0-440-40865-2). Ages 11–14.

Bereft after the death of her aunt May, 12-year-old Summer is terrified that her Uncle Ob misses May so much that he'll die and leave her behind.

Springer, Nancy. *Toughing It*. 1994. San Diego: Harcourt (0-15-200008-9). Ages 13–16.

Tuff's living with an alcoholic mother, her sometimes violent "old man," and a bunch of out-of-control step-siblings is made bearable only because of his relationship with his older brother, Dillon. When Dillon is viciously murdered, Tuff wants revenge.

VIDEOS

ORIGINALLY COMPILED and introduced by former *Booklist* assistant editor Ellen Mandel, the video list that follows includes new material gathered with the help of the current staff of *Booklist's* Audiovisual Materials Section.

Most of today's young adults have been raised with TV. *Sesame Street* taught them numbers and letters, and media advertisements molded their tastes and attitudes. As a result, many teens absorb facts from a TV screen more readily than from a book's pages. When their minds are distracted by serious crises, young people may have even more difficulty concentrating on reading. A TV drama can offer escape from life's concerns while simultaneously counseling, consoling, and advising.

The following list represents some of the best current videos (most released within the last three to five years) available to young people facing personal challenges. Including both documentaries and dramatizations, the selections are suitable for home and school viewing; many are accompanied by study guides to enhance their classroom applications. A variety of factors were considered in determining the suggested age levels, including subject matter, running time, and ages of the characters. Unlike videos that are released solely for home entertainment, these titles are very expensive. Large public libraries and school districts may own a few of them; some may be accessible through public and school library film and video cooperatives; some can be rented directly from the distributor. Cited prices are for the VHS format, and rental prices, when known, have been included to facilitate short-term rental of prints from distributors, who are listed at the end of the chapter. Prices and addresses are current as of the time of this book's publication.

Beginning the chapter are excerpts from an interview with filmmaker Michael Pritchard conducted by Sue-Ellen Beauregard. The conversation can be found in it's entirety in the May 15, 1994, issue of *Booklist*.

Michael Pritchard: Making Films on Subjects That Matter

A former stand-up comic and juvenile probation officer, Michael Pritchard is well known to PBS audiences as the host of the immensely popular video series *The Power of Choice,* for high-schoolers, and the equally well-received *You Can Choose,* for elementary students. In his newest series, *Big Changes, Big Choices,* Pritchard speaks to the middle-school/junior-high crowd on self-esteem, values, parental conflict, and related topics. As funny, warmhearted, and sincere over the telephone as he is on screen, Pritchard, who is known for his wide girth, began this interview by revealing that he suffers from "anorexia ponderosa."

SEB: *What prompted you to incorporate humor in your work with youngsters?*

MP: One of the most important things I realized when I worked as a juvenile probation officer [in St. Louis and San Francisco] with really tough delinquents was that comedy, humor, and laughter were the best ways to breach barriers of fear. I found that when I mimicked, reflected, or teased the kids in an inclusive way, their fear and defensiveness broke down, and they would tell me everything. We need to find common ground through humor. As I say, "Fear is the little dark room where negatives are developed." When you get people past their own fears, then you can move them in a direction they need to go.

SEB: *How much input do you have with production and script writing in your video programs?*

MP: The comedy is essentially me, but the producer is the head of the cattle drive because he puts everything together. He and I work on the questions and go over the things we need to discuss with the kids. Basically, we're marketing the love I have for kids.

SEB: *When you began doing the videos, was it difficult to get financial backing?*

MP: It was difficult, but luckily, after I met the producers at a teen conference where I spoke, one of my corporate friends finally gave us initial financial backing. It's very interesting, though, because even today it's hard to get additional funding. One woman told me that she thinks it's ironic that I have this financial difficulty, even though I'm doing a worthy thing on video. I don't get a great deal of commercial visibility because I'm not selling merchandise to kids.

SEB: *Who decides what schools you use, and who chooses the children in the small groups that appear on the programs?*

MP: Usually the producer picks the schools, and the teachers and administrators have final say on the participants. We always make sure that participation is not perceived by the kids as a reward; we seek inclusion of all types of kids. Sometimes people criticize us because they think we're only featuring the best kids, but that's not true.

SEB: *How much editing do you have to do for a half-hour program?*

MP: I would say we film six hours and edit down to a half-hour. Remember, we're guiding children along, we're not tabloid television looking for the sensational. We are trying to show realistically how kids feel.

SEB: *You're very nonjudgmental with the students. In the newest series, you asked the children if they would shoplift in order to be popular with a certain peer group, and some said they would. Do you ever have to bite your tongue when you hear such responses?*

MP: No, I never bite my tongue because I want the students to be honest. If I come at the children as a parental figure, I can't help them. My unconditional love for them is a very important part of sustaining a relationship of trust.

SEB: *Do you do any warm-up routines before the cameras begin rolling?*

MP: No, we kind of roll and go. I do a few icebreakers, and we let the kids get to know me during the comedy show early in the morning, where I tell them in a heartfelt way that the relationship we have with each other is very important. People tend to underestimate kids, but I listen to them.

SEB: *Do the assembly programs you do at schools differ from the videos, or are they basically the same?*

MP: It's interesting that the students want me to do the same thing they see on the videos; they want me to sit down and talk with them. The consistency is what they're looking for.

SEB: *Have the problems that children are dealing with changed over the years?*

MP: No, the problems really haven't changed. In our society, everybody talks about violence, but nobody talks about anger. Everyone wants the answer to drug and alcohol abuse, but no one wants to talk about the grief and sadness kids feel. As always, the kids say it best. One boy said, "What good does it do if I get straight *A*'s in school yet I still don't like myself and feel like killing myself?"

SEB: *So you see that the most significant problems are still related to self-esteem and self-acceptance?*

MP: Yes, that's the core of it. I don't want to blame television, guns, or schools because blame does nothing. But when we start addressing feelings, we're headed in the direction where our society must go. My videos revolve around feelings; as a society, we don't deal well with feelings. We find ways to distract ourselves from our feelings, ways to deny them or drug them instead of learning to handle them.

SEB: *How do your own children react to your role as a caring counselor?*

MP: My kids are so aware. Recently, my oldest son jumped in the car after a Little League baseball game and told me he hated one of his teammates. I told him that even though the teammate punched and kicked him, I was proud of my son because he was a good sport and didn't retaliate. My boy replied, "I still hate his guts, Dad." And then I asked if I could say something else. My 11-year-old looks at me and says, "Dad, can I just hate the kid for five minutes before you tell me he has a dysfunctional home life!"

SEB: *What are you doing next?*

MP: I really don't know. I've thought about doing a kindergarten series for the little ones. I perform all these cartoon voices and characters so I'd like to work with puppets. If I had the money, I'd build a place where kids could come from all over the country, and we'd film them and give the videotapes away. I'd also like to spend time at a child-development center for kids under 5 years of age. I have so much fun with the little kids. They're very healing to me.

SEB: *How about the older ones?*

MP: Well, I'd love to find a bunkhouse in California with a huge living room and fireplace. We'd fly kids in from all around the country and let them get to know each other for a couple days, and then we'd start filming. I've worked at a camp in New Jersey for the past eight summers. I love it because we bring kids from all cultural and socioeconomic groups together. Initially, they hate each other because they're afraid, but at the end of one week, they don't want to leave. I had one young guy from Newark who told about his hardworking father who was a churchgoer and a nondrinker, yet he was shot and killed on a street corner. He then went on to say that his mother killed herself because she couldn't cope with her problems. Subsequently, he began dealing drugs because he felt it was the only way to make a living. Then a girl from the suburbs gets up and tells how her stepdad physically abused her daily. Because of her stepfather's immense wealth and power, she was afraid to tell anyone about the abuse.

SEB: *Obviously, you see problems that cross cultural and socioeconomic lines. Are there any differences?*

MP: No. I remember once in Washington, D.C., a boy told about being a latchkey kid. I asked him why he couldn't have friends over, and he said he was ashamed. I assumed he lived in a tough section of town but found out he lives in a thirty-eight-room mansion. The housekeeper puts the meal in the microwave oven for him, and every night he waits for his alcoholic parents to come home. As he related this story, the rest of the kids were very silent. I pressed on and asked him why he couldn't have friends over, what it was that he was ashamed of. "I'm ashamed of the fact that I have everything that a kid could want except parents who care about me." Finally, after a long and very awkward silence, another girl responded in an affectionately teasing manner, "Oh you poor, poor baby!" Then everyone cracked up.

SEB: *Again, humor prevails.*

MP: Yes, it relieves the stress for everyone. Everybody is tense, emotional, and close to tears, so when she said that, the room just busted up.

SEB: *Have you had any mishaps or quotes that fall into the "kids say the darndest things" category?*

MP: Oh yes. For example, I asked one boy if he wasn't being too critical, and he said, "I am, but I try not to take it personally." Every therapist should have that saying on the office wall. Another memorable statement was also during a moment of extreme tension. I asked one of the kids what he'd most like to say to his mom and dad. He said very emotionally, "I would tell my father not to travel so much on business." Then I asked the same question to the next boy, and he said he'd tell his dad to "get off the crack pipe." By this time, everyone in the group was crying. Then I moved on to the next student who articulately declared how he would urge his father to get into some kind of drug or alcohol program. I thanked him for sharing that personal moment, but then he blurted out. "Wait a second. I'm not done. I'd also like to tell my mother to please let us know when she's having her period so we can stay out of her way!" The whole tenor of the group immediately changed; it went from the worst tears to the longest laughs imaginable.

SEB: *I assume that segment ended up on the cutting-room floor.*

MP: Absolutely. But it just goes to show that in the midst of all this fear, anger, and pain, life can sometimes still be funny.

SEB: *Do you think that your videos help stimulate or encourage communication between parents and their children?*

MP: Yes. I hear that all the time from both kids and parents. I had a flight attendant chase me down at Chicago's O'Hare Airport. I was lumbering along, and she yelled at me to stop. She said that she just remembered who I was, and she wanted me to know that my series completely changed her son's life.

SEB: *That's a nice story.*

MP: Yes, you have those great moments, and you keep trying your best.

FAMILY MATTERS

The Crown Prince. The Media Guild. 1988; rel. 1990. 38 min., guide, $205. Ages 11–up.

Fifteen-year-old Billy and his younger brother, Freddy, hide in their rooms while their father physically and verbally abuses their mother. Billy wants to guard this tragic family secret, but Freddy tells the school authorities. Before the mother and her sons take refuge at a local shelter, Billy begins to exhibit violent behavior and is horrified to realize he may be growing up to be like his dad.

Daddy Can't Read. AIMS Media. 1988; rel. 1990. 45 min., $99.95. Rental, $50. Ages 11–up.

Although she donates her time to a high-school literacy program, Allison Watson does not realize her own father cannot read. When she learns the truth, she encourages and finally persuades him to attend night school. This effectively worked drama meaningfully conveys the fears and feelings of inadequacy one man experiences because of illiteracy and depicts the power of a concerned and caring family that helps the man help himself.

Families in Trouble: Learning to Cope. Sunburst Communications. 1990. 35 min., guide, $199. Ages 12–18.

Three situations of family crises—child abuse, parental fighting, and teenage alcoholism—are shown to have an impact on teens in the family. Even though young adults in these troubled families may not be directly involved in the incidents, they often feel responsible. Information provided about counseling and other positive coping strategies will reassure and help guide affected viewers.

Just for the Summer. Churchill Media. 1990. 29 min., guide, $99.95. Ages 13–18.

High-school track star Philip is an outgoing teen who suffers when his grandmother comes to live with his family. Grandmother's often unpredictable and irrational behavior, caused by Alzheimer's disease, frustrates and confuses Philip and causes tension for everyone. This poignant dramatization depicts the effects of Alzheimer's from a teen perspective.

Necessary Parties. Public Media Video 1988; rel. 1990. 110 min., $29.95. Ages 12–14.

When his parents announce their plans to divorce, Chris Mills decides to sue them. The teenager, who has looked after his kid sister through the years of their parents' stormy marriage, turns to an auto mechanic friend with a law degree for counsel. In a realistic portrayal of suburban junior-high life, children's feelings about their parents' divorce—especially their desire to prevent dissolution of the marriage—come to light. The reasonable price is a bonus. Adapted from the novel *Necessary Parties,* by Barbara Dana (Harper, 1987).

Nobody's Home. AGC Educational Media. 1990. 20 min., guide, $385. Rental, $50. Ages 12–up.

A patient, effective school social worker slowly wins the trust of 10-year-old Anthony and draws from the troubled child the fact that he is responsible for looking after a younger brother while their mother is away from home working or dating. The unkempt, nervous Anthony is helped to understand his strong feelings about the neglect he endures, and the skilled social worker motivates positive changes in the boys' home situation. This is a fine dramatization of a very prevalent type of child abuse.

Other Mothers. AGC Educational Media. 1993; rel. 1994. 45 min., $295. Rental, $40. Ages 14–adult.

This made-for-television drama about a nontraditional family focuses on high-school freshman Will who lives with two mothers, his birth mother and his "other mother." Meredith Baxter and Joanna Cassidy star.

Surviving Your Parents' Divorce. Cambridge Educational. 1993. 45 min., $79.95. Ages 15–18.

This ultimately upbeat, reassuring program, which acknowledges the emotional upheaval that comes when parents divorce, combines specific coping strategies for weathering the stress with comments from three teens who talk about changes in family roles and responsibilities, being caught between parents, and turning to self-destructive behavior to ease their pain.

Teens in Changing Families: Making It Work. Sunburst Communications. 1989. 25 min., guide, $169. Ages 12–up.

The guilt and conflicting loyalties experienced by teenagers who have both biological and stepparents; the adjustments necessary to live in two homes—one where parents are strict, the other where parents are lenient and even indulgent; and the resentment of discipline imposed by a "wicked" stepparent are among the controversies aired in candid discussions with teens and parents from blended families. Group counseling and family meetings are shown to pave the road to understanding and improved relationships for these "instant" families.

Why Does Mom Drink So Much? Human Relations Media. 1989. 30 min., guide, $189. Rental, $40. Ages 14–18.

The painful emotions of shame, anger, and loneliness tear at children of alcoholic parents, often driving these youngsters to drink or to pursue other self-destructive escapes. This caring production urges teens to realize they have no control over their parents' drinking. The personal experiences candidly shared by young people with alcoholic parents, along with helpful comments from professionals, attest to the value of support groups for comfort and guidance.

SCHOOL: FOR BETTER OR WORSE

Degrassi Junior High, Term 1, 2 & 3. Direct Cinema. 1987–88. 42 episodes. Each program: 30 min., guide, $75. Ages 11–14.

Degrassi High School, Term 4. Direct Cinema. 1989; rel. 1990. 15 episodes. Each program: 30 min., guide, $125. Ages 14–18.

Degrassi High School, Term 5. Direct Cinema. 1991. 12 episodes. 1 program, 60 min.; 11 programs. Each program: 30 min, guide, $125. Ages 14–18.

Degrassi Talks. Direct Cinema. 1993. 6 episodes. Each program: 30 min. Series, $450. Ages 13–18.

With provocative plots attuned to the realities of teens' lives and subplots that intensify viewer interest, the programs in all of these critically acclaimed series center around a group of ethnically diverse neighborhood kids. The Degrassi Junior High series was originally broadcast on television in the 1980s. *Term 4* and *Term 5* are more-recent productions that pick up on the lives of the kids in high school and realistically deal with issues of interest to older teens, such as suicide, homosexuality, and self-esteem. The newest Degrassi series, *Degrassi Talks,* follows several of the actors who appeared in the early programs as they travel across Canada and talk to teens about their lives and their feelings.

How to Succeed in Middle School. Sunburst Communications. 1994. 21 min., $149. Ages 11–14.

In a lively production addressing the often difficult transition from elementary to middle school, four students who've mastered the change interview classmates and give advice to incoming adolescents on everything from managing locker combinations and handling classroom changes to balancing extracurricular activities with homework demands.

Ready or Not. Direct Cinema. 1994. 13 episodes. Each program: 30 min., $195. Ages 10–13.

Like the Degrassi Junior High series, the videos in this fine thirteen-part series are aimed at the middle-school/junior-high age group. With humor and honesty they zero in on the growing up concerns of 11-year-old Amanda and her friend Bizzy, who deal, during the course of the series, with such issues as puberty, sexuality, substance abuse, and smoking. Humor, recognizable characters, and adept production are combined to good effect.

School Colors. PBS Video. 1994. 143 min., $89.95. Ages 14–adult.

California's urban, racially mixed Berkeley High School is the backdrop for this dynamic video produced by students. The program follows teens through the hallways, into the classrooms, to social events, and into private homes, capturing them with their friends, teachers, and parents straightforwardly confronting issues such as school violence, interracial dating, and segregation.

ME: MY RIGHTS, MY FRIENDS, MYSELF

Big Changes, Big Choices. Live Wire Media. 1993. 12 programs. Each program: 30 min., $69.95. Series, $699. Ages 11–14.

Footage of Michael Pritchard putting kids at ease with his stand-up comedy routines sets the tone for this fine new series targeted at middle school/junior high kids. Programs deal with age-appropriate issues ranging from getting along with parents and making friends to being honest and setting goals for the future.

Bring a Friend. What Does It Mean? Sunburst Communications. 1995. 20 min., $149. Ages 11–15.

This film depicts teens who are part of the same crowd coping with various aspects of peer relationships, such as friendship and romance. In one vignette, a friendship is tested when one boy switches allegiances; in another, two students find themselves moving beyond friendship toward romance.

How to Deal with the "Jerks" in Your Life—and Earn the Respect of Your Friends. NoodleHead Network. 1994. 11 min., $39. Ages 11–14.

This well-done program uses junior high students to send viewers a message about peer pressure. Introduced by a high-school senior, five skits, written and acted out by eighth graders, depict various ways teens who are being pressured to smoke, drink, steal, etc. deal with the situations and explore the effectiveness of assertive, aggressive, and passive responses.

Myth of the Perfect Body: Accepting Your Physical Self. Learning Seed. 1995. 21 min., guide, $89. Ages 12–16.

An important developmental task for adolescents, adjusting to one's body image, is the subject here, with the program focusing on high-school-age Jen, whose family and friends are constant critics of what she wears and how she looks.

The Power of Choice. Live Wire Media. 1987. 58 min., $79.95. Ages 13–up.

Much more than an entertaining comedian, Michael Pritchard is a first-rate discussion leader and rapt listener—talents honed while working as a juvenile counselor. In scenes capturing his informal encounters with teens and his performances before high-school audiences, Pritchard amusingly and effectively advises young adults to formulate clear goals, take positive initiatives, and keep things in proper perspective. His unique approach helps young people eye life with a sense of humor, while his advice inspires them to work toward their ambitions.

The Problem with People Pleasing: Improving Relationship Skills. Learning Seed. 1994. 21 min., guide, $89. Ages 14–16.

Problems with girls, grades, and sports are tackled in this live-action dramatization in which Mike's good friends help him redefine his self-concept and replace negative behaviors that are affecting his self-image and his relationships with others.

Say No and Keep Your Friends. Sunburst Communications. 1995. 26 min., $169. Ages 11–15.

A dilemma that touches most young people at one time or another gets serious consideration by a group of students in this useful video that crisscrosses some of the same territory as *How to Deal with the "Jerks" in Your Life.* Young people brainstorm and use role playing to explore the best response to situations in which lying, ignoring no-trespassing signs, and driving without a license are involved.

A Season in Hell. New Day Films. 1989; rel. 1991. 59 min., guide, $208. Rental, $84. Ages 15–up.

Representative media hype about ideal feminine bodies is adeptly combined with interviews conducted over a five-year period in a program that poignantly reveals the influences behind a young woman's eating disorder.

Self-Confidence: Step by Step. Sunburst Communications. 1994. 23 min., $149. Ages 11–15.

What do you do when friends make fun? What do you do when you're convinced you're not going to be able to accomplish something you really want to do? Fine acting makes the stories of three middle schoolers who want to succeed—one at basketball, one in science, and the third in photography—convincing models for explaining how to become more self-confident.

Supermom's Daughter. The Media Guild. 1987; rel., 1989. 32 min., $345. Ages 12–up.

Noelle's high-powered career mom cannot understand her daughter's desire to study early childhood education, especially since Noelle is a brilliant science student. Despite her parent's pressure to choose a more sophisticated college major, Noelle holds to her convictions, showing how she can combine her knack for science with her love of children by inventing a robot "monster buster" to chase away children's nightmares. A professionally polished, well-acted, and meaningful drama, this speaks to teens' need to find their own path in life.

Speak It! Filmakers Library. 1993; rel. 1994. 28 min., $295. Rental, $55. Ages 14–adult.

Blacks are a minority at 16-year-old Shingai's Nova Scotia school, and racism is an unpleasant part of his student life. This program, which will speak to American as well as Canadian youth, accompanies Shingai as he and classmates meet with school officials, prepare a play about racism, and attend a conference in an effort to raise the consciousness of fellow students.

Surviving in the Real World. Human Relations Media. 1991. 3 programs. Each program: 25–32 min., guides, $169–$199. Each rental, $40. Ages 15–18.

Available individually, the dramatizations in this trio of videos advise older teens about some of the practicalities of living independently. *Dollars and Sense* discusses checking accounts, budgeting, obtaining credit, and maintaining a savings program. *Housing and Transportation* helps young adults buy a car and find an apartment. *Lifestyle* encompasses such everyday essentials as insurance, food and clothes, education, and time management.

Take Another Look. Direct Cinema. 1994. 24 min., $295. Rental, $55. Ages 10–13.

Rock music and effectively designed sets add sparkle to a lively story of 13-year-old Sarah's struggle to make herself perfect. A fairy godmother's intervention happily sets Sarah on the right path, but not before the teenager's fantasies take her to an exercise class, a photographer's studio, and a fashion show in search of flawlessness.

When Food Is an Obsession: Overcoming Eating Disorders. Human Relations Media. 1994. 28 min., $189. Ages 11–17.

Interviews with health professionals and a teenager recovering from anorexia, along with voice-over narration, serve to emphasize and inform viewers about the symptoms, behaviors, consequences, and treatments for eating disorders. Neither overdramatized nor preachy, this is a fine complement to the more personal approach used in *A Season in Hell,* discussed previously in this section.

SAFE PASSAGE: AT HOME, AT SCHOOL, IN THE COMMUNITY

Abby, My Love. AGC Educational Media. 1991. 45 min., guide, $395. Rental, $50. Ages 15–up.

Chip Wilson and Abby Gilmore have known each other since childhood. Now in high school, the pair find their affection deepening. But Abby is afraid to commit herself to more than friendship. Chip finally finds out why when a distraught Abby reveals that her father has been sexually abusing her for years. Good editing, fine acting, and the utmost discretion characterize a dramatic depiction of the worst and best in human relationships. Based on the novel by Hadley Irwin.

Alternatives to Violence: Conflict Resolution, Negotiation and Mediation. United Learning. 1994. 2 videos. Each program: 64 min., $150. Ages 15–18.

Conflict resolution through student mediation is the subject of this two-part program, the first of which features teenage hosts and students from a Colorado mediation project teaching peer mediation and communication skills. Part two instructs teachers or adult mediators in similar skills.

Big Shot. Pyramid Film & Video. 1994. 20 min., $295. Rental, $75. Ages 11–14.

This nicely produced, provocative, live-action video sends a stern message about guns. Home alone with his little brother, high-school student Henry gives in to the goading of his friend Skeet, who wants Henry to prove his boast that his dad has a

.357 Magnum. The tragedy that results from Henry's giving in makes this film excellent for prompting discussion of peer pressure as well as the issue of gun control.

Date Rape: Violence among Friends. SRA School Group. 1991. 22 min., guide, $37.32. Ages 14–18.

The comments of a rape-crisis professional and interviews with two young women who were raped by men they knew help illuminate the trauma of date rape. In addition to heightening awareness, this production primes viewers to recognize and to prevent potentially threatening situations and offers guidelines for recovery to those who have suffered sexual abuse.

He's So Fine: Crossing the Line into Sexual Harassment. Media Inc. 1993. 25 min, guide, $325. Rental, $50. Ages 14–18.

Danny thinks he's hot stuff where girls are concerned and treats the opposite sex with little respect, leading his buddies in loud, sexist comments and behavior that makes even his girlfriend, Julie, uncomfortable. He gets his comeuppance in comic yet pointed fashion when he falls asleep in class and dreams of a world in which the guys have to suffer the indignities that the girls dish out.

The Morning after: A Story of Vandalism. Pyramid Film & Video. 1989; rel. 1990. 27 min., guide, $295. Rental, $75. Ages 12–18.

While under the influence of alcohol, four Minnesota youths broke into the local high school and savagely vandalized it, causing one million dollars in damage. In this program, which is documented by newsreel footage, teens try to explain their rampage to viewers. Their words and actions speak volumes about the impact of peer pressure and alcohol abuse.

Out of Bounds: Teenage Sexual Harassment. Coronet/MTI Film & Video. 1992. 19 min., $350. Rental, $75. Ages 14–18.

In a convincing program intended to raise the sensitivity of teenage boys, rock singer Freddie is made to feel uncomfortable by the leers and remarks of the members of a band for which she's auditioning. Between-scene comments from a rapper add perspective.

Reducing School Violence through Ethnic Harmony. AIMS Media. 1994. 26 min., $194. Rental, $75. Ages 14–adult.

Renowned psychiatrist Alvin Poussaint is among those featured in this insightful program in which an ethnically diverse group of high-school students from Medford, Massachusetts, discuss racial confrontation, their fears about escalating violence, and ideas for mediation and effecting change.

Sexual Harassment—Issues for Teachers and Students. AGC Educational Media. 1994. 2 programs. Each program: 18–21 min., $295. Each rental, $50. Ages 14–18.

Although each of the two programs in this series is targeted at a different audience, they share some of the same interviews and realistic vignettes. *Guidelines for Intervention and Prevention* is aimed predominantly at teachers, while *You Don't Have to Take It* is meant to help students understand the issues surrounding harassment in a school environment and to deal wisely with them.

Teenage Crises: The Fateful Choices. Human Relations Media. 1993. 28 min., $189. Ages 14–17.

A candid, ultimately optimistic video uses interviews with social workers and teens to show that desperate situations need not end tragically. An ex-gang member, a former drug user, and a young pregnant mother describe their experiences and what helped them turn their lives around.

Understanding & Resolving Conflicts. United Learning. 1994. 23 min., $95. Ages 11–15.

Acknowledging conflict as a natural part of everyday life, this involving video presents teens with vignettes depicting various ways discord can be handled through better communication skills and compromise.

When Dating Turns Dangerous. Sunburst Communications. 1995. 38 min., $199. Ages 15–18.

In this realistic drama, 17-year-old Lucy wants desperately to keep her college boyfriend Zach happy even though he's totally unpredictable and physically abuses her. His apologies suffice for a time—but when he finally puts her in the hospital, she has no choice but to face up to Zach's problem and to her own emotional dependency.

WELLNESS: BEING SICK, STAYING HEALTHY

Anger: You Can Handle It. Sunburst Communications. 1995. 24 min., $169. Ages 13–17.

A variety of things that trigger angry feelings—from rules to putdowns to comparisons to punishment—are depicted in vignettes that use teenage actors to explore the ways people become angry and suggest how they can cope with their turbulent feelings in healthy ways.

Are You Addicted? Human Relations Media. 1992. 30 min., guide, $189. Ages 13–16.

Presenting good opportunities for classroom discussion as well as independent thought, this no-nonsense production turns the spotlight on three teenagers who've overcome addictive behaviors (compulsive gambling, alcohol abuse, and eating disorders). Two mental health professionals offer necessary medical background and advice.

Breast Self-Exam for Teens. Media Inc. 1993; rel. 1994. 7 min., $225. Rental, $50. Ages 14–18.

In a program that is both reassuring and practical, a woman explains to teens the reasons for conducting breast self-examinations, and three women, one Asian American, one African-American, one white, demonstrate proper examination techniques while standing in front of a mirror and lying on a bed.

Bulking Up: The Dangers of Steroids. AIMS Media. 1990. 23 min., $149.95. Rental, $75. Ages 14–up.

Congenially hosted by Olympic medalist Bruce Jenner, this informative, nonthreatening documentary discourages steroid use. In addition to citing the litany of potential steroid side effects, the program hears from such appealing role models as an NFL trainer, a former NFL football player, a body builder, and retired Olympic athletes to make its case.

Dare to Be Different: Resisting Drug-Related Peer Pressure. Guidance Associates. 1988. 19 min., guide, $79. Ages 12–15.

Kim and Sarah are relay racers and friends, but they take different paths when Kim is drawn into a drinking and drug-abusing crowd. Ultimately, Kim grows bored with her new acquaintances and their one-dimensional interests and returns to racing. This well-produced video addresses self-esteem and the value of friendship as well as the dangers of substance abuse.

Early Warning Signs: Recognizing the Signs of Addiction. Coronet/MTI Film & Video. 1991. 21 min., guide, $125. Ages 12–up.

In this sincere, caring dramatization, families of addicts, gathered in a drug-rehab waiting room, talk about how they failed to recognize their loved ones' addictions. Through flashbacks, individuals recall the denial, anger, and hostility that go hand-in-hand with addiction. Warning signs are clearly summarized in the production, which sensitizes viewers to the needs and suffering of addicts and their families.

Fighting Back: Teenage Depression. Sunburst Communications. 1991. 44 min., guide, $199. Ages 14–18.

In excellently acted vignettes, three young adults display characteristic signs of serious depression brought on by true-to-life crises. In one instance a girl has broken up with her boyfriend; in another, a boy is pressured to attend a prestigious college against his will; in the third, a young woman is forced to baby-sit for her younger siblings instead of living her own life. All three receive helpful intervention from professionals who legitimize the teens' feelings and counsel them toward emotional well-being.

Gambler. AGC Educational Media. 1990. 45 min., guide, $275. Ages 13–up.

Seventeen-year-old Jim is an honor student and star quarterback on his high-school football team. Colleges already are wooing him. But he gambles away his promising prospects by compulsively betting on professional football games. Only after his gambling takes a toll on his grades, causes him to be benched from the team, and costs him most of the things he holds dear do his parents learn the truth. Then Jim begins to get the help he needs to recover. A gripping portrayal of an increasingly serious problem among today's youth.

High on Life: Feeling Good without Drugs. Guidance Associates. 1988. 46 min., guide, $129. Ages 12–18.

Eight students tell how outlets such as wheelchair athletics, motocross, and rock climbing led them to "natural highs" as opposed to drug-induced highs. Despite their own health and emotional crises, these personable youths have discovered positive ways to set goals and to offset discouragement. Their lively testimonies will inspire others to find enthusiasm in life rather than trying to escape problems through drugs.

Just Kids. Filmakers Library. 1994. 26 min., $295. Rental, $55. Ages 12–18.

Jon, 15, and Brandy, 19, have cystic fibrosis; David, 17, and Kristy, 20, have cancer; each also has amazing optimism, faith, and courage. With occasional voice-overs from a physician and a psychiatrist, these teens talk about their treatments and their aspirations in a film that will inspire viewers.

Over the Limit. AGC Educational Media. 1990. 45 min., guide, $395. Rental, $60. Ages 12–18.

After a drunk-driving accident leaves several of his friends dead, Matt determines to find out the truth about who was driving. In the process, he learns much about honesty and loyalty. This film version of Todd Strasser's novel *The Accident* (Doubleday, 1988) reinforces the dangers of driving drunk.

Schlessinger Teen Health Video. Library Video Co. 1994. 15 programs. Each program: 30 min., $39.95. Series, $599.25. Ages 14–18.

Teenagers talk about their experiences while physicians provide counsel for young people dealing with health issues in this series of attractive and effectively presented videos that offer concise, useful information on such timely topics as AIDS, cancer, self-esteem, and teenage pregnancy.

Self-Defeating Behavior: How to Stop It. Human Relations Media. 1990. 40 min., guide, $189. Ages 14–18.
Stress Reduction Strategies That Really Work! Human Relations Media. 1990. 31 min., guide, $189. Ages 14–18.

In a stimulating seminar format, both of these titles deliver practical advice on how to respond to typical teen situations. In the first program, problem assessment and self-diagnosis, techniques for controlling negative thinking, and behavioral strategies are recommended to counter social anxiety, worry, lack of assertiveness, and procrastination. Time management, assertiveness, and relaxation techniques are among the remedies promoted in the second program.

Smoke Screen. Durrin Productions. 1993; rel. 1994. 20 min., $199. Rental, $52. Ages 11–17.

Dave Goerlitz, a model who worked for Winston cigarettes, awakens viewers to the dangers of smoking and the tricks advertisers use to lure young people into beginning the habit. A discussion of his own smoking-related health problems reinforces his message.

Smoking: I'm in Control? Perennial Education. 1993. 15 min., guide, $295. Rental, $40. Ages 13–17.

Although this dramatization carries an unmistakable antismoking message, the presentation is less strident than most. Teenage Alex thinks she has her habit under control, but Alex's best friend, Keisha, disagrees and challenges Alex to give up her cigarettes.

Stress and You. Sunburst Communications. 1994. 24 min., $169. Ages 11–14.

Rachel gets headaches when she faces pep-squad tryouts; Luke is troubled by his parents' constant fighting; Dennis is worried about being shorter than the other kids in his class. Three tense young people learn to manage their stress in a variety of ways—among them, physical activity and relaxation techniques.

Who's In Charge? Teens Talk about Diabetes. AGC Educational Media. 1994. 18 min., $295. Rental, $50. Ages 13–18.

Five teenagers, ranging in age from 13 to 18, talk candidly about living with diabetes—touching on everything from their parents' and friends' reactions to their illness to monitoring and treating themselves and preparing for emergencies in their day-to-day lives. This supportive program will reassure teens who have diabetes and inform those who don't.

Your First Pelvic Exam. Media Inc. 1993; rel. 1994. 6 min., $225. Rental, $50. Ages 14–18.

A good film to pair with *Breast Self Exam for Teens,* listed previously, this straightforward program explains what to expect during a pelvic examination, identifies the placement of various organs, demystifies the instruments used, and discusses the kinds of problems the procedure can identify. Diagrams and models help clarify the explanations, which are presented by a female narrator.

SEX STUFF

Birth Control for Teens. Churchill Media. 1993. 24 min., $295. Rental, $60. Ages 13–18.

Directed to "teens who are having sex," this program uses well-staged vignettes, labeled drawings, and animation to introduce contraceptives and explain how they are used. The footage covers birth control pills, spermicides, foams, suppositories, and barrier contraceptives (including the female condom) as well as implants and injections.

Condoms: A Responsible Option. Landmark Media. 1991. 10 min., guide, $99. Rental, $50. Ages 16–up.

A couple's intimate evening is interrupted by the uninvited arrival of their previous sexual partners, followed by the arrival of the previous partners' previous partners. The resulting roomful of sexually active adults clearly illustrates the narrator's advice about the role of condoms in combating the spread of sexually transmitted diseases such as AIDS. This almost slapstick episode may be the lure that draws older teens' attention to the effective use of condoms and helps them understand the necessity of protection for both women and men. Originally released in 1987, the film has been updated to include additional information on latex condoms and AIDS.

Girl Stuff. 2nd ed. Churchill Media. 1993. 18 min., $285. Ages 10–14.

This update of a classic instructional video uses the comments of preadolescent and young teenage girls and a pleasing mix of animation and advertisements to help blossoming young women distinguish between media hype and their real physical and emotional needs. The result is a well-produced common-sense approach to reproductive maturity and personal hygiene that also promotes a positive self-image.

The Great Chastity Experiment. The Media Guild. 1987; rel. 1989. 34 min., guide, $245. Ages 14–18.

When teens Nicki and Keith decide to try chastity for one week, they find that getting to know each other's true personalities, intellects, interests, and feelings can be harder than having sex. But after a week of quick kisses only, the couple extend their experiment for another week. This slick, made-for-TV drama is certain to cause teens to consider the quality and direction of their relationships.

Homoteens. Frameline. 1993. 60 min., $300. Rental, $75. Ages 13–18.

Five urban gay and lesbian teens are profiled in this thought-provoking video in which the young people straightforwardly speak out about their lifestyles, romances, coming out, encounters with prejudice, and entry into the gay community. A good catalyst for discussion, the program shows teens who basically are comfortable with who they are despite the problems they've encountered.

In Our Own Words: Teens and AIDS. Media Works. 1995. 20 min., $104. Ages 14–18.

This frank, moving program unites five teenagers from different backgrounds, each of whom contracted the AIDS virus from unprotected sexual activity. In voice-over narration, the young people express their feelings about their illness, while footage, including some from the funerals of two of the teens, brings their stories into sharp focus for viewers.

Out: Stories of Lesbian and Gay Youth. Filmakers Library. 1994. 43 min., $295. Rental, $55. Ages 15–adult.

In a supportive program for homosexual youth, the words of young men and women who've come out and footage of them at school, at work, and in other familiar situations combine with scenes of the teenagers in group sessions discussing the reactions of their parents and friends and their own feelings.

The Perfect Date. AGC Educational Media. 1990. 45 min., guide, $395. Rental, $50. Ages 13–18.

Too often teens focus on being the "best." Stephen wants to be the school basketball star, and he wants to snare a date with the homecoming queen. He realizes both these goals. Then, in a series of humorous mishaps, he is stood up by his dream girl, loses his father's car to a tow truck, and finds Bernice, whose sincerity and charm make her a far more attractive date than the homecoming queen.

Sexual Orientation: Reading between the Labels. NEWIST/CESA. 1991. 28 min., guide, $195. Rental, $50. Ages 13–up.

Hosted by a congenial young man named Jeff, this top-notch program mixes insightful comments from parents and professionals with the frankly spoken words of gay and lesbian teenagers to explain the pressures gay youth face today and the various ways they handle their problems.

Teen Contraception. AIMS Media. 1990. 13 min., $129. Rental, $75. Ages 14–18.

In a nonthreatening manner, an unbiased teen host informs peers about the female reproductive system and cycle and about birth-control methods. Commonly held yet often dangerous myths about sexuality and pregnancy are dispelled by this valuable program's explanations. The film is also available in Spanish.

Thinking Positive. Landmark Media. 1993; rel. 1994. 24 min., $250. Rental, $60. Ages 15–18.

Although the setting is a rural Newfoundland seacoast town, this video will have much to say to American audiences. Clips of teen AIDS activist Trudy Parsons, who is HIV positive, sharing her story have been combined with footage of young adults speaking frankly about their sexual behaviors—including reasons why they take foolish chances that can result in death. A film that encourages teens to be responsible—to themselves and to others—this will open the door to classroom discussion and independent thought.

Too Far Too Fast. Film Ideas. 1989. 26 min., guide, $189. Rental, $60. Ages 14–18.

While it focuses on two couples, this comprehensive production incorporates a panorama of teen attitudes about sexuality. Melissa and Josh are at odds over how far to go sexually, while Angie and Hector suspect they've already gone too far—Angie might be pregnant. Some of their friends talk silliness; others talk sense. As this realistic drama unfolds, the teens grow in maturity and understanding.

What Teens Want to Know about Sex. Sunburst Communications. 1994. 29 min., $189. Ages 13–17.

In this instructive, straightforward dramatization, two magazine columnists contribute facts and advice about sex-related matters as they look over letters they've received from teen subscribers. Questions about subjects including AIDS, menstruation, reproduction, and contraception are covered, with animated drawings illustrating the discussion.

ONE PLUS ONE MAKES THREE: MARRIAGE, PREGNANCY, AND PARENTING

Baby Blues. National Film Board of Canada. 1990; rel. 1991. 24 min., $200. Rental, $50. Ages 14–18.

Jason's thoughts are on playing soccer and Kristen's are on a recently won scholarship until the two are distracted by fears that Kristen may be pregnant. Indeed, the anxiously awaited results of a home pregnancy test confirm their suspicions. Through believable scripting and fine acting, viewers become involved in the young couple's dilemma and are alerted to the necessity of taking sexual responsibility. The film is closed-captioned for the hearing impaired.

Discipline from Birth to Three: Guidelines for Avoiding Discipline Problems. Morning Glory. 1994. 52 min., $195. Ages 13–18.

Based on Jeanne Warren Lindsay and Sally McCullough's 1991 book *Teens Parenting: Discipline from Birth to Three*, this multipart video alerts teen parents to appropriate strategies for disciplining their children at various stages of infancy and toddlerhood. Encouraging and supportive, the voice-over narration explains ways to divert children from bad behaviors, how to set limits, and how to give children the opportunity to make appropriate choices on their own.

Flour Babies. The Media Guild. 1989; rel. 1990. 30 min., guide, $295. Ages 13–18.

A high-school assignment in which couples must care for a make-believe baby for three weeks gives Donnie and Carrie reason to reconsider their romantic relationship. Prior to this true-to-life responsibility, the couple was considering having sex. Now, alert to the realities of a baby and to the risks of STDs, they communicate respectfully with one another and are able to set a model for postponing sexual activity. This program is a fictional dramatization. *Salt Babies,* described elsewhere in this list, documents the effects of an actual high-school family-life class project.

Going It Alone: Preparing for Single Parenthood. Cambridge Educational. 1994. 30 min., $79.95. Ages 14–adult.

Single teen mothers-to-be are the target audience of this video. Their frankly spoken comments reveal the satisfactions and disappointments of having a child and the economic hardships of "going it alone." Voice-over narration and the words of professionals contribute to the picture of the responsibilities involved in the motherhood experience.

"I Never Thought It Would Be Like This": Teenagers Speak Out about Being Pregnant/Being Parents. Guidance Associates. 1988. 50 min., guide, $129. Ages 12–18.

Clear anatomical diagrams and candid facts about contraception alert teens to the responsibilities that attend their blossoming sexuality. While the production actually encourages viewers to postpone sexual activity, the thoughtful program features three teens who did not. These girls forthrightly share memories of their pregnancies and deliveries and drive home the fact that parenthood is forever.

Let's Talk Babies! Instructional Video. 1994; rel. 1995. 30 min., $69.95 (schools), $39.95 (public libraries). Ages 14–adult.

Although this isn't a film made strictly for teens, it's full of information young parents may need to have. A child-care professional demonstrates techniques for routine daily care activities, such as feeding, diapering, and dressing, and touches on a host of other child-care basics, including crib safety and dealing with diaper rash.

Labor and Delivery for Teens. Churchill Media. 1993. 28 min., $360. Rental, $60. Ages 15–18.

Designed to prepare expectant teens for giving birth, this supportive program focuses on 15-year-old Hillary and on high-school senior Jessica, following them from prenatal visit to actual birth. Childbirth educators and medical professionals are shown reassuring the young women, explaining anatomical terms, and discussing labor and delivery alternatives.

Salt Babies: An Exercise in Teen Parenting. Human Relations Media. 1990. 15 min., guide, $119. Rental, $40. Ages 14–18.

Diapering, dressing, and looking after a five-pound bag of salt for two weeks is the high-school health-education assignment documented here. As "parents" care for their "babies," their awareness of parental responsibilities is heightened. At the same time, communication about sexual matters is promoted between teens and their parents.

Teenage Father. Sunburst Communications. 1989. 34 min., guide, $199. Ages 13–18.

Spotlighting the young man's point of view, this production introduces three expectant teen couples. Each couple chooses a different way to deal with an unplanned pregnancy: one opts for adoption, another for abortion, and the third has the child out-of-wedlock with the father allowed visitation rights until the mother marries another man. This sensitive, realistic film gives viewers a vicarious opportunity to assess the importance of planned sexual activity.

DEATH: ROMANCE AND REALITY

Empty Chairs. Agency for Instructional Technology. 1988. 30 min., guide, $150. Rental, $55. Ages 14–18.

An empty chair on a dark stage symbolizes the place Kate Keily once filled in the lives of those close to her. In compelling monologues, young and talented actors portray teenage Kate's mother, English teacher, boyfriend, sister, best friend, and even Kate, herself. Their reflections on Kate's life and death deftly incorporate the warning signs of suicide and intervention advice while they express survivors' feelings. The result is a moving dramatization of the far-reaching effects and pain of one young person's suicide.

The Power of Choice: Depression and Suicide. Live Wire Media. 1988. 30 min., guide, $64.95.
Ages 13–up.

Juvenile probation officer turned stand-up comedian, Michael Pritchard calls on his experiences and his humor to help young adults recognize depression and suicidal symptoms. Pritchard's talent for communicating with teens is equally evident in *The Power of Choice,* listed previously, which is aimed at helping teen viewers establish positive goals.

Top Secret: A Friend's Cry for Help. Human Relations Media. 1989. 27 min., guide, $169. Rental, $40.
Ages 13–18.

Karen loves acting and is often on stage, so her close friend Alan can't tell if her confessions of contemplated suicide are legitimate. Because he's unsure of her intentions and because he promised not to tell, Alan is deeply troubled. Should he chance losing Karen's trust at the risk of her life? Though it pauses to let viewers contemplate Alan's dilemma, the sincere yet fresh drama is respectful of both teens' problems.

Distributors

AGC Educational Media
1560 Sherman Ave.
Evanston, IL 60201
(800) 323-9094

Agency for Instructional Technology
P.O. Box A
Bloomington, IN 47402
(800) 457-4509

AIMS Media
9710 DeSoto Ave.
Chatsworth, CA 91311
(800) 367-2467

Cambridge Educational
P.O. Box 2153
Charleston, WV 25328-2153
(800) 468-4227

Churchill Media
6901 Woodley Ave.
Van Nuys, CA 91406-4844
(800) 334-7830

Coronet/MTI Film & Video
Customer Service Center
4350 Equity Dr.
P.O. Box 2649
Columbus, OH 43216
(800) 321-3105

Direct Cinema
P.O. Box 10003
Santa Monica, CA 90410
(800) 525-0000

Durrin Productions
4926 Sedgwick St. NW
Washington, DC 20016-2326
(800) 536-6843

Film Ideas
3710 Commercial Ave., Ste. 13
Northbrook, IL 60062
(800) 475-3456

Filmakers Library
124 E. 40th St.
New York, NY 10016
(212) 808-4980

Frameline
346 9th St.
San Francisco, CA 94103
(415) 703-8650

Guidance Associates
P.O. Box 1000
Mount Kisco, NY 10549
(800) 431-1242

Human Relations Media
175 Tompkins Ave.
Pleasantville, NY 10570
(800) 431-2050

Instructional Video
727 O Street
Lincoln, NE 68508
(800) 228-0164

Landmark Media
3450 Slade Run Dr.
Falls Church, VA 22042
(800) 342-4336

Learning Seed
330 Telser Rd.
Lake Zurich, IL 60047
(800) 634-4941

Library Video Co.
P.O. Box 1110, Dept. B
Bala Cynwyd, PA 19004
(800) 843-3620

Live Wire Media
3450 Sacramento St.
San Francisco, CA 94118
(800) 359-5437

The Media Guild
11722 Sorrento Valley Rd.
San Diego, CA 92121
(800) 886-9191

Media Inc.
P.O. Box 384-B
Media, PA 19063
(800) 523-0118

Media Works
P.O. Box 15597
Kenmore Station
Boston, MA 02215
(800) 600-5779

Morning Glory Press
6595 San Haroldo Way
Buena Park, CA 90620-3748
(714) 828-1998

National Film Board of Canada
1251 Avenue of the Americas
New York, NY 10020
(212) 586-5131

New Day Films
22-D Hollywood Ave.
Ho-Ho-Kus, NJ 07423
(201) 652-6590

Northeastern Wisconsin In-School Telecommunications
Cooperative Educational Service Agency No. 7
(NEWIST/CESA #7) 1110 IS Bldg.
UWGB
Green Bay, WI 54311
(800) 633-7445

NoodleHead Network
107 Intervale Ave.
Burlington, VT 05401
(800) 639-5680

PBS Video
1320 Braddock Pl.
Alexandria, VA 22314
(800) 424-7963

Perennial Education
1550 Sherman Ave., Ste. 100
Evanston, IL 60201
(847) 328-6700

Public Media Video
5547 N. Ravenswood Ave.
Chicago, IL 60640
(800) 343-4312

Pyramid Film & Video
P.O. Box 1048
Santa Monica, CA 90404
(800) 421-2304

SRA School Group
P.O. Box 543
Blacklick, OH 43004
(800) 843-8855

Sunburst Communications
39 Washington Ave.
Pleasantville, NY 10570
(800) 431-1934

United Learning
6633 W. Howard St.
Niles, IL 60714
(800) 424-0362

Author-Title Index

Boldfaced type *indicates videos.*

Subject Index

Boldfaced type *indicates videos.*

A lifelong lover of books, former teacher, and public librarian, Stephanie Zvirin joined the staff of the American Library Association in 1976 as a reviewer for *Booklist* magazine. A contributing editor for *The Best of the Best for Children,* her articles have appeared in a variety of publications, including *Book Links* and the bulletin of the Children's Book Council. Zvirin is currently the editor of YA books at *Booklist* and consultant to the American Library Association's Quick Picks for the Reluctant Young Adult Reader committee. She lives in Glen Ellyn, Illinois, with her husband, Michael, her son, Bob, and two rowdy cats.